Gulag Caledonia

Bruce Scott

Gulag Caledonia
By Bruce Scott

ScottsViewsBooks1@protonmail.com

ISBN 978-1-7396570-0-0

Cover:
Photograph by Clare Scott (2009), Cover design by Fiona Scott (2022).

Contents

Ephesians 6:10-13, King James Version

The Whole Armor of God

Finally, my brethren, be strong in the LORD, and in the power of his might. Put on the whole armour of God, that ye may be able to stand against the wiles of the devil. For we wrestle not against flesh and blood, but against principalities, against powers, against the rulers of the darkness of this world, against spiritual wickedness in high places. Wherefore take unto you the whole armour of God, that ye may be able to withstand in the evil day, and having done all, to stand.

Acknowledgments.

Acknowledgements are never easy. One is prone to think too much and miss so much. Any attempt is always a missed attempt. But one has to try. We are, however, fallen beings. I must thank my wife Clare for all her love and support. My friends and family-you know who are-who stood by me when I was ridiculed, cancelled and scorned. I must say a big thank you to Bridget Gevaux, my proofreader who did such a wonderful job on my manuscript. Fiona Scott for her wonderful cover design-it is always best to keep things in the family! My dog R for keeping me company on those early winter mornings while writing at the computer. A special mention to all my friends in Eastern Europe (Lithuania, Belarus, Russia and Ukraine) whose religious sensibilities were the quickening I needed which had such a part to play in why this book was conceived and born. Last, but certainly not least, my two sons F and I. My first book was dedicated to F, so another book had to be written for I. This book is for both my beautiful sons who have completed my life and who are the lid on my box, but a special mention to I-Daddy has written a book for you too now! God bless you all.

Escape Plan:

Sometimes, a book can be a warning for what is to come in the future, or a look back at the past to help us learn from past mistakes never to repeat. *1984* by George Orwell and *Brave New World* by Aldous Huxley were never intended to be blueprints of how future world governments were meant to run things. It seems that some people feel these blueprints from prophetic writers are being used to accomplish what was warned against.

What can help the children and people of 2021? Preparation.

Often, people who are dying pass on letters to loved ones, to be opened after they die, with kind words of love, but also of warnings and advice on how to live life and to not repeat the mistakes of the past. Books can perform the same function. They can be both a 'key' to the moment or the zeitgeist. Often, reacting to the present can be too late. Indeed, as the totalitarian Soviet or Nazi Germany examples show us, people can be so enmeshed in the cultural narratives that they cannot see the proverbial woods from the trees, and then of course it is too late. People act by 'just doing their job', or are convinced of the moral necessity of the state programme of domination.

People are duped so very easily. Even the great philosophers Jean Paul Sartre and Simone de Beauvoir (like many of the French intellectual set) were deluded enough to think that Communist Russia was a utopia to be revered. The publication of the *Gulag Archipelago* brought to light the dystopian reality of things, and Sartre and de Beauvoir sank into a gloomy old age. 'What shall we do?' asked Sartre in a plea to his lover. 'Where shall we go?' 'A whirlwind is carrying me to the grave and I am trying not to think,' mourned de Beauvoir.

If the clever, the great and the good, as well as the cowardly, are so easy to control, what hope is there? The only hope is to have an escape plan and a paper trail in case things get so bad that those who supported the oppression, and enacted it, can be proven guilty. So, when it happens, you can say 'I told you so'. At least one can save one's integrity, which is something that can never be taken if one holds firm. But that takes courage.

No amount of prophesising is worth anything if there is no courage. The suppression of free speech is one way to deal with people who have courage, but then the person must double down

1

and have courage again to rally against the injunctions against free speech. That is the cross people have to bear if they are to remain free.

Michel Foucault, for all his faults, did have a few interesting things to say. In his ideas on free/fearless speech, he emphasised that the mark of civilization is where fearless speech is allowed and encouraged. In the sick (or dying) days of the Western world, can we truly say that the fearlessness in speech and thought is being encouraged, or is it being eroded? I suspect the latter; I think that is pretty clear for all concerned. Even if one has the knowledge, one needs the added ingredient of courage. Fear is the great leveller, of course. Therefore, fear of the consequences of breaching the barrier, or limits, of the imposed zeitgeist is a great controller for many.

How are we to deal with such fear? In a Godless world, where God has been killed, fear works easily. The cultural Marxist idea of Dialectical Materialism, whereby everything that matters, or is of consequence, can be related back to material conditions, such as status, living conditions, wealth, happiness, resilience, mental health, justice, etc. In such a world, courage is a pretty poor attribute to value, especially when one could lose everything (material wise).

To overcome such fear and lack of courage, one needs something more than the idea of material reality. As Saint Gregory of Palamas describes in his Triads:

'Has it not occurred to them that the mind is like the eye, which sees other visible objects but cannot see itself?'

And so, it is with faith as the Orthodox Hesychasts ascribe, the Nous, beyond the material, beyond knowledge, a *Docta ignorantia* as Nicolas de Cusa would say, that taps into something else – something other beyond our ken, so to speak. But, of course, such things are not taught in schools these days, not encouraged in our citizens, and not given any importance whatsoever. Some, like Father Seraphim Rose and D.M. Lloyd Jones, would describe this as a demonic development. Indeed, it may be. When you cut a person off from the source, you are opening them up to some of the most terrible aspects of human reality and evil. But the powers that be, who want to cut people off from this, who advocate this, and the people who don't even realise they are being cut off, place little importance on this *Docta ignorantia*. They even ridicule it. And, even if they do not ridicule it, they give lip service to it in the realm of tolerance and acceptance like any other part of material reality.

Opinion or syllogistic argument only takes us so far. Some psychotherapies rely upon this formula (e.g., cognitive behavioural therapy, humanistic therapies), while others of a more existential or unorthodox-minded, psychoanalytically inspired therapy recognise, quite rightly, the limits of ratiocination and syllogism. Psychoanalysis, in its etymological roots, is a loosening of the soul from constraints; these constraints are the chains of the anti-*Docta ignorantia.*

So that is the plan. It does not seem much on the surface. It is (as ever) a tough sell. This has always been the way. The world is a vale of tears, right? Well, it might be the case, but it is also much, much more. To live not by lies, as Alexander Solzhenitsyn argued, is a powerful tool, as living in the truth of being a human being, rejecting oppressive totalitarian measures, is an energy in itself which spreads.

This is the escape plan. Use it well.

For my wonderful boys, whom I will love for eternity.

Preface

In the year 2050, some sixty years after the collapse of the Iron Curtain, the supposed fall of communism, the warnings to the West from the great Alexander Solzhenitsyn had gone unheeded. The West had, indeed, forgotten God.

The West had, on the surface, since the sexual revolution of the 1960s, the flurry of Marxist intellectual activity piggybacking on the works of the famous Frankfurt School, and the numerous human rights and civil rights movements, seamlessly entered the age of the internet without a care in the world, believing that freedom, liberty, democracy, and free speech were a given. But it had forgotten God.

The age of sexual 'freedom', coupled with internet access (which included unlimited availability of pornography), was a destructive force which ate away below the surface, deep in the soul, and sowed the seeds of forgetfulness of God.

The forgetfulness reached very far. Parents gave up the most precious gifts, their children, to be corrupted on every level with indoctrination in sexual matters (e.g., masturbation), pornography, and different sexual lifestyles (e.g., polyamory). But, more importantly, the corruption involved pernicious gender ideology which inculcated into children as young as 4 or 5 that they could change sex. And parents, in their forgetfulness, dutifully went along with it, were even proud of it, and some even coerced their children to 'transition' and broadcasted this with glee on social media platforms. The demonic narcissism that fuelled such displays was truly a sight to behold. Celebrity expectant parents, freed from the usual constraints of child welfare concerns, would routinely announce to the world how they would be bringing up their child as gender neutral and would even go as far as not telling people, including family, the actual sex of the newborn child. The delusion reached so deep, like a deep hypnosis, when gender 'activists' would try to convince the world (and themselves, no doubt) that doctors assigned the sex of children by announcing at the birth if it was a boy or girl. And people went along with this as they had forgotten God; 2+2 really did equal 5.

Marriage, family, and heteronormativity all came under sustained attack in many guises, such as the school, the media, political campaigns, and politicians. Marriage had become nothing but a minor contractual agreement that could be annulled with very little difficulty, while parenthood was devalued to the point that, to even suggest that a biological mother and father was an ideal, could result in a person being sacked from their job. You see, parenthood had been expanded and accepted to include many different types of family, including same-sex parents (e.g., two men, two women, transgender parents, etc). Of course, in such cases, a third party would be needed to actually create the child. Moreover, the human right of the child, to have a right to know their two biological parents, was way down the list of concerns of such 'movements'. Parenthood was placed at such a premium that politicians proudly declared that it should be encouraged to normalise and make acceptable fatherless children, ignoring the evidence that fatherless children had the most problems (psychologically speaking).

Even more macabre developments of these Godless times involved the issue of abortion. There were scenes of celebration after the Irish Abortion Referendum in 2017, where many women (and men) were screaming and had tears of joy running down their faces when they learnt that they had won the right to kill an unborn child. In other Western countries, there were debates about the need to be able to abort children (i.e., kill children) up to the ninth month of pregnancy. Even some Scottish politicians were barred from standing as members of parliament as they were Catholic and abortion was against their belief system (and the party line). Abortion on demand was a rallying cry from the radical feminists during this time.

Mental health also was on the hit list of this Cultural Revolution. Many on the left were encouraged by historical developments from the 1960s from the likes of the anti/critical psychiatry movement to make mental health treatment more humane and ethical; lobotomies and electroshock became rare, or even obsolete, and mental health hospitals were closed to be replaced with 'care in the community'. The development leading on from this was a huge industry with the birth of new psychiatric diagnoses and new drugs to treat these diagnoses. Indeed, Scotland had the highest rate of anti-depressant prescriptions in Europe. The cause of this problem lay in the rise of therapy culture and the manufacturing of mental health victims. When one lives in a world which has forgotten God, one only has recourse to man as an object, and any 'suffering' one encounters has to be faced with recourse to amelioration at any cost. Psychic well-being, therefore, became a cult along with an obsession with Adverse Childhood Experiences. Of course, an obsession with child experiences was a perfect opportunity for state involvement into the lives of families and their children. A whole industry of saviours was born offering 'trauma-informed' healing. Everybody could be identified as having trauma and, in turn, the manufacturing of passive victims became a cultural phenomenon; nobody can resist such a career path when it is the only solution to a world where God has been forgotten.

Ironically, the aforementioned burgeoning mental health industry rose in tandem with an increase in male suicide rates (especially amongst young men) aided and abetted by an anti (often white) men and boys agenda. The mainstream media and social media were awash with the pernicious narrative of 'toxic masculinity', of how men and boys were intrinsically flawed and how their 'masculine essence' needed to be rooted out and changed to become more feminine.

Of course, this development arose with the virulent fourth-wave radical feminist discourse. Bearing the banner of desiring equality, in reality it became a war against men and boys; a veritable game of 'Top Trumps' on any issue from wages to sexual pleasure. The twisting of words and statistics to fit any feminist narrative became almost an art form, and it led to a mass unconscious incorporation of believing the lie, without question, that men and boys were bad, toxic and that women were victims. The irony, however, was that when men started to fight for their issues through various men's rights movements, opening up about their emotions and feelings (as desired by the feminist dictate), men were lambasted for their 'male tears' and misunderstanding of the issues, even if they were highlighting the very real issues of male victims of domestic abuse, male suicide, or poor educational attainment in education relative to women.

Alongside these issues was the thorn of free speech. It became almost impossible to speak about these issues in a critical way without being laughed at for being backward, for being a bigot or fascist, or 'phobic' of some kind.

A deep paralysis crept into the psyche of peoples, a darkness that Solzhenitsyn experienced in his home country of Russia during his time. A creeping paranoia infused the interactions of everyday discourse; for example, was one politically correct, was one being inclusive and diverse enough in one's thinking, and was one assessing the 'risk' about certain issues enough?

As a barometer of the times, social media was extremely informative. People were wary (in person) of saying the wrong thing or were blatantly frightened of committing a crime against social justice. Scarily, it went in the other direction. Some people openly defended the destruction of the biological unity of the family, killing children at nine months' gestation, championing puberty blockers and invasive surgical procedures for children to change sex, teaching about pornography to children in schools, burning books written by white men, white guilt, toxic masculinity and the demonisation of men and boys. It was like the bullies had taken over the world and, if one put up a fight, one quickly found out that the authorities were on the side of the bully.

This was amply demonstrated by campaigns to stop sending women to prison for committing crimes (even though women comprised only five per cent of the prison population), by not treating criminals as criminals, but by treating them as victims of childhood adversity (as if the causality for individual cases could be shown), and by allowing an obnoxious, vacuous social justice discourse reign without let or hindrance, which was as Godless as they come. If one challenged this discourse, ridicule was the main remedy.

Obviously, there was the COVID-19 'thing'. A great opportunity for those in power to accelerate their power grab and political overreach to usher in a globalist technocratic totalitarianism, a global panopticon where ordinary people became livestock.

Ultimately, God had been forgotten and consigned to the historical dustbin. This was the ultimate objective of the cultural Marxist war on the West. It drove people underground. Some were driven underground to hide; others were driven there by public shaming and a quasi-juridical process, where witch-hunts and lynch mobs did the master's bidding.

This is the background; the scene is set which frames the stories from the Gulag Caledonia. This is a possible story about Scotland, of a dystopian future, in a time not long from here.

Chapter One

Glasgow, Scotland 2050

Looking out of his window, far out to the spire of an old church reaching towards the heavens and the divine, David Campbell took a long drag on his insipid nicotine vaporiser and peered into the grey, damp and murky early morning. Having slept little the night before due to having experienced a terrifying cannabis-induced panic attack, where he thought he was dying and could not stop shivering and shaking, he had eventually got to sleep at around 4 am, only to be woken by his alarm at 7.30 am to get ready for his back-to-work 'mental health' assessment at the Department of Work and Well-Being (DWW) at 9.30 am. It was an appointment he was dreading. If he played the 'game' with the assessor, the best outcome would be that he could keep his monthly universal basic income allowance. If not, things could become very, very tricky.

You see, in these times, work, well-being and 'mental health' had become intrinsically linked in a very insidious way. Being out of work, or not being able to find work, was seen as not just a result of the poor job market, it was seen as a 'mental health' condition – or, at the very least, one's 'mental health' was the prime factor why one was out of a job. It was, therefore, imperative for the DWW to take a perverted interest in the mental world of its jobseekers. The methods of assessment were based on traditional cognitive psychology, for example negative early maladaptive schemata (e.g., abandonment, enmeshment with parents), conditional and unconditional dysfunctional attitudes (e.g., 'I am a failure if I don't succeed'/'I am a failure in life and will never succeed'), and negative automatic thoughts (e.g., 'I am shit').

There were also intensive and invasive investigations into one's past and family life, namely 'Adverse Childhood Experiences' (ACE). This was a scheme (or scam, if you look at it in a different way) whereby the Scottish government, in the latter part of 2023, assessed the risk of every individual to later develop mental and physical problems and also substance misuse issues. The scheme was implemented into every aspect of daily life such as nurseries, schools, hospitals and the workplace. It was pseudo-scientific, clairvoyance, and 'pre-crime' science fiction. If your parents had divorced, and you were poor, you were picked out for mandatory 'treatment' to rectify the 'trauma'. There were no 'ifs' or 'buts' – psychosocial re-education would be prescribed. This could range from removal from the parents and family to a foster home if one was a child, mandatory treatment to treat 'trauma' if one was of working age and working in a public institution, or, if one was self-employed, mandatory assessments at regular intervals. If one refused, one could be stopped from working or taken into a treatment facility, because one would be at risk at a future time of being 'ill' and therefore a burden on the state. The ACE scheme ultimately functioned as a social and mental credit score algorithm. It was a great way for the state to collect data on all individuals and a very successful way of controlling a population from the cradle to the grave. There were no aspects of one's life where the state could not reach, and one could not venture anywhere, in life or virtual space, without there being surveillance and constraints placed upon you. It was, as they say, a truly dystopian Orwellian nightmare.

David Campbell had accumulated enough nicotine vapour and took a shower, dressed quickly and drank a quick cup of coffee before leaving his 6th floor apartment. Taking the elevator to the ground floor, he made his way to the Department of Work and Well-Being, which was some 45 minutes away by bus. His apartment block was on the south side of the city and was indeed an imposing and bleak sight to behold. His block, in the middle of six miles of similar blocks, housed a mixture of multi-cultural peoples and families, as well as many single people, all educated, poor, with little hope of ever moving out of the block, or escaping the uber surveillance of Digitised Universal Basic Income (DUBI), or improving their lives. If one was unemployed, the state would contribute to the cost; or, if one worked, the rent would be extortionate enough to make life barely liveable. But, of course, housing further up the social status scale was out of reach of most of the population.

By 8.10 am, David was standing at the bus stop, outside his apartment block, shivering on this dark, dank morning. There were several other people waiting with him – two children, of primary school age, with their very fat, harassed mother who was lecturing the children in an Asian language David could not recognise, an old man with a bandaged hand who was engrossed in his phone, and a very pretty young woman dressed in an extremely short leather skirt reeking of perfume and her face caked in makeup. What a rag bag of people. David mused about the lives of these people and how miserable must it be for them, as it was for him, living or existing here – but this was life, life for most people.

This was a life with an erased past. Social justice warriors from the sexual revolution in the 1960s up to the early 21st century had destroyed the remaining remnants of Western culture, Christian heritage, and traditional values, including the positive notions of the family, marriage and the cherishing of children. This was the communist dystopia that the great Russian author Alexander Solzhenitsyn had warned would come to the West if it did not make preparations. Well, the West did not prepare and the world became an open prison, or digital panopticon, very quickly. David Campbell's insertion into this was an easy process by the prevailing cultural forces that blew his way. There was very little choice. There was no freedom.

David was a 'white cis male' which indicated that 1) he was an oppressor of 'liberty' of civilization due to the colour of his skin, that he was male, and, worse of all, he was a white heterosexual male who identified as a biological male. This hateful narrative towards the white cis male was gradually introduced during the late 20th century and became common-day parlance amongst the social justice warriors and mainstream media in the early 21st century. So much so that universities in their droves started 'decolonising' their curriculums, including the 'great' universities such as Oxford, Cambridge, Edinburgh and Glasgow. This entailed getting rid of any white male authors from reading lists, on the premise that they were outdated, worthless, and oppressive. Out went Plato, Shakespeare, Dante, Montaigne, Kierkegaard, etc. Great works of literature were consigned to room 101 of banned texts. And, of course, there was affirmative action; institutions, workplaces and universities operated on a system of positive discrimination, whereby they would actively hire females, black and ethnic minorities, and LGBTQI+ people for jobs. The latter groupings also were favoured for university student places as well, which resulted in a populace where white cis men made up the majority of low-paid, manual jobs and the unemployed. Appeals to the powers that be by men's rights activists, that men and boys (especially white cis men) were being dealt an unfair hand, received increasingly more sophisticated measures.

Counterterrorism operations were defined and redefined to create categories of 'hate crimes' that were liable to extremism and terrorism. Of course, hate was defined as anything that contradicted the cultural Marxist narrative or attempted to bolster traditional ideas of marriage, family, or child rearing (by two biological parents). Offensiveness was a key idea, in that to promote or celebrate any such of the aforementioned lifestyles was tantamount to hate.

David fitted into the white cis male category very, very well. Standing by that bus stop, David thought back to his previous life and how he had got to this point. You see, David, several years earlier, was a promising post-doctoral researcher at St Andrews University. His topic of research was political activist groups, their structure, functioning and hierarchies. He was based in the department of Political Anthropology, in the School of Social Sciences. After a promising PhD researching the Occupy Movement and its offshoots Extinction Rebellion (climate activists) and ANTIFA (Anti-fascists) of the early 21st century – movements which essentially helped the world governments usher in digital technocratic totalitarianism – David landed a fully funded 3-year scholarship at the University of St Andrews to study political activism in the areas of gender and climate.

The reason he was awarded the scholarship by the University was that they were greatly impressed by how he had lived in one of these Occupy encampments and took on the role of an organiser or manager of the camp's hierarchical structure, to make it more inclusive of black and ethnic minorities, LGBTQI+, and more feminist friendly. It was basically an experiment to see if the members of the camp would accept hierarchical change (by dictate) and adapt and function. The outcome was a success. Traditional romantic couplings took a libertarian turn; women shared men as sexual playthings, polyamory flourished, and children were shared amongst several care givers (children were deemed not to belong to any one man or woman, e.g., biological man or woman). Gender neutrality became commonplace, both in appearance (i.e., clothes) and in roles. Inevitably, the camp disbanded. It was not a sustainable existence to live in tents in a city centre.

David's uncomfortable conclusions were not welcomed by academia and the wider world; the huge prevalence of mental ill-health amongst certain kinds of political activists and damaged children was attributed to the state by the activists and they always demanded more from their master, and they got what they asked for – being mastered over. Amongst the activist community, little importance was made of the traditional building blocks of human society, namely a loving relationship other than using a person as a masturbatory device, a mum, a dad, a home. Indeed, things moved into desperate places when researchers started blaming fatigue (or general malaise) on late-stage capitalism – a lazy and unverifiable hypothesis which fed into a childish desire for self-entitlement, narcissism, nihilism and even more hysterical demands to the state. The state licked its lips in glee. In the great 'pandemic' of 2020, the world governments used demands of climate activism and other kinds of hysterically fed activism (e.g., race, gender, etc) to usher in political overreach to keep people 'safe' and to 'save' the world.

David came unstuck, so to speak, when researching anarcho-communist activist groups in Glasgow. He discovered a virulent toxic feminist totalitarian hierarchy, whereby men were outlawed from speaking, having an opinion, or having men-only groups to discuss issues (where they could discuss how to be better feminists). All these activities were oppressive, a function of the patriarchy (according to the feminists). David met and interviewed the male victims of such a hierarchy and he could not contain how repellent he started to find these toxic and aggressive groups. Many of the men found themselves on the verge of, or having or experiencing, mental breakdowns through the guilt and shame they were burdened with. For many, the worst punishment was expulsion from their respective activist groups. Many men committed suicide as a result. David brought these issues up with his supervisor, Professor Karin Whorton-Smith. She initially viewed his concerns about these male activists as unfortunate side effects of the political organising and dismantling of the 'patriarchy'. However, this did not satisfy David. He truly began to feel that these men were victims of a group dynamic as pernicious and toxic as the 'schizogenic' families described by the psychoanalyst R.D. Laing in the 1970s, where double binds and poisonous family dynamics drive people insane. David became increasingly irritated, angry and upset at the rebukes by his supervisor and the dismissal of his emotions and his ability to open up about his emotions on the topic (which was a virtue of shedding one's toxic masculinity); but it was an opening up of the wrong kind.

David's supervisor became increasingly distant and less involved with his post-doctoral work until, one day, an email arrived (during a summer break whilst he was on holiday) from human resources at the University. It stated:

15/10/2041

Dear Dr. Campbell,

We are writing to you as it has come to the attention of the University that you broke your terms of employment as set out in 2.1. of the terms of your post-doctoral tenure within the University, namely that you have engaged in hate speech which has been of a misogynistic and transphobic nature. This is not in keeping with the University's ethos of inclusion and diversity. Further, your views have been extremely offensive to your supervisor and other work colleagues within the department of Political Anthropology, in the School of Social Sciences.

As a result, the University cannot support your 3-year post-doctoral tenure at the University, nor is you supervisor, Professor Karin Whorton-Smith, willing to supervise your work. We have informed your funder, the Bellingham Scholar Trust, who funds our post-doctoral programme within the School of Social Sciences. They have now cancelled further salary payments with immediate effect.

The contents of your office have been searched for any offending material and any relevant items have been passed to Police Scotland Hate Speech Department. Police Scotland will contact you in due course if they feel the need to. The rest of your possessions (books, clothes, trinkets, photos, etc) have been stored at the University Works Unit; you can collect these items at your earliest convenience. If you do not collect these items within 14 days of this email message, these items will be destroyed.

The University regrets this eventuality, but wishes you the best in your future career. Please find attached a list of charities and government agencies that offer help, support and guidance on social justice, diversity and inclusion which may be of help for your continued professional development.

Yours sincerely

Beth Edwards, BA (Hons), MSc.
Manager of Human Resources
University of St Andrews

13

And so, that was the letter that ended his academic career. There was, as per University policy, no recourse for appeal; hate speech was a non-negotiable issue. Police Scotland never got in touch with him; the police rarely did contact people in similar situations. The punishment had been delivered – expulsion from one's job and career. David's name went on 'black lists' amongst all universities (several global lists) which highlighted his 'crimes'. He was, therefore, unlikely ever to get another post at an academic institution again. It was game over.

David never did attempt to get his possessions back from the University. He had very little in his office, anyway – just a few books that he would never need again, and an old rain jacket.

That was nine years ago. David was now 38 years old, on Digitised Universal Basic Income, and now off for his 'mental health' assessment at the Department of Work and Well-Being. The worst part was that, due to the social credit scoring system, his wife felt coerced and forced to separate from him, for the sake of their two children, two boys aged 4 and 7. As David was considered a social pariah, the prospect of him staying with his family would have meant heavy (or heavier) state involvement and could have entailed the state taking his children into care. The best thing was for David to leave. Such was the force of the state.

The bullies had taken over society. When bullies take over a society, there is no justice and there is nobody one can turn to for help, for the people who are meant to help are the bullies.

The bus arrived at the bus stop. It was already pretty full from previous pick-ups en route. Standing room only. Every grey, miserable face on this veritable meat truck taking them into the city centre for their menial, meaningless jobs told a story. Stories that would never be told and never be heard.

David boarded the bus and it took off down the wide boulevard towards the city. A sinking feeling overwhelmed him. He had never before felt such a feeling. His legs felt weak, his mood was utterly bleak and hopeless, and he cared nothing for the world or even his own life. But worse, as the bus trundled towards the city centre for his appointment, he experienced a feeling that this would be the last time he would board this bus and make this trip to the city.

The bus drove towards the city centre along the left-hand side of the triple carriageway, stopping every so often. The landscape was one of a non-changing, homogenous grey, bleak, infinite landscape portrait. One mile was indistinguishable from the next. You had your apartment blocks, which were all built exactly the same – ten floors high, ten apartments wide. Situated on the ground floor of the blocks were mini supermarkets, some open for twenty-four hours, where you could buy anything from drugs, alcohol, phones, food, and widescreen televisions, etc. There was, of course, the enormous variety of fast-food restaurants and takeaways selling the latest artificial protein-based, and insect-based, protein foodstuffs, as well as artificial processed vegan varieties.

Interspersed along the route were bars, nightclubs, and erotica shops, where you could buy all manner of sex toys, sex dolls and pornography. One could also buy a plethora of drugs to enhance sexual enjoyment and stimulation. For the gender fetishists, one could purchase cross-sex hormones; if one fancied 'becoming the other gender' one could pop some inexpensive oestrogen or testosterone, or some synthetic copy. Chest binders and castration devices could be bought for very little.

The bars and nightclubs along these vast expanses of social, cultural and community obliteration were places where time could be wallowed away in a haze of booze and pills. People would often meet their dates at these places, whom they had 'met' online, for meaningless pursuit of sexual pleasure. Sex had become a hobby. Sexual liberation had certainly reached its zenith. To hook up with someone had become nothing more uncommon than ordering a takeaway or food delivery from a supermarket. Some of the bars and nightclubs doubled as brothels, which had become legalised. Sex as a career (for women), thanks to the efforts of political activists a decade earlier, had made the attraction of fucking people for a living a viable life goal. Interestingly, many of the sex workers worked in the area of sado-masochism.

The mile after mile of indistinguishable human habitation, shops, eateries and adult entertainment was the culmination (so far) of the globalist dream; a landscape devoid of culture, tradition, values, morals and community. People just existed, existed for the state to feed off; for their labour, for their data (to control them further).

The state fed on and fed the passions and desires of the people; drugs, sex, pornography and fantasies were all promoted and legitimised by the state. It was, as Aldous Huxley described in *Brave New World Revisited*, as if these vices and passions of the people were fed by the soma. To keep people in chains is one way of controlling people, but it's not very efficient, as people can rebel; but when people willingly put on their own chains, then that is a whole different ballpark. The populace becomes as docile as a kitten, as it exists in a hypnotised state towards their own enslavement, a meaningless life and their inevitable death.

Chapter Two

Department of Work and 'Well-Being'

The bus arrived at the Department of Work and Well-Being on Humza Yousaf Avenue (a politician from the 2020s who ushered in the most draconian and abusable hate crime/thought crime laws in the democratic world) at 9.15 am. Plenty of time for David to empty his bowels, which were now rumbling and telling him a shit was impending. The DWW building was an imposing 6th floor, square concrete building with lots of tiny windows and a small door on the front. At the back entrance to the cube, reminiscent of the Star Trek Generation Borg cube, was delivery access for tradesmen and the like. However, much more sinister, there were also the cells for holding people who became rowdy, violent, or who were deemed in need of some state intervention. State intervention could include being shipped off to a local or national psychiatric hospital for treatment, which could include intensive cognitive and emotional remodelling coupled with psychoactive psychiatric drug treatment to aid the process. This could last as little as thirty days, or months, or even years for some people. There was no volition or consent involved; this was all done for one's well-being and for the greater good of society. More likely, one would be sent off to some far-off rural area to work on the wind or wave energy farms, or the protein/insect farms. Rural areas were, for the most part, commandeered by the state, for state use only under ecological laws. In essence, the psychiatric or work placements were partly re-education to correct the wrong thinking that a citizen was displaying, and often such wrong thinking was often extracted with very little provocation at the Department of Work and Well-Being. Sometimes, people needed to be prodded more than others; but, if you had violated any social justice laws on the outside, the department would know about it and try its hand at exposing you. The human labour was also a bonus to run the new-age ecological religion which, disguised as altruism to 'Mother Earth', was an excellent way to control human beings.

David rushed inside the entrance and joined the line of people waiting to go through one of the five security ports that led into the building. These ports comprised full-body x-ray scans. All pockets had to be emptied and shoes, belts and other metal objects had to be removed. David found a tray and emptied his pockets.

The contents included his wallet with credit cards and some cash, which was hardly used or accepted in any outlet or shop nowadays. The only place one could use cash was on the black market, rogue mobile food vendors on roads, or in seedier parts of towns and cities. And, of course, cash was not illegal, as sometimes it was necessary to use when the networks went down and electronic transactions could not be used. He also had his identity and history card on his PERCD (Personal Electronic Record and Communication Device), which included all his data from birth to present, such as infancy well-being scores, school reports, family history and background, medical records, education and work history, travel history, social internetwork records and political activity/involvement. This information was also contained in electronic sensors implanted in one's body – under the armpit, just under the skin, in the buttock and in one's wrist. These communicated with one's PERCD and the outside network.

David had now arrived at the security port. A stern-looking but attractive, heavily tattooed and pierced blonde woman in her 30s beckoned him forward into the x-ray scanner. She barked at him to put his arms above his head and stay like that until the green light in front of him flashed. He did as he was told and then exited the port. The woman growled at him to collect his belongings and shoes and make his way to his appointment on the 3rd floor. The bull ring piercing through her septum in her nose was very commonplace as a fashion accessory. It was highly aggressive and symbolic of being a cog in a chain, a mere tool for the smooth, efficient running of the state machine. Nothing but a mark of livestock, embraced and celebrated by so many.

After fetching his belongings and putting his shoes back on, David rushed to the elevator to take him to the 3rd floor. Luckily the door was about to close and he was able to squeeze, just in time, into a crushed elevator cubicle with around thirty other people. The elevators in this building were fast, furious and frightening what with the jolts and bangs coming from the mechanisms. Luckily, there were no stops en route to the 3rd floor; the people travelling with him were all 'customers of the state'. The ground floor was primarily for building security purposes, while the 1st and 2nd floors were general administration. The people who worked there did not do front of house or dealing with the public. The 3rd floor was for Work and Well-Being interviews and assessments, the 4th floor was dedicated to psychiatry and social work, the 5th floor was the legal and police department, and the 6th floor was dedicated for Management. On the very top of the building was a helicopter pad. The basement held accommodation for those who were about to be processed and shipped off to the energy/protein farms or psychiatric hospitals.

The elevator doors opened and David rushed out into a large, open-plan waiting room. He spied the signs for the toilets in the far left-hand corner of the waiting room. He was getting desperate. His bowels were churning and it was getting close. All toilets were 'gender neutral' as no distinction was made on biological sex in most contexts in society. On entering the toilet, there were no urinals; public urinals had been banned in Scotland since 2023, as those is power felt that urinals were male-centric and that everybody should piss sitting down. I mean, why should a man be allowed the patriarchal privilege of pissing standing up, with no shame in front of other people? Men would have to wait for a free cubicle like everybody else and he would have to sit and submit like everybody else. The ban on urinals was also justified in terms of public health as a good way of stopping the spread of disease.

He tried all ten cubicle doors, but they were engaged. 'Shit!' he muttered, hoping for some relief soon. Luckily, one of the doors opened and he was greeted with a huge hulk of a woman in a yellow floral-pattern summer dress and ginger, curly hair. The 'woman' smiled at David as she exited the cubicle. The cubicle toilet bowl resembled a sewage overspill nightmare. The unflushed turd and brown water lurking in that toilet made David feel like vomiting. But sit down he did as he let his bowels empty like a champion. The relief was exhilarating. His joy soon turned to disgust when he looked over to his left to grab the toilet paper, when he saw that there was very little left on the roll on the holder. *She could have warned me*, he thought. Luckily, there was just enough toilet paper left. He quickly exited the cubicle, without flushing, as the handle was broken, and washed his hands in the sink. Fortunately, there was a full soap dispenser.

Returning to the vast waiting room, he approached a central information point with a telescreen. He placed his identity card upon it and it spat out a piece of paper with a number on it: 281. He looked up at one of the several large number counters dotted around the room. His heart sank. It was only 253. This meant they were probably overrunning; well, they were always overrunning. A 9.30 am appointment normally meant that you would be seen thirty minutes later, sometimes longer. They were thorough at the Department of Work and Well-Being.

David sat down on one of the straight rows of seats overlooking the window. He glanced to his right and to his left; a real gaggle of unfortunates waited with him. Four men and one woman. Well, David could in his mind categorise them as men and women, but he would have been wary of vocalising it out loud; referring to biological sex was potentially a hate crime in Scotland. The demonisation of using biological sex first started in the schools around 2019, when pupils were expelled and/or refused entry to school if they did not adhere to the gender ideology that was force-fed into them. It proliferated into all walks of society and public life with great force. The Third Gender Recognition Act in Scotland of 2027 finally made it legal for someone to be recognised as a woman or man if they simply decided, without medical dictate or medical/social intervention on the part of the person who was transitioning. Of course, this caused a major ruckus with feminist groups who felt this was an erasure of (real biological) women's rights and an invasion of their female-only spaces (e.g., changing rooms, sports, hospital treatments; everyone can have a cervix if one says). The ruckus from the feminists came to nothing, anyhow; such hate groups (as decreed by the government) were outlawed in the ultra-devolved Scottish government (from the UK parliament). Indeed, in many European countries, simply being a member of a critical transfeminist group could result in imprisonment. Women had had their voices and bodies essentially erased by the state. The curious thing was, it was embraced by many women.

Whatever the gender of David's companions in the waiting room, they all looked as miserable as he did. They, like him, were all waiting for their 'interrogation'.

A loud 'beep' signalled a jump in the queue. David and the other people on his seating row, and everyone else in the waiting area, all looked up toward the nearest number counter like well-conditioned Pavlovian puppies to see the progress to their allotted slot. 264. There was no rhyme or reason to the count and how it reduced. Sitting in this situation facilitated wild indulgences in fantasy. What was going on in the interview rooms off to the side of the waiting room? These fantasies were encouraged by the steady stream of poor, beleaguered souls who exited the main door from the interview rooms.

At that point, what appeared to be a middle-aged, Middle Eastern-looking woman with a headscarf exited the interview room. She was carrying a huge bag with God knows what in it. She was followed by two young children around 5 and 8 years old. The woman was crying and muttering to herself in a foreign tongue. No doubt the interview had gone badly. David felt anger rising in him and pity for the woman and her children. Most probably, she and her family had come to Scotland to start a new life after Western nations had gutted her country of origin, then invited her with open arms to settle in their lands as humanitarian repatriation. Some welcome that was! To live in a tiny apartment in a high-rise in a huge, sprawling grey city, to live on Digitised Universal Basic Income, where no sense of community existed. It was indeed dire. It was merely existing to die. So many displaced peoples from wars and Western nations' interference had resulted in many people ending up with the same fate.

David caught the eye of the woman as she passed. She gave him a haunting look. It was a knowing look between two people consigned to the 'existing to die' waiting room of life. But, paradoxically, in that intimate moment, each recognised the other as a human being in the Syphian struggle to get through it all. In that moment, there was a glimmer of hope amongst all the grey and grime. Or was there? He would never know this woman, know her family, participate in her customs and traditions. But, of course, that was irrelevant. Both his and her traditions, heritage and backgrounds were nothing but a distant memory for both of them. She and her family had been forcibly uprooted from her homeland by war and economics. Similarly, David had had his Scottishness erased and outlawed by successive governments pushing a social justice, cultural Marxist agenda; both their lives were socially engineered by globalist powers, whereby they had been coerced to live in a homogenous, monotone, grey, cultureless, tradition-less, family-less, amoral, hyper-sexualised society. This included living in a non-rooted, community-less sprawling metropolis, in a tiny flat, which was actually a prison because the state could monitor everything about a person's life, from how many shits they did (digital water monitoring devices), to social media devices use, sleep time, physiological changes – and your conversations, of course. You did not know your neighbours and they did not know you. The state kept close tabs on you. For example, a next-door neighbour of David's had a heart attack during the night, and as he was being monitored the emergency services arrived to revive him and kept him alive. His neighbour was still alive and well today after an operation to put a stent in his heart; he was back working at his job at the protein processing factory on the production line. The state 'cares' so much they monitor to get you back to work and keep you there; poverty management for profit. A society of prisoners.

David watched the struggling woman and her two children walk off towards the elevators, huffing and puffing. In his mind, he wished her well. She was as much a victim in this as he was. And her poor children? Future fodder for the machine. They deserved far better. The world that had been created was a giant crime against humanity, but there was no Court of Human Rights to appeal to.

A flurry of beeps rang through the waiting room. David looked up and saw that several numbers were shown on the counter: 259, 260, 261, 262, 263, and 264...

David's heart missed several beats when he saw his number appear on the counter. No doubt his physiological responses were being monitored by technicians in the building, and could be used in the interview that was about to take place. He would just put it down to anxiety, but even admitting to suffering anxiety could be used against him as being 'unstable'; there was little use for recourse to reasoned argumentation within the state bureaucracy. The state had borrowed well from the methodology of the dogmatic application of psychoanalysis; when the state told you something about yourself, any attempt to refute its assertions would be met with the accusation of the use defence mechanisms and a diagnostic intervention.

David rose wearily from his seat and walked towards the door where the interview rooms were situated. As he walked slowly across the floor to the door, several fellow poor souls looked up at him with pity, and he opened the door.

Directly inside the door was a reception booth where one had to type in your appointment number. Then a message appeared on the screen: GO TO ROOM 32. David walked along the long corridor past all the numbered doors until he came to a beige door with the number 32 on the centre of the door. He knocked. A voice shouted from the other side.

'Come in.'

Chapter Three

The interview

'Hello, my name is Mr Smythe,' said the man sitting behind the desk in the small, windowless room. On the desk was a computer and some papers. He was an insipid-looking man of around 40 years old, dressed in a grey suit that looked too big for his puny, sun-deprived body. His greasy mop of jet-black hair, swept to an annoying long fringe to the right of his brow, set off the look of emancipation and submission to the bureaucracy.

'Hello, I am David Campbell,' replied David.

'Sit down, let's get started,' Smythe retorted. He punched some keys into the computer and brought up a file on the screen. 'It says here that you have been out of work for approximately one year. Your contract from your post at the University was terminated over issues to do with misogyny, and making female staff members feel uncomfortable, which was against the University policy.'

Boom! Go for the guts on the first question, thought David.

'Well...' he began to explain. 'That's not quite how I see it. I raised concerns about my research and how male political activists were being abused within their activist community. I came to some conclusions of how an abusive dynamic was being played out within such a community and how it was affecting the mental health of its male members.'

Smythe looked uninterested and continued to stare at his computer screen, but David continued. 'I raised these concerns with my supervisor, as I felt it was an important finding in my research. It was something that had not been mentioned in the research and was not something openly discussed within activist communities.'

'Nevertheless,' Smythe replied smugly, 'you made your female supervisor uncomfortable with the misogynistic language you were using.' He went on, 'Are you aware that the University records indicated that you were looking at websites about men's rights on the internet?'

'What is the problem with this?' replied David. 'There are many sites about men's rights, about men who are abused by women. It's nothing groundbreaking, surely? I was investigating these sites to see if any research had been done, as feminist groups were unlikely to research such topics.'

'Seems like you are saying that women cannot be objective or conduct proper research?' Smythe argued. 'It sounds like you are operating with a bias in your thinking, which is quite negative towards women.'

'It's research, research to find out things,' said David. 'In research, some things lead to dead ends, one follows leads, one has hunches, one forms ideas, and one looks for the existence of evidence. The men's rights sites provided evidence, from testimony of men, that many men had felt abused by women in social-political groups. This backed up my observations and interviews within political activist groups in Scotland. It's hardly rocket science. Some men get abused by women, and its cover is feminist rhetoric within the political group. It's essentially mystification through dogma.' He was becoming more exasperated and angry by the fact that he was encountering such cognitive dissonance from Smythe.

'Nevertheless,' said Smythe, 'the levels of distress you induced in your supervisor and other colleagues were indicative of toxicity, of problematic toxic masculinity that had not been dealt with. This was corroborated by your superior, your supervisor who is an expert in the area you were studying. Indeed, from your medical records, I see that your male hormone levels have been deemed problematically high. You have never considered hormone suppressants?'

'No!' replied David. 'Why would I mess with nature? My ex-wife was a biologist specialising in endocrinology and she knew the research on such things. There was nothing wrong with my hormone levels.'

'Ah, yes,' Smythe remarked gleefully. 'You were married and had two children, but your wife left you and took custody of the children. Or, rather, the courts deemed you to be unsuitable for their gender developmental trajectory, amongst other things, of course.'

'That is not quite true,' quipped David. 'After I wrote a few blog articles on my thoughts on the abuse of men in activist communities, my wife was harassed by anonymous people, online, at work, and even in the street. When the press found out about my expulsion from the University, my supervisor and others *so*

24

bravely went public and trashed my name. I was hung, drawn and quartered, sentenced without trial, by a lynch mob. My wife had a breakdown and went to live with her parents. Then the courts decided I was not to be near my children, my two boys, for fear I might be a negative influence on their lives. In the end, my wife had no choice but to leave me, otherwise the children would have been taken off her. You ask her. She will back me up. It was a *fait accompli*, so please don't pretend otherwise.'

David, by this point, was starting to perspire badly. He felt sick, dizzy, as if he was going mad. There was no way of talking to these people. They – the University, his supervisor, the courts, and Smythe – had a discourse that was deliberately obtuse, mystifying, bullying – and, of course, certain that they had the truth. The truth in 2050 was a very strange thing. Truth was whatever those in power wanted it to be; and, if one deviated from their version of the truth, one was accused of hate speech or extremism, especially so if it offended the other person. It was the perfect schizogenic-inducing double bind so famously described by Gregory Bateson in communications theory. The psy-op par excellence.

Smythe sighed. 'You see, this is how we here at the Department of Work and Well-Being see it. We are attempting to help you become integrated into society, to be productive, to find meaningful work, to be healthy. To help you see that, in order to fit in, you have to understand how destructive your behaviour patterns are and how they affect others – and yourself, of course. Interestingly, I note from your childhood developmental adversity records (CDAR[1]) that both your parents were substance abusers, namely alcohol, that you experienced poverty, and you displayed high levels of attention deficit in your early school years. This is indicative of a risk for future adult emotional deregulation. This fits

---

[1] The acronym associated with the Scottish government's monitoring system of children's well-being, a risk-preventative psychosocial policy. It was based on the pseudo-science that certain factors in a child's life would lead to adult dysfunction (e.g., ill-health, drugs misuse, dysfunctional and destructive relationships). Such ideas regarding the direction of fixed causality had been debunked by many researchers in the field for a long time, but of course such ideas were suppressed and buried; these ideas did not add to the matrix of social control that was desired by the government.

with the pattern of interpersonal conflict at the university, with your supervisor and colleagues, your dismissal from your research post, your marriage breakdown and your unsuitability to be a parent, as deemed by the courts. It would seem that you have not dealt with many issues that affect your well-being and they are having a detrimental effect on your life. Things are not going well; this is clear. You are in a chaotic situation and things have spiralled out of control. You have little insight. Ok. We have decided to send you upstairs to psychiatry and social work. You are going to have a chat with a couple of people who are going to advise you on the next steps to get you back on track. We can do this, Dr Campbell.'

Smythe pushed a button on his desk. The door opened and two men came into the room. One of them announced, 'Please come with us, Dr Campbell.'

David felt sick to his stomach. His worst fear was being realised. The state was now about to get its claws into him. He knew it would come eventually. It was only a matter of time. He got up out of his seat.

'Ok, let's get on with this shit show,' he said.

'Goodbye, Dr Campbell,' Smythe said. 'I hope it works out well for you.'

David stared at him blankly and walked out the room, followed by the two attendants, who would take him up to the 4th floor for the next part of his ordeal.

Chapter Four

4th Floor: Psychiatry and Social Work

It was not an unexpected turn of events that David was now being transferred to the shrinks. From what he had heard from others, from people who had heard of people being transferred there, from people who had been there, even from people who worked there, the whole *modus operandi* of the Department of Work and Well-Being – nay, the entire state apparatus – was to problematise being. To borrow a phrase from Aneurin Bevan, a 20th century socialist politician, it was to problematise being or human life 'from the cradle to the grave'. The aim of this was not the altruistic aim of caring for the populace, but ostensibly poverty management for profit (and control of the masses), hyper-monitoring of people's activity, the manufacturing of victimhood through this rise of 'therapeutic culture' and encouraging the governance of the self.

The sexual revolution in the 1960s gave rise to the therapeutic culture (e.g., encounter groups, Eastern mysticism, cognitive therapy, and all types of wacky one-to-one psychotherapy). Accompanying this was the increasingly negative view of Christianity, the family, and marriage, which led to the breakdown of Western civilization. Self-improvement, and state involvement/governance of one's private life, gutted the last vestiges of Christian spirituality from the soul of Western peoples.

The result? By 2035, the 'self' had become nothing but a project, an object to be handled, improved, therapised, and polished. Much to the chagrin of the German philosopher Martin Heidegger (writing in the 1960s), therapeutic culture had devalued the human being to the level of a technicised object. Of course, as the utopian upsurge of sexual liberation, coupled with the denigration of God, had led to the universally accepted idea that the self was seen as solely a project, this had dire consequences for civilization. The world had walked into a trap. It was a fait accompli. The easiest way to control people is to get them to desire the chains that enslave them, rather than impose the chains on them. Once they have willingly put on their chains, then the state can start the real work of moulding the world they want. Offer the people the answer to their lusts, desires and sufferings. Take things like family, marriage, religion, values and community, and replace

27

these with sterile, transient, meaningless relationships. Celebrate freedom in the guise of being single, childless, 'independent' living, with the offer of all kinds of intoxicants, chemical and psychological, to placate the desire.

By 2050, this had created a world of mass neurosis, or perhaps even mass psychosis. With the self as a project, and passions and desires (sex, consuming goods, food, drink, drugs, pseudo-spirituality, etc), it was just something to pursue and attempt to satiate the dead individual. It fails because, ultimately, one has been tricked away from the transcendent to buy into the Faustian pact of the material, selfish self; the self which can never be satiated. And, as the great 20th century psychoanalyst Jacques Lacan warned, when people become unsatisfied, and demand satisfaction, eventually demanding from the state, the people will get a new master. This kind of system culminates in the transfer of people to the 4th floor of the Department of Work and Well-Being: Psychiatry and Social Work. What else does one expect to do with a faulty machine? If one is just a project, an object, a machine, then one must return to the factory to be fixed. The factory was always full of people to be fixed.

And so, in the long line of machines to be fixed, here was David standing in the elevator going upwards to the 4th floor with two attendants.

'So, what is the plan for me up here?' David asked them.

Attendant 1, a man, replied, 'You will be assessed to see if you are fit for societal re-integration, or to see if you need Intensive Social-Cognitive-Emotional Restructuring.'[2]

Attendant 2, a female, added, 'And you will be questioned on your social history records to verify if you need legal intervention.'

David felt a chill go through him. He knew this meeting would be life defining. He was quickly realising that he was being 'set up' for the big 'set-up'.[3] They would have been, and will be,

---

[2] The acronym for this was ISCER. ISCER was a programme developed around 2035. It was a holistic approach involving every aspect of a person's life – their private life, social life and psychological life. Each aspect was interrelated and 'treatment plans' had to target each one, and a person had to be 'balanced' in each aspect before they could be considered safe enough to be successfully re-integrated into society.

[3] A term used by people and victims of the state social/psychological

going through his records, often with powerful computer modelling algorithms, to predict 'risk' which selectively picked out pieces of information that fitted the set-up, but which had little bearing on reality. However, thanks to the brainwashing into mass psychosis by state propaganda, this illogical way of thinking had become mainstream in government and governing – global totalitarian technocratic societies of control.

The elevator came to stop and the matt silver metal doors slid open. The three of them walked out.

'Turn to the left,' said Attendant 1, and they walked down a bare, windowless corridor for what seemed like an age until they came to a black door with the number 21 on it. The door opened automatically and they walked in. David had entered another windowless office where two people were sitting behind a large, metal desk. On it was an assortment of papers and two computers. Behind these two people were several filing cabinets, two standing lamps, and an intercom point on the wall to his left. The man was in his mid-40s, with short, black, swept-back hair, with shaved back and sides, black suit, white shirt and pink tie.

'Please sit down and make yourself comfortable,' said the man. 'My name is Dr Mallory. This is...' looking to his right 'Ms Jones, my associate.'

David sat down; his two attendants remained standing either side of him. David looked at the name badges of the two people sitting opposite him. Mallory's badge said 'Psychiatrist', while Jones' badge read 'Clinical Associate in Work and Well-Being'. Jones was mid-20s, slim, with long black hair. She wore a black, sleeveless dress cut very low into her cleavage, and very fashionable spectacles. She looked the epitome of pseudo-

---

'diagnostic' machine. The methodology of the 'set-up' was not an objective process where actual evidence was gathered to reach a conclusion, where reasonable doubt of the conclusion could not be used to refute the conclusion. The facts were spuriously selectively gathered and, much like a hysterical child, touted as the ultimate truth. No opposing facts would be entertained, however convincing, if they did not fit the 'set-up'. Social media discourse of the early 21st century had acclimatised people to this way of thinking, as well as pernicious ideologies and government propaganda, which infiltrated society and became normalised.

professionalism, while he looked like a heartless psycho-bureaucrat who dealt with human beings like they were on a conveyer belt.

'Ok,' said Mallory. 'We have a problem, don't we? Chronic unemployment coupled with serious social disintegration. It looks like you have really gone off the rails. We are here to help you with that. Myself and my associate have been analysing the data from your social records history, which includes online activity, occupational and educational history, and CCTV[4] from over the years, and it appears from our modelling predictions that you are a danger to yourself and society. Your behaviour has all the hallmarks of looming future ill-health and dysfunctional relationships.'

Mallory turned to Jones. 'Could you show the montage now, please.'

Jones turned the computer screen around so that David could see it. 'Here is a short audio-visual summary,' she said, 'of some of the things we found from our analysis that give us real cause for concern, and that we feel require intervention.'

David knew the technology existed for such invasive scrutiny of one's life. He, like many others, however, felt that the likelihood that it would show up on state radar was highly unlikely. A sinking terror began to flood every fibre of his being as Jones turned the screen on and pressed a few buttons on the keypad opposite her. There was, at this point, no recourse to a defence. This was it. They were the judge, jury and executioners all in one. This was the culmination of social justice, 2050 style.

'As you can see,' continued Jones, 'from the list there are several issues that are highly worrying.' She began to read from a list, a summary, on a piece of paper in front of her, which David

---

[4] CCTV; close circuit television. The technological advances of this system by 2050 were quite spectacular. The system was digitised and was integrated with the internet. Powerful face recognition technology and complex algorithms could bring up 1000s of hours of footage of an individual's past, whether in public or at home, e.g., walking in the street, shopping, sitting in a cafe or bar, speaking to a woman in a nightclub, speaking on the phone at home, sleeping, etc. It also had audio capability whereby the system could filter out any noise and focus on what the individual was saying. Big Brother was really watching you, and hearing you.

could also see on the screen alongside examples of where, when etc:

1) Numerous approaches to women in public spaces, bars and nightclubs over a period of ten years which indicate inappropriate sexual harassment without consent.

2) Online social media activity, in public forum and private forum, indicating political leanings which indicate a risk of radicalisation.

3) Being a member of social media groups and attending meetings which disseminate, discuss sexist, misogynist, racist, homophobic, transphobic and inappropriate religious articles. These indicate a danger and propensity for extreme radicalisation.

4) During nursery and primary school years (age 3-5 years old, and primary 1 to primary 5 especially) you displayed biased sexually stereotyped play, preferring rough and tumble games with other boys, solitary building play (e.g., with blocks, Lego etc). You refused to engage in non-stereotyped activities, which indicates an unhealthy bias, and that your parents did not help with your gender identity trajectory in a healthy way.

5) During primary school years, you refused to participate fully in the Social, Cognitive, Sexual and Emotional Resilience Development Programme.[5] You refused to

---

[5] The Social and Emotional Resilience Development Programme (SERDP) was a national curriculum subject taught to all children from nursery age to age 18. It essentially functioned as a group therapy/encounter group within the classroom where children would dish the dirt on their emotional life, their home life, and their parents (and the parents' emotional struggles, mental ill-health, etc). Sexual education would include the plethora of sexual activities/lifestyles in the alphabet, from A to Z (e.g., Anal, Feltching, Fisting, Rainbow kisses, Rimming, Scat to Zoophilia). Gender ideology would inculcate to children that they could be born in the wrong body; that they could be a boy or a girl really, or that they could be one of

31

participate in group sessions where you discussed home life, your emotional and cognitive state and worries, and ideas of sex, gender and sexuality. It was noted that your parents were encouraging you to not co-operate in these aspects of the curriculum and were instead inculcating you with inappropriate radical ideas. Indeed, your father was questioned by police on several occasions for objecting to these aspects of the curriculum. The teachers and parent-teacher council found his behaviour highly offensive, transphobic and extremist.

6) You attended meetings of subversive radical political parties/groups that were on the state's list of 'groups of concern' which might lead to radicalisation.

7) You objected to psychosocial sex education given to your children at their school. It was noted that your objections were felt as threatening by schoolteachers and other parents.

8) The culmination of your life experiences and development, and subsequent employment problems with

---

110-plus different genders on the gender spectrum. This programme effectively turned the classroom into a mental health clinic (by manufacturing mental ill-health) and a sexual grooming/indoctrination centre, as many children were traumatised by the programme and by the damaging levels of social and cognitive introspection required, which were highly age inappropriate. What was more undermining for children's sense of self and grounding was the constant undermining of the role of the parents (by the school via the ethos of the programme). The curriculum instilled the idea that parents, especially married biological parents, were 'lacking' and that, if the children told the teacher things about home life or their parents, they could discuss it safely with the teacher and the teacher would not tell the parents. Many children were removed from the family home as a result of the testimony that children coughed up (rows in the family home, diet, reinforcement of sexual stereotypes, etc). Overall, the parent(s) were only a bit part in the agenda of the state when it came to children. Their importance was no greater than any other part (e.g., school, council, government agency). It was truly horrific.

your supervisor and colleagues, indicates from our modelling and predictions that things have gone awry and that your trajectory needs to be taken in a different direction.

'So, as you can see, Dr Campbell,' continued Jones smugly, 'the evidence suggests a dysfunctional developmental trajectory. It would seem that you could be at risk of further mental and physical ill-health if you do not receive treatment. You could be a danger to yourself, to others, and might need treatment in the future that could be avoided.'

Mallory then interjected with a more serious tone. 'You see, where we are at is this... taking into account all the evidence, from a counter extremist perspective, your actions from the past, the ideas you have espoused, have all been analysed and it seems it may be that you are at a tipping point, from pre-crime into crime. I mean, let's be frank, much of your activity is drenched in hate and extremism, which many would consider to already be actual hate crime and/or extremism. You are obviously in need of help. All the modelling suggests that, if we don't intervene now, you will have a very unhappy life. Do you have any questions?'

David sighed, rubbed his eyes, straightened himself up and slowly looked at both his interrogators in turn. He then looked upwards to the ceiling, almost as if he was about to appeal to God for strength for what he was about to say.

'Would a defence be of any use in this current situation?' he said. 'No. Would a breakdown of why I feel that I could justify my actions and explain them in their entirety lead you to see me in a different light? No. You see, I am well aware of the algorithm that you have fed my data into. It is black and white. The algorithm cannot assess the relative merits of a human life or the nuances of good and evil. Most importantly, it cannot know who created the programme and for what political ends it was designed for and for the people it was designated to condemn. The algorithm suits people like you, especially Ms Jones, the power-hungry types who would burn their grandmother to keep warm. You see, I have an algorithm; it's called a bullshit detector and I detect bullshit. Like most people do. But they are just too frightened. You see, this is the society that has been created. In the past, it used to be an economic disparity between rich and poor. But that was not a secure system. Poor people could get angry, organise and try to effect change. Nowadays, the disparity is between people who are allowed to say certain things, and those who are not. How can people rise up and fight against that? How can people rise up and speak the truth, if the state comes after your children as a first port of call in the pseudo anti-extremist bullshit?'

David paused for a moment, but the two people sat silent in front of him.

'So, you either buy into it, or get a boot in the face,' he continued. 'It's funny, there was a time in history when, if the state was feeding pornography to children, killing children in the womb for the reasons of sex selection, or just as a convenient form of contraception, for demonising the male sex, for telling children they can change sex, for feeding the population propaganda about climate emergencies, with no way of checking the validity of these claims... in another time, people would kick up a fuss. But not today. Parents stand, sheep-like, at the school gates scared to say a word, parents who dutifully go down to the medical centre to get vaccinated with shit and let their kids be diagnosed with invented disorders which necessitate medical intervention... psychotherapy, pills, even fucking castration or double mastectomies... for fuck's sake.'

David started crying, sobbing with his head in his hands, but quickly composed himself and looked up again at his interrogators. As he did so, he saw the utter glee and pleasure in the eyes of Ms Jones at what she was witnessing. She was getting 'off' on it.

'So, for what it is worth,' David continued, 'any questions I have will fall on deaf ears here, of that I am sure. But let me quote somebody, who lived in a different time, who was very wise and who saw all this coming.' David rummaged in the left pocket in his jeans for his wallet. He took it out and opened it. Inside was a small piece of paper. He took it out and unfolded it. David began to read from the piece of paper.

'I have spent all my life under a Communist regime, and I will tell you that a society without any objective legal scale is a terrible one indeed. But a society with no other scale but the legal one is not quite worthy of man either.'

He then folded the piece of paper and put it back into his wallet.

'That was,' David continued, 'from the great Russian author Alexander Solzhenitsyn, who lived under the oppression of

34

totalitarian communism. This was one of many of his warnings to the West. The West did not heed the warnings. So here we are now, in a room with two people obeying an algorithm designed to obliterate any notion of a human being, any appreciation of ethics, and any consideration of dialogue. And Ms Jones sitting there, with glee in her eyes befitting any psychopath, is well aware that all this boils down to power over the other, in a sadistic way, that benefits those who want to control others. It has nothing to do with social justice. It has all to do with the obliteration of human ethics towards the other, the complete opposite of the state-desired objective. So no, I have no questions. I refute what you are asserting. Conducting research about abuse in activist communities, chatting up women, objecting to pornography and gender mind fuck ideology, and not acting in desired ways as a child in school is not wrong, and it's not an indication of pre-crime or extremism. What is extremist is obeying an algorithm, or the output of computer modelling, designed by the state to shut people up and take away all the rights of defending themselves. The system excludes the idea of defence; one is only obliged to accept or perish. That is not justice or ethics. It's a double bind. It's abuse on a societal level and the bullies are in charge. Congratulations. You got me. Do what you fucking will.'

David stared at Mallory and Jones with utter contempt. His tears had dried up, but his rage lingered. Jones stared back. Mallory shuffled some papers and cleared his throat.

'It is our opinion at the Department of Work and Well-Being,' he began, 'all things being considered, that it would be best for you to enter our Personal, Social and Occupational Rehabilitation Scheme.[6] You will be sent to the Western Isles

---

[6] The Personal, Social and Occupational Rehabilitation Scheme (PSORS) was a venture created by the European Union and United Nations in 2025 as a result of the post-COVID-19 global financial collapse and the fabricated climate emergency policies. Due to high unemployment globally, lowering of wages and increased costs of living, many found themselves unable to work, earn money, pay rent or buy food. Homelessness was becoming a huge problem, as well as suicide (especially with men). Governments created a digitised universal basic income which functioned simultaneously as a social credit system and medical/well-being surveillance system. The PSORS scheme involved a myriad of work programmes whereby one would work on one of the

section to work on the protein farms. There, you will have all the occupational, social and psychological input to help you get back on track. Then, you can return home for two months, where we can review you and see if you can gain employment. So, we will take it from there. We can see you are in distress and in need of some immediate help, so you will stay with us for a couple of days until your departure date to the Luskentyre camp on the Western Isles. We will take care of your flat and fetch a suitcase with your clothes, etc. You have nothing to worry about. These people will take you down to your room now.'

The same two attendants who brought him to Mallory and Jones returned to the room. David felt light-headed, but managed to get up on his feet. He had not really been listening to what Mallory had been saying. His words sounded kind of distant and detached. David felt confused; so much so that he felt, at that very moment, that he might be going insane. This was the desired effect of this system. To drive people mad via menticide and a schizogenic social system. A crime against humanity. More words from Solzhenitsyn flooded his mind:

'It is almost always impossible to evaluate at the time events which you have already experienced, and to understand their meaning with the guidance of their effects. All the more unpredictable and surprising to us will be the course of future events.'

'Goodbye, Dr Campbell,' said Mallory, while Jones still sat with that smug look on her face.

---

government schemes, to be able to retain one's digitised universal basic income, and be housed (rent free, of course, usually in shared accommodation, barracks, or, if one was lucky, a self-contained flat, and have food provided for free). One would receive a small amount of money to be able to purchase essential items like clothes, toiletries, alcohol, drugs – all of which were rationed, of course. Usually, this would entail six months on, two months off, where you could return home for a period to see how you functioned back in society. One was closely monitored by the authorities. If you were unsuccessful at finding a job, which included most people, one would return to the work scheme. Some worked indefinitely on the schemes. These were the factories of the era.

David replied, 'I don't think you will meet me again. I will be gone, not of this world.'

David did not really know what he meant by the sentence, but he felt it sounded apt. He did not feel particularly suicidal, but he felt that a change was in the air that might precipitate an ending of some kind. Whether it was positive or negative, it was not clear. He did not have a clear head, so anything could be possible, including his own death. All he knew was that he was going down to the basement to the holding cells and he would be going on a trip to the Western Isles, which would be his new home for God only knew how long.

One of the attendants pointed towards the door to indicate that it was now time to exit the room. David turned around, facing the now open doorway and uttered to Jones and Mallory as he walked out, 'Not sure how you two can sleep at night, ruining people's lives for a living.'

David and his two attendants walked slowly down the long corridor to the elevator, which would take him down to the basement.

Chapter Five

Basement Dwellers

The short ride in the elevator down into the basement of the Department of Work and Well-Being was the logical conclusion to being a very small cog in the machine, or a faulty machine that needed to be sent away for repair. In the reified totalitarian atmosphere that Scotland had become, everything that was done to you, or everything that had happened to you (e.g., childhood and your experiences), was justified by the state, either because you needed help by the state or you never got the help that was needed by the state, but you need it now to rectify the situation, to fix the faulty machine. The linear line of process, from point A to point B in the Aristotelian sense, doused with the magic ingredient of causality propelling you from point A to point B, was the underlying logic of a 'risk preventative' state bureaucratic social policy method. Everyone, from the cradle to the grave, was seen through this reductive lens whereby any semblance of free will, personal volition, motivation, or desire was excluded. And, for the most part, the masses had willingly put on these anti-human chains a long time ago.

This 'philosophy' was drip fed into the masses over decades, with propaganda targeted at the children 'market', mental health, substance misuse, and crime. Children, parenting and childcare were targeted so as to undermine, first and foremost, the idea that a child 'belonged' to the parent; instead, the state was the most parental influence. The parent was regarded as just a convenient childminder and the state inculcated into people that this responsibility could be revoked at any time. The state had a list of hierarchies of childhood adversity (or prime causes) which led to children becoming faulty adults (e.g., divorced parents). Of course, divorce could cause a child discomfort; but, even before any 'damage' was shown or any problems became apparent, the state would intervene and 'rectify' the situation (e.g., take the child off the parents and place them in a foster home). The sinister reasoning was only one of a myriad of ways to undermine the role of the parents in society. The excuse used by the state was that this was for the 'greater good'.

Mental health propaganda was also drip fed into the minds of children and adults constantly for decades. Ordinary

38

human existence, thoughts and emotions had been pathologised and taught to be feared. In schools, children were taught to obsess over their anxieties – for, if they did not, their anxieties would hurtle out of control and overwhelm them. The same logic was applied to other human emotions, such as sadness, boredom, excitement, panic, fear, etc. The same ideas were targeted at adults. There were signs, in the very early 21st century, that adults were obsessively observing their 'self' and their emotions and thoughts in a way never before seen in human history. This became apparent in universities, whereby certain texts were banned as they might upset students (i.e., trigger them), university counselling centres were flooded by students who could not handle their emotions or moods, and certain guest speakers and topics were banned from campuses for fear of upsetting people, or were demanded to be shut down by students as the topic or speaker upset them. In 2050, approximately seven out of ten adults and children, at any one time, were taking some form of psychiatric medication such as anti-depressants, anti-anxiety or anti-psychotic medication. Children and adults were indoctrinated into becoming perpetual victims in need of assistance from the state as they could not handle ordinary human existence.

The same ideas were integrated into the notions of substance misuse. Problematic drug use was attributed solely to childhood trauma. Any link to the prevailing culture of hedonism, which the state encouraged via hyper-sexuality, gender bending, the music culture and media, all encouraged a person to 'be free'. Sexual liberation and hedonism became the new religion. When this failed to 'hit the spot' and satisfy the existential need of a person, there was nothing to fall back onto, except more drugs, prescription drugs, therapy, and leaning on the state for a solution; the state had created the problem of victims and victimhood and the state became the solution. The prevailing ideas of mental health and substance misuse, whereby difficult human emotions and thoughts were automatically pathological, and drug use, which alleviated the existential malaise (that was induced by a reductive mindset where people could not deal with emotions and thoughts), made people feel that every negative experience from childhood and adulthood was pathological. When a drug user started experiencing feelings of difficulty (when not using drugs), automatically their existential response was to put it down to illness, created in childhood trauma, and thus were in need of treatment. The state had created the perfect victim and perfect prisoner. The state did not direct the masses to the idea of humans as existential beings, where the innumerable emotional and cognitive experiences of being a human could be seen as ordinary, commonplace and necessary for a fully functioning human being.

Indeed, this is why, over many decades, religion was gradually denigrated for being a regressive, conservative and backward facet of the human race. The state knew that the inherent wisdoms in Christian religious thought, the necessity of difficult experiences, the wisdoms of the 'dark night of the soul', would direct people to an opposing insight into human existence whereby they would be freed from their chains of victimhood. The state could not let this be. Religion and religious thought were, therefore, seen as subversive and threatening to the status quo. Hence, in 2050, religious thought was suppressed, banished and just barely tolerated, with a thin inauthentic veneer of 'tolerance'. Religion, for the most part, had been driven underground and was tolerated as a historical oddity practised by mentally ill people. But the state kept a watchful eye.

Exiting the elevator, David entered a bare room with windows that had bars on them, and a counter with a tray filled with some toiletries and a towel. A man was standing behind the counter. The man beckoned David to him. David stepped forward, still accompanied by his two attendants. The man, in his late 40s, had a name tag stating:

Calum Short
Holding Facility: Transfer Manager

'Dr Campbell,' Short began. 'You will be held here until your transfer to the Western Isles. All your needs will be taken care of. Here is a pen and paper. Please list all your belongings that you wish to be picked up and collected at your apartment. You will be given a receipt for all belongings to check. On your return, you can take an inventory at your apartment to verify everything is in order and nothing is missing.'

Short smiled to himself and David took the pen and paper.

He continued. 'Now, please give us the electronic key for your apartment and we shall see that your requested items are brought to us here before your departure. You are allowed a

40

maximum of twenty kilograms. We prefer no material relating to religious or spiritual issues, but we will not object to one or two books. The reason being that, during your placement, you will be receiving intensive individual and group self-development and growth. Our programme providers suggest as a matter of course that spiritual and/or religious ideas may confuse things, or get in the way of truly getting a benefit from the courses available. It's only a suggestion, of course, but highly recommended, as people find their progress is severely hindered by indulging in materials which deviate from the course materials. The outcome of one's progress, for example when somebody returns home for societal re-integration, or gets holiday leave before a return to their placement, or indefinite placement assignment, is entirely up to the participant and his progress. Many people end up returning home for good after a year or so – those that have participated fully, that is. Please take this tray with some toiletries and a towel.'

The chilling words from Short echoed in David's brain. What was being described to him in the most 'kindest of ways' was that, in order to participate fully in the 'programme' which he was now being inserted into, he was to give up any dissenting ideas. If he did not, then his stay at the placement might be ongoing, or indefinite. This scenario was like a prison guard telling a prisoner, 'Here is the key… you can take it if you want and leave the cell, but you must believe this "truth" about the world, as the "truth" will set you free. The choice is yours.' Two and two must make five.

'Ok,' David mumbled.

'These two attendants will take you to your room, which has an en-suite facility,' said Short. 'Please take your tray. There is also a public games room and televisual entertainment room if you wish some down time. You can also use the gym and swimming pool. We hope your short stay here is comfortable before your transfer to the Western Isles.' He spoke as though it was some script that he spouted many times per day.

The two attendants indicated to David to walk with them towards a door which led, yet again, to a long, brightly lit corridor with many doors with numbers on them. They stopped at room number 37. One of the attendants gave David an electronic key to open the door. He inserted it into the slot and the door swung gently open. The attendants wished him good day.

41

David's room had a single bed with a desk and tabletop lamp, chair, and a small wardrobe with coat hangers. There was a small en-suite wet room with shower, sink and toilet. A small fridge contained some water, sparkling and still, milk, orange juice and tomato juice. Next to the fridge was a small table with a kettle, cups, tea and coffee. On the desk was an electronic menu for meals: breakfast, lunch and dinner. David was instructed from the menu to tick his choices for meals and press enter; his choices would be sent directly to the kitchen. Meals would be brought to his room. There was a television monitor above the desk where he could access the internet and television channels. There was no phone, and his own phone could not receive a signal in this building. The window was small, with six vertical bars on the outside. It was quite dark in the room as this level was in the basement. Light tunnels funnelled light from the upper levels into the room.

David filled out his food request. It was almost 10.45 am, and lunch was served at 1 pm. He chose the vegetable soup and cheese savoury sandwich and apple pie. For dinner, he ticked the option for quiche, baked potato and salad; for breakfast, cereal and toast. He pressed enter, sat on the bed, and stared at the ground. Then, for the first time in a long time, he caught himself thinking longingly about his two children. Tears welled up in his eyes and he crawled up on the bed and sobbed into the pillow. He felt broken, helpless and condemned. A free man in a world where one could only be really free if one followed the state-ordained truth.

He lost track of time crying his lonely, anguish-ridden tears. However, for a while, he must have fallen asleep as he was suddenly roused by a knock at his door and a shout of 'Lunch'. David gathered himself and opened the door. There was a young woman with a tray with his lunch, and also a male, who looked like a nurse.

'May we come in, please?' the nurse asked.

David waved them inside, where the young woman put his lunch on the table.

'We observed you were crying,' said the nurse. 'We are concerned for your well-being. Is there anything we can do to help? We realise it is a shock to the system to be here and have your life changed in such a short space of time, but we have medication to soften the blow. Would you like some medicine, to help you out?'

42

'No, thank you,' replied David. 'I am quite fine. It is just a shock, that is all. I am quite fine, really.'

'Ok,' replied the nurse, 'but we will keep an eye on you. We have heard that you may be moved in less than twenty-four hours, but we will see. If you need us, press the buzzer on the communication panel on your headrest on the bed.' And, with that, the nurse and young woman left his room.

Fuck, David thought. *They can even watch me crying on my bed. Is nothing sacrosanct!* This was nothing less than a panopticon, as described by the 20th century philosopher Michel Foucault.

Chapter Six

Basement Panopticon

Three days in the basement of the Department of Work and Well-Being, living in a small room in the middle of a long corridor, where the corridor led to a labyrinth of basement sections containing a gym, a swimming pool, TV lounge, etc, may sound quite relaxing. However, in the Basement Panopticon, one was always accompanied by a sense of being watched by the constant cameras dotted around the basement and in one's room. A sense of freedom was kept far from one's mind.

The loneliness was also a strange encounter. The only people David and the other basement dwellers saw were the kitchen staff who delivered the meals to people's rooms, and the occasional visit from a sickly, though nice, staff member who would ask him how he was feeling today. David received a daily visit from a psychiatrist, who would try to convince him that he was 'mentally ill' in some way or another, that he needed some 'help' and that there were ways 'they' could help him be lifted out his malaise. Nothing he said to this psychiatrist hit the spot. It was like speaking to a brick wall, a computer. The psychiatrist just spouted out an algorithmic answer in response to David's protestations that he was alright:

'Mmm… you sound distressed. We could give you some medication.'

'Looking at your records, you may have unresolved trauma.'

'Perhaps we can help you reformulate your past trauma to help you have more insight and meaning.'

'It's ok to feel sad and to want to cry… Often, as men we feel we should not cry, but gender is fluid and men can and should be vulnerable and cry.'

Etc *ad finitum*.

This barrage of inane pop psychology did not stop at the daily visits. David also received audio communication in his room from various people, day and night. These messages often woke him up from his sleep. David felt that they were trying to slowly drive him insane with sickly sweet 'kindness' and trying to brainwash him into believing he was sick.

44

He encountered two other 'residents' in the basement; two men, in their mid-30s, from what used to be Syria (before the Western nations had bombed the fuck out of it during the civil war). They had come over to Scotland to be resettled as part of the great immigration crisis, which took off big time around 2015. They were nice chaps. David met them in the TV lounge. Their English was not bad, and they laughed together while watching some stupid celebrity reality show nonsense. They joked that the TV company should come to the basement to film them.

David gathered from his conversations with them that both their families had been killed in Syria and they had relocated to Scotland as children. They had been adopted by two Syrian families who were already settled in Scotland. Both were unmarried and had worked on the public transport network before being brought in on 'charges' of harassment. This involved speaking to white women in a nightclub. They (Rahim and Abdul) had been out drinking together and decided to go to one of the city's top nightspots, 'The Celestial Hedonist', located in Glasgow city centre, just off Sauchiehall Street. They had just bought their drinks and were standing at the bar, when two white women approached them. Both the women were drunk and asked the two men if they would buy them a drink. Rahim obliged. Two vodka and cokes. Rahim and Abdul and the two women chatted away for a few minutes, discussing where they were from and what they did.

After the first round of drinks had been consumed, the women asked if the men could buy them another. Rahim explained that he was a bit skint until payday, so could not oblige by buying another drink. Abdul repeated the sentiments. The two women suddenly turned; the men were subjected to a torrent of verbal abuse, which included racial slurs. Then, one of the women grabbed Abdul's glass and smashed it over his head. Luckily, Abdul suffered only minor cuts to his head. Abdul and Rahim then grabbed both the girls – who, by this time, were attacking them bodily by throwing punches and screaming and trying to bite them. The two men managed to wrestle them to the floor and they shouted to the barman to get security. When security arrived, the women screamed that they were the victims and said that the men were lewd, and they had asked them for sex in return for buying them a drink.

The police were called, statements were taken, and Abdul and Rahim were taken to the local police station. The two women were allowed to go home. Abdul and Rahim were given the choice of criminal charges of 'harassment' or social re-education with a work placement provided through the Department of Work and Well-Being. Of course, they chose what they thought would be the lesser of two evils. The sentence would probably have been the same, either way; six months or more in the Western Isles to wise up, get with the programme, or spend repeated six-month blocks far away from home. This was social justice 2050 style. After decades of feminist propaganda, anti-men/boy propaganda, indoctrination in schools and society at large, even men approaching women in public places could be deemed as sexual harassment.

David had plenty of time to ponder his past, present and future in the basement. The past and how he got to the present seemed like a blur. It was like he had not been fully aware, that he had been aimlessly floating through life without realising the seriousness of life, and now it felt too late, that he had missed the boat and he was a condemned man. And then the future? That was unknown. He had a vague idea of what the work placement would involve: work, education, psychosocial work, sent back home, then see how it goes. If he was not 'reformed', he would have to do another stint. It was (officially) not seen as punishment or anything to be ashamed of; but, in reality, there was great social shaming associated with being engaged in the work/re-education placement scheme.

It was all part of the state's plan to nurture good citizens. Everything was presented by the state on the plate of altruism, coupled with the threat of shame. It was a big double bind. If you did not conform, the re-education and work placements would go on and on, indefinitely. It was an open-air societal prison; there was no escape, as there was nowhere to escape to. It was the perfect prison; a prison whereby one, eventually, willingly placed the chains on oneself. There were certain pleasures and rewards for putting the chains on, for example drugs, meaningless sex, mind-numbing social media, financial rewards for towing the line (bonuses at work for not stepping out of line). But there was no nirvana at the end of it. The sameness of existence just went on until one died. One was just a cog in the machine. Meaninglessness.

The sense of meaninglessness infiltrated David's mind during the time he spent in the basement. It offered him time to think about the many memories over the years, to daydream, to ponder and to think. He made a concerted effort to recall in a way that was like a biography and commit it to memory. He felt it was an important task. People had ceased to remember their past, history, culture and identity. The state operated solely on the present for the idolised dystopian future.

David started to remember…

Chapter Seven

Memories

....*my father. He had taught me so much. Imparted so much wisdom and wise words. He was my companion, my guide, my mentor. He was a gentle man, who was not afraid of being utterly maternal in his care for me and my brother. He did not see it as a feminine quality, but, in actuality, a real masculine quality. My mother told me that, when I was born, after they brought me back from the hospital, he slept with me on his chest all that first night, sitting up in bed holding me, only handing me to my mother when I needed to be fed. He was protective and my mother told me that if anybody had come near me with malice, my father would have fought to the death to protect me. He would have volunteered himself for death to save my brother and I. I always marvelled at such preparedness for death. As a child, death scared me. The thought of it terrified me!*

My father told me that, when one is born, one is born into death, dying. What tragedy! Of course, death is usually far from the mind of a child. The endless possibilities of existence seem such a promising and infinite joy to come, that death is usually far from the minds of children. Well, of course it is, but as an adult the reality of the facts of life and death become very apparent. Before I was born, my father had been ill and rushed to hospital with a vicious viral condition (pericarditis), where his heart lining was so infected it stopped his heart beating. He recalled to me how he became 'conscious' during this period, and saw his body on the hospital bed and the doctors and nurses furiously trying to get his heart to start circulating blood around his body. He realised he was dying, but was not sad. He was only sad that the people he would be leaving behind, his parents, his brothers, would be sad. But he so wanted to impart to them not to be sad. He was at peace.

He told me how he had travelled out of the hospital ward, where his body lay, into a corridor and out through the ceiling, into a dark tunnel towards a light. He said he was willing and ready and off he flew. Off he flew he did, and up the dark corridor to a great light. Once in the light, bodiless, he was part of the light. He realised where he was and felt compelled to ask the big question to the big Man! He asked God, 'What is life all about?' Not in human language, of course; human language did not exist in such a place. The response was immediate and utterly simple, yet utterly complex all at the same time. The profundity of what was said was difficult to convey in human terms, and my father often had difficulty trying to get me or other people to understand. The message from God was 'Love'. In that moment, my father

48

knew, really knew, what he, God, meant. The message of 'Love' utterly and completely transcended the human language conception of love. It encompassed a supernatural ethics that was an antidote to human folly, human passions and human evil, that delivered man from his fallen state. It was a love which was sent to the world in the guise of Jesus Christ.

I remember when my father recounted this tale to other people, which he did not do very often, often prompted by somebody else, to his great reticence and embarrassment. He sensed the unbelief and/or the growing bemusement of his listener. He would often wink at me when he told the story, as a kind of secret code that he knew. I knew what he meant and the dumb person he was telling was not ready, or was unable, to really understand what he was saying. But, of course, I sometimes doubted whether I could understand my dad's wonderful, exotic, supernatural tale.

He was fond of reciting passages from the Bible to illustrate how human reasoning only took our sense of existence only so far, and that true understanding came from our heart, not our minds:

And he said, The Things which are impossible with men are possible with God. (Luke 18:27)

For this commandment which I command thee this day, it is not hidden from thee, neither is it far off. It is not in heaven, that thou shouldest say, Who shall go up for us to heaven, and bring it unto us, that we may hear it, and do it? Neither is it beyond the sea, that thou shouldest say, Who shall go over the sea for us, and bring it unto us, that we may hear it, and do it? But the word is very nigh unto thee, in thy mouth, and in thy heart, that thou mayest do it. (Deuteronomy 30: 11-14)

But this tale of my dad exemplified his eccentric nature and character. He was not one to follow the herd, to submit to the mass or deviate from his convictions. He was a man who was well travelled, geographically and psychically. He had studied psychology, Buddhism (Zen, Tibetan), Sufism, Shamanism, Marxism/Socialism/Communism, Anarchism, Continental philosophy, postmodernism… the list goes on. He had even been a member of political parties and secret underground Socialist/Activist organisations. This had all been an education to him. Valuable in some ways, a smokescreen in others. He felt that his own education had been some kind of subtle indoctrination, whereby the fabric of his own reality had been pulled over by a smokescreen of deception which blinded one to really thinking… I mean, really thinking, or beginning to think in the sense that the German philosopher Martin Heidegger was wont to argue.

My father told me, and as I later read from one of his books from his vast library, that thinking, as Heidegger argued, is in the first place not what we call having an opinion or a notion. Thinking is not even the notion of representing or having an idea about something or a state of affairs. Further, thinking is not ratiocination or developing a chain of premises which lead to an effective deduction. Thinking, for Heidegger, was not a method in the way that one uses to build up a preliminary body of doctrine after deconstructing earlier doctrines. Questioning was, rather, a way of thinking that a person must clear the path himself; there is no clear destination in mind. Heidegger likened it to making a path in the fresh snow with skies. Questioning and thinking are not a means to an end; they justify being as praxis, for the sake of being itself. The praxis of being, doing and activity for the sake of the activity, about which my father droned on many a time, contra the idea of process (i.e., in the Aristotelian sense, getting from point A to point B) was something that the modern world had forgotten, was in the process (literally in process, rather than praxis) of forgetting, destroying, covering up, putting down the memory hole like in George Orwell's famous novel '1984', where history was rewritten.

My father was, amongst other things, also a trained psychoanalyst. Another profession that had been obliterated by totalitarian state technological 'advancements'. Freud's golden rule, or free association, of speaking what comes into one's head, had been long condemned as politically incorrect, and a waste of time. People had been reared to be constant censors of their every thought, to double-check before speaking. Essentially, a psychic prison, a prison with no walls, no bars, imposed on people themselves. Anyway, my father told me many stories about his experiences of psychoanalysis, which were fascinating. Much richer than cognitive-behaviourist 'Nudge'[7] social policy-engineered treatments for the masses. He told me of a dream he had while in analysis. It was so rich, terrifying, and completely unbelievable; one would never think such a reality would come to be. A quite nightmarish scenario.

My father was in analysis with an elderly English gentleman. Harrow educated, Cambridge, the real deal, the full works, a real wisecracker who did, indeed, deviate from the norm and did not give a fuck… Sadly, one of a dying breed. He was 'one of the last', as my father used to sadly say, his voice

---

[7] A sinister organisation called the 'Behavioural Insights Team' (BIT), also known unofficially as the 'Nudge Unit', which was in operation around the 2000s onwards. It was a social purpose organisation that generated and applied behavioural insights to inform policy and improve public services. BIT worked in partnership with governments, local authorities, non-profits, and businesses to tackle major policy problems.

trailing down to a whisper with his head bowed down, holding in the tears. This old analyst, I was told, cleared the fog of confusion and the lure of inauthenticity. He basically gouged out your bullshit and narcissism and presented it to you on a plate. Painful, but well worth the effort. Like all confessions, repentance, real repentance, is a necessary road to travel. Not many travel this road nowadays.

Anyhow, in this dream, my father's analyst was sitting in his old armchair in his consulting room, but it was at the end of a railway track on a platform in London – Marylebone station, I think. He was dying. He was one of a dying breed, being pushed out, forgotten, thrown on the trash pile for the sake of this Brave New World. At the end of this track, there was not the station, but a bland, concrete jungle of high-rise buildings, a grey sky, no sun, no grass or trees. People were walking around like drones with dead eyes, with no hint or glint of humanity in their eyes. The people did not even see my father, acknowledge him or the elderly analyst sitting in his battered old armchair. My father's soul wept at the death of mankind, the end of days, and he sank to his knees and cried. On his knees, on the concrete ground, big tears dropping onto the concrete ground, he noticed a crack in the concrete. In this crack was what looked like soil. 'Actual soil!' he thought in surprise. Even more surprising was that, within this crack, a few small blades of grass were growing and shooting up and searching for life. My father realised then that all was not lost, that there always was a way and that the spirt, or soul, whatever you wanted to call it, would always find a way.

Another experience which he recounted to me, when I was 17 or 18, was from his first analysis. It was with a woman, who also bore him rich ripe fruit which defied quantification of the algorithm, or manualised 'psychotherapeutic' treatment – although, to be fair, he feared she did not realise her effects, beyond the analyst's persona, gaze, theory or role. Never mind, many psycho-technicians, especially of the modern age, don't see beyond these handicaps, either.

My father's experience of this analysis that he recounted to me was approximately after one year that he had been having sessions with her. She invited him to lie on the couch, rather than sit in the armchair facing her. He immediately obliged, but was nervous, shit scared. He felt vulnerable, exposed, ashamed, pathetic. But he forced himself. He found himself lying there, alternating between euphoria, tears of sadness, being uncomfortable, shy, and feeling completely at one with himself, not having experienced himself like that ever in his life – apart, perhaps, from when he was a child. He then 'let go' and the couch became a safe haven, a womb. He could lie there, three times a week for fifty minutes, and drift and then become animated, and cry, and laugh. It was truly liberating and it was a re-education of what it was to be a *human. But this was not the end. Nearing three years of analysis with his analyst, as he lay on the couch, opposite the big bay window of her consulting room, he was looking at the big oak tree, which he could see from his position on the couch. He realised that he had seen that tree in all the four seasons: spring, summer, autumn and winter. He had seen it shooting buds in spring, full bloom in summer, shedding its leaves in autumn and bare in winter. This was now winter. It was a stormy day outside. The rain was lashing down and the wind was howling. That old tree was just swaying in the wind, solid in the ground because of it deep roots, but able to take the vicissitudes of its existence, stoic in its existence, and unashamed in its state or trials.*

In that moment of looking at the tree and becoming aware of it in all these details, my father's eyes welled up with tears. The tree, the world and my father… there was something far bigger going on that he could not imagine, or really articulate. From some religious writings, some would say that he had been opened up to the holy spirit; from my father's description of the experience, it certainly felt like something in that realm. He knew, in that moment, that he would be ok, that he would never in his life need to fear the black dog of depression, or that he never needed to feel ashamed of who he was. It was a revelation to him. He told his analyst what he was experiencing, but she did not get it. She just wittered off some psychoanalytic bullshit that being distracted by the outside was an escape from the negative transference that my father had towards her. That was ok. He could even forgive her in that moment. He even felt that he loved her in that moment, even in her imperfections of being unable to 'meet' him in this poignant moment that he was experiencing. That was ok. He supposed that, too, was a healing, being able to deal with the ambivalent feelings!

Yes, my father was indeed interesting, to say the least. He regarded his family, me, my younger brother and our mum, as his church. He regarded the family as a cornerstone of society and culture. It was something to be defended, cherished, fought for, and for the rights of parents to be held as invaluable. But, in his time, as he described to me, when I was just a child, global movements, very sinister in nature, were in operation to change the nature of parents, family, to bring them under a more totalitarian state control system.

When I was a young child, there was already ongoing a huge drive by the UK and Scottish governments for queer theory and gender/transgender ideology to be taught in schools. To children. It came from the globalist/United Nations drive for population reduction, population movement, to deconstruct nations and nationhood, to dilute cultures, including the family. It was a concerted attack on the idea of biological parenthood, or the necessity or importance for a child to have its biological parents as parents; the state could do that and any old Tom, Dick and Harry (or Sue, and Annie) could be the parent of a child, a child incubated in a stranger's womb, then sold to the highest bidder, or through sperm donation, egg implantation, etc. The whole state philosophy was a battle against heteronormativity in all its guises.

The most sinister aspect of queer theory was its disdain for reproductive futurism; to change society, so that childrearing within a family context and child reproduction itself was being engineered out of daily existential reality. The reality that was being engineered was one of people living alone, having sterile, transient sexual 'meetings'; sex as a hobby, sex as just for pleasure, sex as a human right. People lived and moved where they could get work; family and cultural networks dissolved; allegiances to history or nation became meaningless, and individuals just functioned as worker drones and sexual/hedonistic creatures. That was my father's (and many like him) take on it. And it has indeed become so by 2050.

My father told me the story of how he challenged this zeitgeist. He challenged the schools for the queer theory clubs promoting anti-reproductive futurism. He wrote articles for non-mainstream media news outlets discussing what went on in schools and society at large. He caught a lot of flak, from colleagues, friends and even family. They could not hear, or bear to hear, what was occurring to their society.

He gave an example of how the world was changing like this when he described to me and my younger brother, when we were old enough to understand, how the local nursery became an indoctrination centre. My mother and father took my younger brother when he was 3 years old for a visit to one of the local nurseries. When they arrived, the nursery manager, a lady, enquired as to who my parents were (in relation to my brother). My father, slightly puzzled (as they had informed the nursery that they were coming), replied that they were the parents. The manager replied, 'Oh, we have to check as we have such diverse family structures these days.' My father replied, 'Well, I am his father, a man, and this is his mother. A woman. And this is our son, a boy.' Her response was priceless. She said, 'Well, just to let you know, we are very LGBT friendly here.'

When recounting this tale, he always shook his head in utter disbelief when he described the manager's comments. He would shout and swear and exclaim, 'How the fuck can nursery-age children be LGBT? How the hell can adult staff be LGBT friendly in relation to nursery care of children?' Of course, my father was correct. It was the imposition of adult experience, behaviour and lifestyle on children who were unable to understand such things. In effect, it was state-enforced indoctrination and grooming for a life where children were primed through education to pursue the state's agenda on what an adult human should be, how to act, live, and what to believe.

This was a great tragedy carried out by gross interference from the state. My father explained how United Nations directives, which were revved up during the turn of the millennium after the year 2000, were all-consuming attempts to disrupt the sacred bond between a child and his or her parents. Separation from the parents, psychically, was dressed-up child human rights. Every policy subtly had a slimy predatory underbelly, which insinuated that anybody could be a good parent to a child, no matter the biological link. Indeed, the importance of a biological link was so underemphasised that many people began to feel that the state was becoming predatory, and one had to keep a watch out for the state trying to intervene in a negative way.

My father recalled to me how state schooling was an obvious start, where the great schism between parents and their children was enacted. Child human rights, of autonomy and well-being, were inculcated into children from nursery age. Minor physical chastisement (a smack on the bottom) was outlawed. Not that hitting children is necessarily a positive thing, but it was twisted so that any 'control' over one's child was deemed as affecting the well-being of the child and, therefore, the parent was deemed as an abuser of human rights. The state was right, the child was right, and the parent was an abuser. My parents did not use physical punishments on us. They did not agree with hitting children, but they did not agree with the idea of turning parents into criminals for a smack on the bottom. Such a law was just a ruse to get at the parents and to undermine them.

My father and mother used to sit at our kitchen table in our little country cottage where we lived and debate the issues of the day, especially when it came to parenting. I remember my father discussing the underhand 'ethical' dummy pass (the 'no hitting children' law), and the state's 'logical next step' on the issue of parenting and the rights of parents (or, who the state deemed could be a parent) in the early 2000s. My father described this as being so far stretched beyond laws of logic, that some very strange things became tolerated and normalised which came under the umbrella of parenting, or the possibility of being a parent.

One such development that became tolerated and normalised was the idea that one biological part of the dyad of parents was not even being considered an important factor in the human right of the child. This was an astounding development. One female lesbian politician announced to the world that she thought it was a good idea to encourage more fatherless children. In other words, a variety of different 'parenting set-ups' were actively encouraged, whereby the adult's desire or want for a child overruled the biological necessity of parenting; that, having a biological mum and dad was not an important issue. Consequently, same-sex parenting (e.g., two men or two women) were actively promoted by the state via propaganda. Of course, two men or two women may well have been kind, caring and able to raise children, but this set-up omits the glaring question of the right of the child; the right to be brought up by, know and have, both of his biological parentage. Research showed that children from adopted parenting set-ups and same-sex parenting set-ups developed a nagging longing to know where they came from and who they were; adopted parenting, single mothers/fathers or same-sex upbringing, where one biological parent was missing for some reason, introduced a lack that could never be filled.

Politicians, celebrities, social commenters all celebrated and encouraged the idea of more children being brought up in fatherless or motherless situations, even though the research showed that, outside a biological mum and dad parenting set-up (especially boys without fathers), children were more likely to have 'mental health' problems, substance misuse problems, criminal activity in adulthood, suicide, etc. Not only that, children brought up in same-sex couplings were more likely to experience and witness domestic violence, substance misuse, promiscuity amongst parents, and the relationship breakdown of the parenting coupling. So, it was clear, the risks outside a traditional biological parenting set-up (a man and a woman) were higher. A biological parenting couple, especially if they were married, was the gold standard of parenting and of child welfare. But the state did not promote this. It denigrated this set-up via numerous policies and constant propaganda. The state hated this idea.

The macabre narcissism which infused the desire to be a parent, forgetting the right of the child to know, and preferably know and live with, both his/her biological parents, was essentially the commodification of children; it was nothing really to do with helping people become parents. The state did not care who the parent was, as long as the child belonged to the state. Even the LGBT lobby was duped by the state on this issue. This facet of the issue was lost on the left of the political spectrum, which was infected with the politics of political correctness and identity politics. Of course, as my father reiterated on almost every occasion when he talked about these issues, if one voiced opposition regarding the stretched definition of parents, one was attacked as being a bigot, homophobe, a Nazi, etc. But he always returned to the point of the right of the child – which was to be able, if at all possible, to have, to know and to be reared by, both their biological parents. My father was well aware of instances of single parents, parents who adopted, and same-sex parenting set-ups which were indeed loving, caring and nurturing, and sometimes life circumstances dealt this card, but he always returned to the child and the right of his or her roots and parentage. It was something to be cherished, fought for and, where possible, should be the default position where possible. The reason he argued this was because he saw in the deviation and the stretching of the definitions of parenting, darker and more sinister motivations; the rise of designer babies through DNA and other technological advances, rearing children in artificial wombs in laboratories, children becoming commodities for those who could afford them (e.g., the fees for surrogacy, medical costs, child sales from medical or other establishments). If parenting was a free-for-all, ethically and technologically, then children would not belong to anybody and the society as we knew it would dissolve into a society of atomised individuals with no connection to anybody else. Family, culture and community, as realities taken for granted in the good old days, would just become some strange phenomena that were a little bit romantic and definitely contra freedom, liberty and the Brave New World. By 2050, my father's warnings had come pretty much true.

In 2050, only 15 per cent of people were married or in co-habiting relationships. Polyamory and open relationships (same-sex and heterosexual) were very popular amongst the 20-50 year-olds. Singledom was the destiny for many people after the age of 50 when reproductive potential was past its best-before date. Indeed, people in polyamorous living arrangements often lived alone and house hopped. No worries, though, as they had the state hedonistic/pleasure dictates to guide them in their course of life. There was no real need for parents; in 2050, there were 'fantastic' childcare facilities provided by the state. From early morning to night, children just out the womb (or laboratory womb – a plastic bag functioning as an artificial womb) could be cared for by a plethora of carers. Childcare even extended to overnight services so that 'parents' could go out and 'party'. In 2050, individual, hedonistic pleasure would not be disrupted even for a child. Getting wasted on the wide variety of psychoactive substances that were freely available and meeting fellow revellers for orgasms would not be interrupted by children. God forbid! The value of children, the cherishing of them, their vulnerability – their very souls – were nothing. This became the reality in 2050. My father warned me that this time could possibly come.

He recounted the legalisation of abortion even up to the moment of birth – another ghoulish development that occurred in the early 2020s. The cry from fourth-wave feminists, which became increasingly loud after the turn of the second millennium, disregarded the importance of the right of the child in the womb. Indeed, the great abortion referendum of Ireland in 2018, which resulted in abortion being legalised, was noted for the ecstatic shrieking celebrations for the right to kill children. These were dark days.

But, of course, human nature is very unlikely to be supressed completely. Discontents and malcontents are always liable to surface in any society when the state tries to control biological nature. That is why you have to give free rein to such a society and their narcissistic desires, their search for pleasure and hedonistic outlets, and selfish demands. This is why so many people willingly put on the chains of oppression rather than contend with the *reality of existence and challenges of daily life, including biological and material reality. And, of course, with the state allowing this, it hollowed out the spiritual nature of man so that he (or she) became just a husk, a walking dead person with little thought of the ramifications of his actions, on his being, or his very soul. The state was in league with the demons, the devil. So were many people; but many did not even realise it. Some, however, did know this was the case.*

So here I was, in the basement of the Department of Work and Well-Being, a husk of a man that had lost his children, his wife and his job all through the madness of the state. I had now become a commodity for the state, standing reserve for the government's apparatus. I had no choice, and no real liberty in the situation; refusal would simply make things difficult and the 'treatment' more prolonged. I was going to be healed by the state, nurtured and moulded by the powers that be, to become more the man they wanted me to be, as that was the correct way; any protestations would be regarded as a sign of illness in need of a cure. For a quiet life, many just went along with it and lived out their life until their insignificant death. But the state did not bank on the human capabilities for searching out meaning to nullify insignificance. Everybody knew, deep down, that the existential sense of meaning was there; it haunted one in the night when lying in bed, unable to sleep, or when dragging oneself to work and seeing somebody in trouble (a homeless person) whom the state had decided to leave alone to die in misery.

Most especially, meaningfulness came to one in dreams; images and pictures of what seemed like past times (or perhaps an imagined time), where families sat together round the table, laughing and rallying together in this thing called life. Pretty countryside vistas, with trees and hills, helping a child climb to the top of a rocky summit to see the view, or jumping into the sea on a frothy, choppy day, where the waves swept you back on a crest of a wave and a cacophony of innocent joyful laughter. These human moments were slowly erased from the consciousness of people over many decades to be replaced by a grey, grim emptiness, where mere survival and a hedonistic 'hit' were all that people lived for. We had fallen from grace for sure. But humans had suffered similar fates in other times, so perhaps there could be a possibility for redemption? Or had the globalist state mindset simply refined and improved on previous failures to gain a better grip on any resistance, or at least contain it?

There were rumours, or myths, of people or peoples who slipped through the net, who lived as dissidents, freely, who could not be contained. I had never met one… yet. The genie was out of the box. It could never be put back in; I realised that from the help of my father. Much of the cultural conditioning had not brainwashed me, which had led me to question and, latterly, challenge the status quo of cultural state indoctrination. It led to me losing my wife and children, and it led to me losing my job; and now, sitting in

57

the basement of the Department of Work and Well-Being, it was leading me to some godforsaken prison island to atone for my sins. Had it been worth it? Was it preferable to be living, half dead, conforming to the state dictates of the time? Or was it a blessing in disguise that the game was up and I was free to be who I was, in exile, indefinitely, if I did not shape up and start towing the party line? I could not come up with a definite conclusion; this was still a work in progress, as is often the case. The only thing I was sure of was that a trip on a boat to the Western Isles would be a welcome relief and change to this sterile holding cell. I was at least open to the experience of going into the unknown, my parents had taught me that. The state could never take that away from me.

The great irony or synchronicity in all of this was that I was being sent to the Western Isles, the Outer Hebrides; the Luskentyre camp. Ironic because, my parents, before I was born, went to the Western Isles on their honeymoon in an old VW campervan. They drove from South to North. In those days, the islands were a veritable paradise on Earth; clean air, sea breeze, mountains, deserted beaches, and a sense of freedom that had long since been eroded out of existence. They stopped and wild camped on many beaches – one of them was the beach at Luskentyre. My parents raved wildly about the two days they spent sitting by the beach, under a clear night sky where they watched the stars, discussing the future, their dreams, of raising children.

It was as remote and peaceful as could be. My parents cooked their meals on the little gas stove in the van, drank red wine and smoked cigarettes and were blissfully happy and in love. Life could not have gotten any better. They had always encouraged my brother and I to visit there, but as the years went by the whole of the Western Isles changed greatly, with the development of wind and wave farms and protein/grub/insect farms, with what became known as the Highland and Island clearances of the 21st century. Globalist directives and government policies gradually made it so that people were herded out of the rural areas into huge metropolitan areas for work. It was made impossible for most people to sustain a living of any kind in rural areas. Those who managed to escape resettlement lived a harsh existence, but the stories I heard were that they could live relatively free from the tentacles of the state, as long as they did not create too much of a problem. These people were essentially like those in the old USSR, living in eternal exile.

So, the irony of ironies, the place where my parents honeymooned, where my existence was helped to be cast into the history of the world, was where I would be sent to be 'rehabilitated'. A place, from the account of my parents, exuded an aura of freedom, bliss, happiness and possibility. And now this place had been desecrated. It had become a factory and psycho-educational rehabilitation centre for the likes of me, borne of the spirit of freedom, from the experiences and dreams of my parents.

My father, who had visited the countries of the old Soviet Union and other Eastern European countries, which historically were under totalitarian communism, told me some wonderful and amazing tales of these journeys. One wise man he met was a psychiatrist from Lithuania, who started his own underground version of Christian-inspired psychotherapy, which was illegal under the regime of the USSR. He told my father that, when he lived as a boy in the old USSR, language was supressed; one had to be careful what one said and how one said it in case it offended the 'party line', on whatever topic one was discussing. It was so pervasive that it seeped into every single part of life: family, social, school, and university. This old psychiatrist told my father that, once the Iron Curtain came down, and people became freer, there was a real appreciation for the ability to be free in language, and also a heightened perception of deception in language and communication. Of course, this influenced the Eastern European methods of psychiatry and psychotherapy in very liberatory ways, in relation to 'mental health'. It has to be remembered that religion was severely oppressed under the USSR and other communist regimes. The totalitarian communist mindset was pro-atheism and anti-family. Anyhow, the conversations my father had with this psychiatrist and his friends about developments in the West caused great alarm in them. They felt, much like the dissident Russian authors Alexander Solzhenitsyn and Vladimir Bukovosky, that the fall of the Iron Curtain would only precipitate the spread of cultural Marxism and totalitarianism. Many in the West at the time scoffed at such notions and called people who thought otherwise conspiracy theorists. Well, how silly those sceptics look now.

My father visited Kiev in Ukraine once. It had a profound effect on him and his spirituality. He met a monk of the Kiev Pechersk Lavra monastery. In his conversation with this monk on many topics relating to issues in the UK at the time, such as the soaring abortion rate, the queer theory and gender/transgender agenda in schools, the monk went silent and his steely blue eyes locked with my father's. They faced each other in silence for what seemed like a blissful, poignant age, then the monk said to my father, 'How do you cope and live day to day in such hell?' In that moment, my father felt truly met by another human being; he felt heard, and he felt that the monk understood deeply the demonic ills that the world was entertaining. The monk blessed my father and gave him a gift of some small pictures of Icons and some jam. It was a profound moment. It was a moment which transcended the human realm and entered into a Godly one.

My father – or, at least, my memories of him, or more specifically the memories of the darkest times of the 2020s of my existence with him – haunted my dreams, my waking hours, even before my arrival in the department. These were truly unprecedented events that changed the course of *global politics forever, especially in advanced Western countries, but specifically the United Kingdom, Canada, Australia, New Zealand, Europe, and the United States of America.*

In the winter of 2019, a virus erupted from Wuhan, China that quickly spread from there to Italy, and to virtually every part of the globe. This virus was known as COVID-19. Some said it was some kind of virulent strain of influenza, others thought it might be a man-made biological agent that was released on purpose, or by mistake. Others thought many other different things. It was a time when it was very difficult to get a hold of accurate information on what the virus was, how it worked, and how infectious it was. Many esteemed scientists criticised the governments for the excessive lockdown measures, which they argued were not justified as the virus was comparable to a very bad seasonal flu. Economists scratched their heads in disbelief as the world economy went into meltdown, willingly created by governments who all seemed to play the same tune in lockstep. The World Health Organisation (WHO) was very much implicated in the global lockdown dictate. They had rich financiers pushing a global vaccination agenda, and technologists developing applications for tracing, monitoring, and surveillance at unprecedented levels. Lockdowns and restrictions went on for many years, until the situation became intolerable; the mental and physical health of people deteriorated, there were food shortages, mass unemployment ensued, and riots erupted in most countries. The armies of several nations were on the streets to control the revolts.

Most countries went into lockdown; basically, house arrest. Some countries had initially more harsh lockdowns than others – it varied over many years. People were at times only permitted to leave their homes for exercise or shopping, and were to work from home if possible. The closing of non-essential businesses (shops, bars, restaurants) varied in their opening/accessibility over several years. Many businesses went to the wall, never to return. Most industries were eventually nationalised, old Soviet style. Most governments created state-run services, such as bars, restaurants, food, clothing, pharmaceutical, tourism. Tradespeople were subsumed under the state as workforce to carry out joinery, plumbing, glazing, roofing, and miscellaneous building works, as 85 per cent of those businesses went bankrupt during the months and subsequent years of lockdown. A bland monoculture of state-run services emerged with little flare, vitality, colour or taste. It was as if, in the space of a few years, the world had gone from one having a colour TV with many channels to a black and white set with three channels.

The supposed death rate of COVID-19, in reality, did not reach the levels of a bad seasonal flu (globally), yet the world was essentially shut down and a kind of global communist totalitarian techno-state was introduced. A cashless society was introduced, people were forced to carry immunity

60

passports, tracing monitoring on their smart (mobile) phones. This eventually evolved to microchips, which also recorded biochemical and physiological reactions/activity.

Big pharma ruled the roost, with the likes of financiers and the WHO pushing mass vaccination over the globe. The vaccines were pretty useless – but, of course, they made lots of money, and a significant percentage of people experienced side effects, for which there was no possibility of compensation; the drug companies were made exempt from liability.

This is where my recollection begins to fail, through the painfulness of it. This is where my life took a dark turn. In 2023, when I was aged 11, the WHO implemented a mandatory mass vaccination programme for COVID-19 of all children. Children were virtually untouched by the effects of the virus, but were supposedly excellent carriers of the virus and, thus, this issue had to be solved; they had to be immunised. My father was against the immunisation programme. It had already been carried out in other countries and I overheard him speaking with my mother about this. The vaccines for COVID-19 were responsible for millions of serious adverse reactions, including blood clots, brain damage, infertility, spontaneous abortions and many deaths. The WHO and governments of the world downplayed the risks and pumped propaganda to counter the bad press. However, the rationale was that the risk was acceptable for the greater good of society. Many people fell for the propaganda; not my mum and dad, though. They were adamant that my brother and I would not be getting the vaccine and that they would never consent. This is where it gets painful. The UK WHO vaccine department sent my parents several letters requesting them to attend the local health centre for the whole family to get vaccinated. They ignored these letters.

Eventually, a vaccine team arrived at our house accompanied by several police officers. A terrible argument ensued between the officers and my father. They started manhandling him, demanding that he allow them to carry out the vaccinations as instructed by state mandate. They immobilised him with a taser gun and handcuffed him.

My brother, my mum and I were vaccinated against our consent. My father screamed in rage at what was happening to us and then they injected him. He was arrested and taken away. The police charged him with endangerment to public health, child abuse (for resistance to vaccination), and assault to police officers. He was jailed and then tried (without a jury, as Scotland had done away with trials by jury) and he was imprisoned for ten years.

I remember my dad's eyes when he was taken away. He was broken. Tears streamed down his cheeks. He knew he was losing everything that he held dear. My brother and I managed to get one last big hug from him before he was put into the police van. He held us close and looked at us both intently. I will never forget what he said. It was what he always said when he was being serious. 'I love you boys, and I always will. Never forget that.'

Things went blank for me after that, a kind of unconsciousness. My mother became a shell, too. I developed intermittent rashes and eczema from the vaccine and picked up every infection going. My younger brother developed hearing problems and terrible tinnitus. We were not allowed to visit our father. We could video call him once a month for a few years. Eventually, all contact was stopped. The state essentially informed us that my father was an extremist and a danger to our welfare and well-being. He had not renounced his convictions, that the vaccine was dangerous and that he did not consent to his children getting it. They told us that he had been moved to a secure psychiatric institution for treatment. Indeed, I subsequently learnt that many people who did not conform to the state's COVID-19 narrative had disappeared into the psychiatric system. These were dark days. I am not sure how I held myself together. Life became quite blurry. I operated in a kind of automatic mode. I was numb. Life was essentially quite meaningless; school, home. No holidays of any kind involving travel were allowed. There were no events or entertainment allowed that could risk groups of more than fifty people; playgrounds, fairgrounds, swimming pools, etc, were distant memories.

Swimming. My father, before the COVID-19 era occurred, took my brother and I swimming every week for years, ever since I was six months old. He loved it. We loved it. I loved it. I was swimming without aid when I was three and a half years old. My brother was three-and-a-half when the lockdown started and he was almost swimming without help. We also went cycling and fishing. There was so much freedom where we lived, and we lived in a country rural place; but even lockdown could stop that freedom.

My father, my brother and I had a secret spot where we would get off our bikes and lie on the grass; we'd look up at the sky and chat and joke around. I felt so close to him in those moments. I could sense a deep love emanating from him that penetrated my soul. That feeling has never left me, nor my brother. It was a feeling of being 'held' in a fundamental ontological way, of being recognised at a deeply profound level, which was healing and other-worldly, supernatural even. This presencing was not something that could be taught through reason or calculative thought; it was on the spiritual level. My father believed that there were some fundamentals that could not be taught or which the state could perform. One of these was parenting. On one of our cycling trips around the farm where we lived, we stopped to look at the calves in a pen. The mother cows were separated by a fence. When we approached the pen, the mother cows became very agitated and frightened, as did the calves. We passed a small lake, where a pregnant swan was nesting, waiting to give birth.

Her mate was circling the nest, very cautious of our presence. My father remarked on these two incidents by explaining how it was nature's way for a parent to be protective of their young. It was an instinctive reaction. Humans, he said, had in some respects 'fallen' and lost sight of this force of nature. The state, he told me, wanted to subvert this innate force of nature and constantly undermined it, meddled in it and reprogrammed parents to feel inadequate, and in need of state guidance and state experts. This was the age of science, where science, instead of adding to progress and enlightenment, degraded and destroyed the natural order, or logos. My father told me that you don't need experts for many things that the state assumes they have expertise in. He warned that you have to be wary of claims to expertise that human and animal evolution did/does without. In fact, he went so far as to say that the imposition of science, wittingly or unwittingly, into the realm of the natural order of parenting and childhood was quite sinister; it was as if, he said, it had satanic roots. It took many years for me to truly grasp this, that state meddling into such things was more than purely political ideology. It was spiritual warfare.

This spiritual nature that my father instilled into me burnt in me always. All through school, into high school, university, my PhD and into my postgraduate studies. I often felt, like the Sufis my father told me about, that I was in the world but not of the world. The world order when I was growing up was of an extremist materialist nature, whereby the self, one's identity and one's rights, were essentially a limited, reductive and narcissistic affair. It was, in some sense, a base and lower-brain behavioural stimulus-response reality, where very little mattered apart from basic needs of food, warmth, sex, entertainment and intoxication. Life, with the aid of science and political ideology, had been reduced to its basics and de-humanised people to automatons. The 'God' in this case was science, the parent was the state, and the roots were satanic. The human race had been taken off course. It was nothing other than a battle of Good and Evil. The frightening thing, however, was how willingly many people took to the path of evil. But, of course, as history showed, the ease with which people sided with the evil path, of 'just doing my job', was very common. Man was a fallen creature, and vigilance of logos had to be maintained, and not taken for granted. It was, as my father solemnly warned (from his writings that he left), something that had to be considered and faced in all its fragility and huge responsibility which it represented. Otherwise, chaos, disorder and evil would reign.

It was on this bedrock that my father's whole philosophy of existence lay. The world had been corrupted by science and led aground, spiritually by science. Science used man, not the other way around, which was what was supposed to happen. The COVID-19 eruption of 2020 brought this stark reality to a head. My father never wavered in his conviction, believing in the

63

path of Biblical Job: that faith could never be relinquished, no matter how much one was ridiculed or shunned by society.

In the months and years to follow in the post COVID-19 era, a Brave New Normal World agenda was accelerated at double-quick pace – where, before COVID-19, the pace was like a small stream trickling like a country brook. Post COVID-19, it was like a raging torrent – orchestrated at a global level. This was accelerated even more with the supposed climate crisis, which also helped limit and control human life and behaviour. Of course, there was no science behind this raging torrent – only science fiction.

New hate crime and extremist laws, essentially enacted in law, forbade people from speaking against the government narrative. It became increasingly difficult to speak the truth, or an alternative truth. Members of the public were enlisted via government propaganda to pay attention to social media and activities in their communities which violated government guidelines, not just during the COVID-19 era but on a plethora of other issues, such as concerns of childcare, concerns of adults' mental health, physical health, or suspicious activity (e.g., extremists). This could include hateful ideas involving transgressing the queer ideology inherent in the LGBT/Trans agenda, such as showing concerns about 4-year-olds being taught that they could change sex, or that pupils were being educated about the ideas and technique of analingus or rimming. Parents who expressed concern to other parents about these issues increasingly found themselves being interviewed by local government officials and being reprimanded about hate speech laws and incitement to hatred.

Dark days ensued. People gradually stopped communicating with each other at any meaningful level. People rarely socialised. Any kind of public gatherings or meetings (e.g., council meetings open to the public, or parent-teacher council meetings, hospital meetings amongst colleagues) were tense occasions. People were fearful of saying the wrong thing or expressing their real opinion. It was easy to tell when somebody was expressing the government narrative; they would spew forth the spell words and phrases of 'new normal', 'transphobic', 'children's rights', 'saving lives', 'they say', 'risk of extremism' and so on.

In previous times, like under the old USSR regime, people also became very careful and fearful of what they spoke, who they spoke to and how they spoke it. It was the reason why dissident psychotherapists set up illegal meetings to speak freely without the constraint of the regime of Big Other breathing down their neck. These dissident Soviet psychotherapy types knew the value of being able to speak freely without hindrance or constraint. Indeed, in ancient Greece, the notion of parrhesia, or fearless speech, was the mark of a civilised society. With fearless speech there is the danger of upsetting somebody, or even of angering somebody so much that there is a risk of conflict.

Nevertheless, parrhesia and the right to be at risk is the liberty of each and every human being. The modus operandi of the modern post COVID-19 state increasingly involved people operating at a level where all risk in speaking fearlessly was discouraged and frowned upon.

For many, it became second nature. For many others, a reality opened up where they moved around and operated in a surreal world, where they felt utterly alone amongst people. People were estranged from each other; children grew up not knowing what it was like to be around others in a genuine, open relationship. A nightmarish, alienated, castrated, and handicapped way of relating became the way people related to each other. This was no big society, no sense of community, no sense of belonging.

And the intellectuals, the academics, the mental health professionals, the cultural celebrities, the artists, musicians, the press and the majority of politicians went along with it without so much as the raising of a squeal.

Many of the same people who, looking back at history, e.g., Nazi Germany, would proclaim that history should never repeat that dark period, who would say 'I was only doing my job' while being complicit in genocide and the oppression of peoples, were now complicit in exactly the same thing. They were just doing their job. They did, however, see the irony in their position and even tried to argue, in the beginning, that it was not the case, that they were not as accused, selling their soul to the devil.

One of the great ironies of this period was the attack on religion and religious gatherings. Of course, in all totalitarian regimes, the church was always attacked. In all humanistic movements, the Church was always attacked. The cognitive dissonance during the COVID-19 outbreak was plain to see. Supermarkets and abortion clinics were kept open. In such places, people mingled with little hindrance, yet several people gathering in a church was deemed unnecessary, dangerous and ultimately against the law. Queuing for the holy sacrament during the Divine Liturgy was illegal, while queuing for food was allowed. Going to a clinic to kill a child in the womb was necessary.

There were many within the religious world who capitulated to this hypocrisy and double standards. There were many who objected and flaunted the rules. Many priests, reverends and parishioners were arrested. Some churches were classified as extremist, commandeered by the government and closed. The darkness of the Brave New Normal World heralded the microchipping of citizens; this microchip contained an individual's data and the authorities could monitor physiological activity and geographical movements. It was mass population control and mass data control. Data was power, knowledge was control, control was control of production of an individual's societal output. The ultimate cog in the machine, a machine where one could not really opt out of, except in one's soul.

Historically, people said – and I remember them saying it, teaching us in school – that what happened in Nazi Germany would never happen again. People would say, 'I would never go along with such evil' or 'I would never take orders and follow them blindly' and such like. But, as the COVID-19 crisis and subsequent climate crisis of the 2020s showed, such sentiments were shallow lip service to an ideal that most people could not, or would not, live up to. In the United Kingdom and the United Sates, the governments encouraged people to snitch on their neighbours or people they saw breaking the 'rules' of virus prevention or climate control.

So, the faux bravado of many, who said 'I would be a resister to tyranny', was a weak-willed lie. It showed how many, at the behest of a government, would give up and go along with a totalitarian charade. The children that grew up in this era knew no better. How could they question if they knew no different? How could they imagine a world without microchips, contact tracers, immunity passports, limited travel opportunities, food shortages, and limited human relationships?

The reality that young people grew up with was one where they had very little contact with neighbours, no sense of community or cohesion with their neighbours, an education that was tailored to a cultural Marxist diet of indoctrination of anti-family, pro-queer theory, pro-gender fluidity, pro-feminist, and anti-male. Any questioning of this non-nourishing diet would be noted as resistance, or extremist, and parents or carers could expect a visit from the authorities. If they felt that the parents or carers were influencing their children, the children could be taken into state care. This dystopian state interference into the lives of children and families was decades in the making, but the COVID-19/climate crises of the 2020s ramped it up to 10 decibels within a few years.

Those on the left politically embraced the lockdown and diminished freedoms. They saw this as an opportunity to implement the Green deals; policies which would implement more environmentally friendly laws and whereby people would receive universal basic income. It was a ploy to tackle the huge unemployment as private businesses and enterprises had been economically destroyed through mafia-like criminal precision. There was a catch, though; one had to work for one's money. Redeployment to work on state projects was compulsory; they included agriculture, sanitation, building work, administration, energy projects, etc. People became slaves. Brave New Normal.

I remember during the COVID-19 crisis of 2020, during lockdown (house arrest), my father would say to me with a glint in his eye, 'Come on, let's break the law and go for a cycle.' One evening, we cycled through the farm where we lived and up through the fields where we reached the road. The road was deserted. We carried on to a small hamlet where there was a church in the shadow of a huge mountain that had once been a volcano thousands of years ago. We sat on the wall (not permitted in lockdown – during exercise, one had to keep moving) looking at the wonderful view on that tranquil, sunny evening at the end of April. There was utter stillness. The only sound was that of the birds singing. The sky was empty apart from a few clouds. There were no planes. My father said, 'We are so lucky to live here… so lucky.' He had a sadness in his voice and his eyes almost looked tearful. At 8 years old, I could not understand really what was going on, and I could not understand what might be going on in my father's mind. The peacefulness, although in some ways was idyllic, felt very eery. In the cottages of the hamlet, everybody was locked inside. We did not see a soul, not even at the windows. I overheard a conversation between my mother and father, where my mother feared that my father and I would be reported to the police for breaking lockdown regulations, or for raising suspicions or concerns for being out and about in such a quiet area. My father felt that it was possible, but what could one do? Become a fearful prisoner under tyranny? It was not something he was prepared to do.

But these were past days, a lifetime ago. I wondered how a world, a life, one's freedom, one's liberty could be so utterly destroyed at a whim. Many in the religious world would argue that satanic forces were an integral part of what was going on in world history; that the world, especially during the COVID-19 crisis and climate crisis after, was a direct result of the forces of evil. It was something I thought about often. It was extremely easy to conceptualise things as the result of greedy and/or corrupt politicians who had a love of power. And one could also rationalise things as a result of nasty people (e.g., paedophiles) infiltrating groups, lobby groups, political parties, etc, so they could act out their perversions. But, during my moments of thinking on these issues, just placing the blame on opportunistic individuals, who were a bit greedy, and bit perverse, or a bit nasty, often felt insufficient to explain the extent of what had and was happening in the world. These thoughts often took me into religious realms which resonated with me more and more. It stirred me up to revisit the Bible, to try to understand what may be behind the religious ideas and claims of the battle between good and evil. It struck me that there must be signposts in the Bible, explanations that had been erased from the consciousness of people over several generations to this present husk we called humanity…

*****

David's daydreaming of his past, his family and his father, was suddenly interrupted when a female voice burst through the intercom:

'Your scheduled transport to the Western Isles from the Department of Work and Well-Being is scheduled for 6.30 am tomorrow morning. Please make sure you are ready to leave. Somebody will come to your room before the 6.30 am departure.

Chapter Eight

To Oban

David was lying on his bed at 6.15 am waiting for his escort to arrive to take him to Oban. From there, he would board a ferry for his onwards journey to the Western Isles.

There was a knock at the door.

'Good morning, David. How are you? Are you ready for your trip?' announced some middle-aged, shaven-headed guy, who looked like a prison guard with black boots, cheap black nylon trousers and white shirt with the sleeves rolled up, revealing army tattoos.

'Oh yes, thank you. I am so excited for the off,' David replied.

'Good, oh!' said the man enthusiastically. 'Here are your escorts, Danielle and Stephan. They will accompany you on your journey to Oban. I wish you the best of luck and hope things go well on Harris. You will get all the support, help and rehabilitation you need. Goodbye.'

'Bye, bye.' David sing-songed his words to indicate what he felt was the fairyland reality of what was happening. Rehabilitation? From what? Wrongthink?

David rose from his bed, grabbed his bag of belongings and accompanied Danielle and Stephan out of the room, down the corridor and into the elevator to take him to the back entrance of the Department of Work and Well-Being. As they exited the building, they were greeted with the most ghastly of days; a cold wind blew, with rain pouring from the darkest of skies.

Lovely day for sailing, thought David.

A small minibus was waiting for them. David boarded and sat towards the back, while Danielle and Stephan sat in front with the driver. Danielle informed him they would be picking up a couple more people en route to Oban. The journey would take about two and a half to three hours.

The minibus pulled away to the security gates of the large, walled courtyard, the top of the walls lined with security cameras and electrified barbed wire. The driver stopped momentarily and then the large gates opened to let them exit. And they were off.

Driving through the windy and wet streets, David sank into an anaesthetic daze. He felt nothing. This is, he thought, how

69

people under totalitarian regimes become; hollowed out, alienated, numb and unable to really think any more. Not wanting to think; menticide. Such regimes want people not to think any more, to be unable to comprehend their own manipulation and to be unable to critique it with their thinking. This was a dangerous way to be. Such people could be very dangerous. Ethics and morals go out the window. There is no framework to guide the social world, other than the state dictates – but, if you don't go along with the state, the main option is numbness.

What could one do? What could one say? The truth of the regime is set in stone. There was no other way of seeing or conceptualising the world. If you disagreed, you were, in effect, ill. Societal discourse was one big double bind designed to drive people insane. The numbness induced was catatonic in nature. A catatonia, where there was no past and no future. Only the numbing present, where immediate needs (and indoctrinated desires) were of any importance; food, sleep, sex and drugs. Rats. Just like rats, rats in a Skinner box. Skinner, the famous psychologist who carried out conditioning experiments with rats. Unthinking humans. Just reacting. Reacting to a stimulus. A problem like hunger or thirst is obviously solved through eating and drinking. No other thought process is needed. However, limiting overindulgence of food via willpower or constraint was not a popular idea The problem of low mood is ameliorated by a drug from a doctor; no consideration is needed. A sexual desire is met with an immediate reaction for this desire to be met, as it is doused with the absolvent of human rights. No risk or negative consequences are needed to enter into the debate of human behaviour or existence. A world of perfect commitment to human rights, but with no commitment to the past, the future to come or to someone else. Totally alone. In 2050, almost any impulse was catered for, promoted and celebrated. Rats, rats in a box. But, equally, you were made neurotic, psychotic, with methods taken from that other behavioural scientist, Ivan Pavlov, who made perfectly healthy dogs insane and physically unwell. The waves of fear and then hope made life a misery; the only option for many was to self-medicate with fantasy, substances, and withdrawal into psychosis.

That is what people had become. A vile caricature of what it was to be human. Some of the viler stuff, the dark philosophy, starting with the promotion of queer theory in the early 2010s, was the drive against reproductive futurism; the devaluing of families, reproducing children, and the future. Then there were the cries of 'love is love' and 'love has no age', which were straight out of the MAPs (minor-attracted persons) and paedophilia network agenda. Many queer theorists in the early years of the 2000s were promoting gender transition for children, which involved puberty blockers to stop normal puberty and the development of secondary sexual characteristics. This made children sterile and unable to reproduce. Queer theory was obviously openly promoted in schools, and advocates of this thought it to be perfectly normal for children to learn about sex, sexualities and sexual relationships and behaviours, of all colours of the rainbow. Perfect for the queer theory agenda. However, a more sinister agenda arose out of this. Some sick people advocated that, if children as young as 9 years old were able to agree to stop their puberty, destroy their fertility and adult sexual reproductive self, then children were old enough to consent to sexual relationships. What a dark defence.

By 2050, it was difficult to know the extent of how MAPs' desires were catered for. Sex tourist destinations had existed for many decades, where such deplorable behaviour existed; but, as such ideology had become more mainstream, subtle acceptance of such behaviour was evident. MAPs acquired human rights to be treated with respect and equality. The argument went that they were born that way, it was their sexual orientation; that, although they would not engage with a minor in sexual activity without consent, they believed that it was possible for children under 16 to have meaningful sexual relationships.

As the minibus drove through the streets of Glasgow toward the A85 and on to Loch Lomond, they passed several schools where parents and carers were scurrying with children towards classrooms, which no doubt would fill the pupils' heads with state-controlled narratives – that boys can be girls and vice versa, that sex was purely a materialistic and pleasure-orientated activity. Lessons would include masturbation, sexual techniques such as anal sex, rimming the anus, the use of sex toys, etc. The body was situated as an object of desire and a tool for fulfilment; a limited tool of fulfilment. Children would be taught to view their minds in an equally objective way. Emotions, thoughts, feelings and fears were to be tackled with 'scientific' precision. The mind was a faulty object to be monitored, noted, measured, dissected,

71

interrogated, and ultimately supressed by techniques derived from the mists of time from the likes of behaviourism and cognitive analytic psychotherapy. Children were taught to see their minds as diseased, in need of cure, and ultimately something to be vigilant of. The disease of a crippling, obsessive narcissism was borne from this educational revolution.

As they passed the town of Alexandria, they were soon onto the banks of Loch Lomond. Thirty years previously, the loch had been a haven for tourists, sightseers, boaters and water sports lovers. Those days were long gone. Boating, water sports, as well as hiking, walking and wild camping in this once great national park, part of the Trossachs, were highly restricted due to supposed public health reasons and climate conservation. Only with a special permit or attained social credit privileges (which were rarely, if ever, awarded) was one able to bypass these laws. One could often see the elites of political society sailing, without a care in the world, on the deserted loch, parking up at islands in the middle of the loch and having lunch with friends and family. No such luck for ordinary people; the countryside in 2050 was banned for most people.

David looked over at the far side of the loch, which, for the most part, had no road. He recalled how his parents had walked what was then called the West Highland Way. An approximate 100-mile hike from Bearsden on the outskirts of Glasgow to Fort William. David inwardly felt envious of the time in history his parents lived. *Why did the adults stand back and have their freedoms and liberties stripped away in front of their eyes?* he thought. *Why did they act complicitly to let this dark fascism sweep the land? And why did so many embrace it?*

Philosophers, for hundreds of years, had warned us about alienation, being seduced by the god of science, the commodity, of merely *existing* and being turned into a commodity; the world of love, relationships, work, and labour being turned into a commodity. The journey from formal to real submission was of crucial importance from the late 20th century to the totalitarianism of 2050. Formal submission is based upon the juridical subjugation of the worker, on the formal disciplining of bodies. Real submission, on the other hand, means that the worker's life has been captured by the authoritarian narrative, and one's soul has been pervaded by techno-linguistic chains. In other words, in formal submission, people grudgingly accept following the rules for fear of punishment; we go to work because we have to pay the bills. In real submission, work is our whole life, our character, our *raison d'être*; it defines us. People embrace the regime, believe it, can imagine no other reality. This requires several generations of demoralisation and indoctrination of totalitarian thought. By 2050, most people could not remember the freedoms of the previous generation. The horizons of most people had been stunted to such an extent that they had become nothing more than finely tuned animals, reactive to the stimulus-response formula. This is why the education system had gotten the children to become so obsessed with monitoring their own minds, like a computer. It disrupted the usual self-self, self-other interactions of ordinary human functioning. People just could not act socially together like they did in previous generations. The powers that be knew this, and that was why they disrupted these social processes.

The standardisation of the masses started in schools over many decades. Schooling was orchestrated to deprive individuals of being freethinkers. The individual mantra contained in the educational system was a deliberate ploy to subjugate children (and the adults in the adult context) to make them into robotlike machines which think, act, and react in the same pattern. One prime example was that of the RSHE programmes relating to mental well-being in the early 2020s. Children were subjected to derivatives/hybrids of Ivan Pavlov's neurism theory and Aaron Beck's cognitive behavioural theory for mental disorders; one's emotions, moods, thoughts were inculcated to children as being of a universal nature, that we could be our God of our own making, that anything discomforting, or 'negative', in these realms could be alleviated by techniques and 'rationalisations' which would sweep away any lingering negativity. It was the most reductive and brainwashing of doctrines.

Of course, such manipulations of the population had their historical antecedents. In the early days of the Soviet empire, in the early to mid-20th century, in the planning of how to control the masses, the Soviets believed that man could be reduced to a chain of conditioned reflexes, and therefore the population could be standardised. Horrific as it may sound, such techniques were alive and well in 2050. Essentially, it was a doctrine that eradicated the idea of individuality. Herd thinking in 2050 was truly a sight to behold.

Danielle, who was now sitting in the back with David (Stephan was up front with the driver), was staring at David in a self-righteous, self-satisfied way.

'What lovely countryside,' David said to her.

'Is it?' she retorted.

'What I mean to say,' replied David, 'is that it is pleasant to look at. Nature has been carved through millions of years, and to eyes it can give so much pleasure, far outweighing what man can create. It is quite astounding that nature can give us this, ground us, to help us transcend ourselves, and yet we are so restricted from fully participating in such a free gift from nature.'

Danielle chuckled disdainfully. 'What people like you don't realise, people who question too much, is that you won't accept that the rules we are asked to follow are for the greater good, for the people. Oh yes, we could all go out and walk around the hills and the mountains, but think of all the risk; spreading disease to others, to animals, damaging the environment. All for what? A pleasant experience? A nice memory? What does that contribute to society? We don't have the resources to cope with the demands that such unregulated activity would have on our health and law and order system. Humans can be just as parasitical as locusts.'

David laughed out loud. 'How old are you, Danielle'?

'Twenty-seven,' she replied.

'Ok, born in 2023. Born in the age of COVID-19. The problem is, you see the world through one lens, a lens of post freedom, of post truth. There was a time when your parents, your grandparents…'

'I have no parents or grandparents,' Danielle interrupted. 'I was adopted. I never knew my biological heritage. It's not important.'

'Fine, but your DNA heritage lived in a time when things were very different. That has not gone away. You don't know it, but it's in your bones, it runs in your blood. It's just that you were brought up to disregard it. There was a different time, during my great-great-grandfather's time. He lived in a cottage in the hills near the English border. He had no electricity, no running water, no gas, no central heating – just an open fire. My great-grandfather was born there, in the house. His son, my grandfather, roamed free in the countryside as a boy, playing, free. My own father used to cycle with a cycling club through the hills of the Scottish Borders,

74

stopping for swims in rivers on sunny days, cooking chicken legs on fires in sheltered forests. Adventure, freedom, education. Risk. Ah, yes... risk. You, Danielle, were born into the age of risk aversion, the outlawing of risk, as was I, more or less. We have betrayed our history. We now live in a husk of an existence of what once was, of what could have been. The future is not what it used to be. That is for sure.'

Danielle looked infuriated. Her tight, slicked-back, blonde ponytail flinched with her furrowed brow, the unconscious misery of her life etched into her young face. No joy, no humour, no adventurous spirit. She was the type of woman that sucked the life out of any joyful occasion.

'That time, that period of history, was incorrect, selfish and highly irresponsible,' she replied. 'I mean...' She smirked with an air of arrogance. 'Look at the diseases that were spread in those days, the risks that we now prevent. The infections that were passed around people. Our age prevents this. We are safer. What is bad about that?'

David just shook his head. This was the predictable response from somebody soaked and indoctrinated in the ideology of risk aversion and safety-ism. It was like talking to a drone, a robot. So lonely. You see, the relations between men and women had been eroded over many decades up to this point. Conversations between the sexes had deteriorated to a passive aggressive argument, a battle to be won. The I-Thou, so wonderfully described by Martin Buber, had transformed itself into an I-It scenario, or rather It-It. Danielle had all the hallmarks of such a transformation, like many women, like many men. People were God, their own Gods, part of the herd collective.

'Life... to be a truly human life, there has to be risk, the right to be at risk,' David tried to explain. 'Human society and its achievements were borne through risk. Our risk-averse society now paradoxically creates a risk that we cannot see because of our blindness... we now risk our soul, the death of our soul... it cries and folk like you laugh in the face of death, you laugh in the face of people like me. You have your place in the sun, yes. It is comfortable... but meaningless. It has no meaning... it only serves a means to an end, to keep the status quo of the state. An individual's freedom and the desire of the state... never the twain shall meet. You and I both know that. Can I ask, do you have – or want to have – children?'

'Goodness me, no,' Danielle guffawed. 'I hate children. I love my freedom to much.'

'Ah!' retorted David. 'You say you love the greater good of society and humankind, but you hate humankind because you hate children, because you love your freedom. But you have no freedom. You don't have the freedom to choose, because freedom does not exist. You hate humankind, and you embrace enslavement by glorifying not having a choice. It makes you a subhuman, alienated from your true nature. To suffer in anxiety over choice is the highest of human givens. To be truly free, we are in a position where there are many choices in our life; we have to make a choice, because, if one does not make a choice, one will be suffering constantly because we will not be free of the dilemma of choice. We may feel that there are too many choices, so much so that we cannot decide which way to go, which way to choose. But we are condemned if we don't make THE choice. And if we choose, take a leap of faith on a choice, to forsake all others, we are condemned to that choice. It might be a mistake, it might work out alright, but at least we are free then. And then, of course, after we make our decision, we have to learn the hard fact of life that infinite choice is a hell, and that living with a choice having been made can be hell... What is one to do? How does one orientate oneself to one's life to mitigate suffering? The practice of ordinariness or extraordinary ordinariness. What is that, I hear you say? Realising that life can be hell faced with choice, that making a choice can be hell. There is no cure for life, as there is no cure for human nature. But nature is there, all the same. And what is that, that is there? It is what the state has killed; it is what people like you have killed, and it is what you don't even know exists.'

'Oh, come on now,' said Danielle. 'I can see now why you lost your job and ended up on the programme. A stint on the Western Isles will do you good. It will get all that nonsense out your head.'

David looked at Danielle and shook his head. She had given him the double barrels of 'I am not going there' narrative. The great refusal of the 'liberated' man and woman. The turning the other way when choice is presented. This kind of refusal summed up the *modus operandi* of the educational system; blind adherence to dogma, unquestioning and huge foreclosure of aspects of human experience. The unhuman.

Looking at Danielle, her face indignant, as though her stunted world view was beyond reproach, he noticed a strip of tablets poking out of her trouser pocket. He recognised the medication immediately; it was Exeortain, a mood enhancer/anti-anxiety medication, which many people took. She could not have been that happy with her life, after all. The attitude was just an act, which was common. David felt sad that there was such an edginess to their conversation. Conversation was just a battle to be won for people like Danielle. They feigned interest and/or concern in ordinary human interactions, but under the shallow crust of such 'meetings' lay an awful narcissism, swinging between arrogance and self-doubt and pathologisation of their every emotion and thought.

The rise of the inhuman was monstrous. A whole society cut off, stunted by an ideology which was essentially a willed self-amputation of the soul by so many. At least Nietzsche, despite his wavering and doubts, was on to something. But it drove him mad, so they say. Yet, this was the commonplace, the norm, the *raison d'etre* of the herd. It made for a lonely world. The loneliness of the herd. It was what the state wanted. It did not desire for beings to be connected in any way, in any deep and meaningful way, and it did not want people to be connected to their own nature in any profound manner. Many argued that such ploys were satanic in nature. So subtle. Only in temptation could one sell such a barbaric soul operation. Temptation as old as biblical times, Adam and Eve, the fall, the dirty rotten apple. That is how the state seduced people, children, by their desires and passions, where no checks were put in place. Giving full reign to such things was encouraged from infancy, arousing curiosity in matters way beyond their years of maturity (e.g., sex, pornography, the mind). Such things had taboos for a reason. They were dangerous. It was like the world had become a topsy-turvy caricature. Some things the state had deemed dangerous, e.g., being a human being with real, authentic relationships with oneself, others and the world, but this was stopped for reasons of caution, safety and risk. Meanwhile, the riskiest thing of all, annexing the soul from one's very existence, was deemed quite the thing.

After retreating from the non-conversation with Danielle, David returned to looking out the side of the minibus window. He recalled his time as a researcher and his meetings with similar people as Danielle in the activist communities. Their sexual lives were of great interest to him. Monogamous relationships, although

77

they did occur, were quite rare. Polyamorous groupings were more common; open relationships, and self-partnered sexual relationships, were very favourable – in other words, masturbatory relationships with sex toys, sex dolls, pornography, or with virtual partners online. The overarching tone of mid-21st century sexuality was one of the body being a temple of pleasure, that the flesh of the body was to be used in any way which one saw fit as the zone of pleasure. This was all that counted. Nothing more, nothing less. David often felt strange in the presence of such people. He could not put his finger on it. It made his skin crawl. It was like being alongside the living dead. There was a sense of contamination, of purification of the flesh in some sense. There was also the sense of danger, that somehow these people were risky in the sense of being unhinged in some way, of instability of being troubled, of being cut off from something. Of course, they were all searching, forever searching; never happy, always analysing their relationships, how their sex lives could be improved, what was wrong with their performance. A kind of dangerous, narcissistic, obsessional sexuality resonated with them and their very flesh did not sit right on their very being.

David gazed out of the window and thought of times and histories past and wondered how they had gotten to the present point. Sitting in a kind of liminal/dream state, he was pleasantly aware of a 'presence' of some kind, that held him in the cradle of his being, which gave him some kind of strength. He felt he may be needing some strength. He even felt slightly panicked at the thought; was this the serenity that came over those who had decided to end it all? But he decided to go with it, into the anxiety of it, the madness of it. It was so easy to retreat from such feelings; it was the way of most people. The psyche of people in these days had reached a point where they could not endure any suffering whatsoever. This was not the way of human culture, where medicine, science and culture obsessively strived to eradicate any psychological discomfort. Any such suffering was perceived as essentially pathological, or at the very least a nuisance that got in the way of life. Most people strived to experience the 'ultimate' happiness, whatever that was meant to mean.

The fool's gold of happiness, driven by medico-technological human engineering, had driven many people insane. Psychiatric hospitals were full to the brim of people who had short-circuited from sanity into a permanent state of seeking for

Shangri-La. The appeal, or hysterical demand, for the state to deliver the goods became the only lighthouse in a dark and bleak ocean of a world. Many became shipwrecked on the rocks within a psychiatric hospital, or on a cocktail of prescription drugs for life, sometimes bolstered by recreational drugs of choice. Life expectancy of these people became lower than those of people who grew up in the late 19th/20th century, where people were comparatively poorer and where the comforts of life were much less in force.

Yes, the shipwrecked human casualties in the technological wasteland were an incredible sight to behold. The culmination of centuries of human endeavour in the realm of science, medicine and technology, from the wonders of the renaissance and the enlightenment to hyper-speed advances in the 20th/21st century, had failed to fathom the complexity of the human psyche. It had failed to cure the human condition. The lack of negative capability (*a la* Keats, the poet) had been ignored at its peril.

David recalled his father telling him that he once worked at a psychiatric hospital south of Glasgow, called Carstairs. This was a high security hospital for forensic patients. Some of the most damaged people in society ended up there. Broken childhoods, child abuse, drug and alcohol abuse, crimes of passion, and just plain born evil were the profiles of people who ended up there. He recalled the story his father told him. Whilst walking through the grounds of the hospital with a colleague, his father came across a shaggy, grey-bearded old man who was playing some sad blues on a mouth organ. As his father and his colleague passed, the old man abruptly stopped playing and looked at them.

'Excuse me, my man, are you an undertaker, by chance?' asked the man.

My father replied, 'No, sorry, I am not. Why do you want an undertaker?'

'I am looking to take the one-way journey out of here.'

His father's colleague explained to him that this bedraggled, bearded fellow had been in the hospital for thirty years and was highly unlikely ever to leave. He would die there.

David's father told him that there were many lost souls like this at the hospital, hidden from society. People on the outside world (of the hospital) used to think that insanity was contained

79

within the barbed wire, electrified fences and walls of such places. However, as his father often used to tell him, the boundary between inside the hospital and the 'sane' world was very thin and very porous. Indeed, it could be argued that insanity, so to speak, was very much alive outside the hospital, contained in socially acceptable ways, bolstered by highly practised and indoctrinated cognitive dissonance, that the world was very much operating in the sphere of insanity.

One such example, where insanity erupted and became clearer, was during the 'pandemic' that never was; the COVID-19 scam of 2020.

In Scotland at this time, the First Minister, Nicola Sturgeon, had mandated in July of that year that face masks had to be worn by couples who were getting married. Incredibly, the registrar, vicar, or priest who conducted the ceremony did not have to wear any kind of face covering. Then, in October, when there was supposedly a resurgence of the virus, and restrictions were being tightened again, she declared all of a sudden that people getting married no longer had to wear face masks. This dictate made no sense in terms of logic, science or sanity. The married couple would be spending the night together, so why would they need to protect themselves from each other with the wearing of face masks during the ceremony? Meanwhile, during this same period, gatherings of people were seriously regulated. Major multinational supermarkets were open for business, but bars and restaurants were closed; brothels were open, but churches were closed; primary school children could not sing in school, but politicians could shout at each other to their hearts' content in parliament buildings unmasked. Logic had left the building. And people were meant to believe and adhere to this nonsense, and politicians had the audacity to demand that their ludicrous dictates be obeyed.

This eruption of state-sanctioned insanity, along with measures which did make people mentally ill (self-isolation, house arrest, not being allowed to work, or meet family or friends for the risk of spreading COVID-19), depicted and predicted the future of a medico-technological totalitarianism based on the lie.

Living by the lie: a feature of totalitarian societies, where logic had been obliterated. This kind of society was warned about by Alexander Solzhenitsyn. In his famous novel *Gulag Archipelago*, he wrote:

'The Lie as a form of existence. Whether giving in to fear, or influenced by material self-interest or envy, people can't nonetheless become stupid so swiftly. Their souls may be thoroughly muddied, but they still have a sufficiently clear mind. They cannot believe that all the genius of the world has suddenly concentrated itself in one head with a flattened, low-hanging forehead. They simply cannot believe the stupid and silly images of themselves which they hear over the radio, see in films, and read in the newspapers. Nothing forces them to speak the truth in reply, but no one allows them to keep silent! They have to talk. And what else but a lie? They have to applaud madly, and no one requires honesty of them.

The permanent lie becomes the only safe form of existence, in the same way as betrayal. Every wag of the tongue can be overheard by someone, every facial expression observed by someone. Therefore, every word, if it does not have to be a direct lie, is nonetheless obliged not to contradict the general, common lie. There exists a collection of ready-made phrases, of labels, a selection of ready-made lies. And not one single speech nor one single essay or article nor one single book--be it scientific, journalistic, critical, or 'literary,' so-called--can exist without the use of these primary cliches. In the most scientific of texts it is required that someone's false authority or false priority be upheld somewhere, and that someone be cursed for telling the truth; without this lie even an academic work cannot see the light of day.'

Living by lies had become an ingrained way of life, increasingly so by 2050. The logic bypass, with ludicrous dictates by the state that made no sense (which were not followed by those in power, anyhow). People had been indoctrinated into slave adherence to the illogical nature of reality. But they had been cut off from even greater realities that had been banned from circulation. Hate crime laws had outlawed religious books and texts for fear of offending certain groups of people. In essence, however, it was to cut people off from other rich sources that might wean them off the teat of the state. The state wanted people to suckle the breast of the state, to get their fill of well-being, hope, and logic. Any wisdom that got in the way of that was frowned upon, or even ridiculed.

One such piece of wisdom (which was censored/silenced/hidden in 2050) was from the Christian philosopher Soren Kierkegaard and his book *The lily of the field and the bird of the air: three Godly discourses.* Kierkegaard's book (which David's father had given him and his brother as a gift to treasure)

81

was Kierkegaard's short masterpiece commentary on Jesus Christ's Sermon on the Mount as described in the Bible in Matthew 6:24-34, where Jesus tells his followers to let go of earthly concerns by considering the lilies of the field and the birds of the air, as they have much to teach people about how to deal with the human condition and how to commune with God.

Generations of people from early childhood had been taught only a solution-focused, technical approach to human suffering. This included developing an acute sense of discomfort with any kind of physical or mental suffering, especially mental suffering. Any kind of 'negative human' emotion was pathologised from nursery school age, and this was nurtured throughout primary and high school, as well as university. In the first couple of decades of the 21st century, universities became increasingly like extensions of high school, where adult supervision of students and welfare infrastructure became an ever more increasing part of university life, even though the youngest university students were classed as adults at 18 years of age.

The infantilisation (or, one could say, totalitarian control) of students showed itself most clearly in the transformation of campus security, from staff/older students acting as wardens, to universities hiring security guards/private security firms to police the campus. Indeed, these new-style guards did become a kind of fascist army on campuses. Their presence infantilised the students. Any minor emotional trouble (e.g., an argument with a boyfriend/girlfriend, or homesickness) could result in security being called, so the poor student could have an impromptu counselling session with a burly security guard kitted out in military-grade clothing and stab vest. Student populations (from nursery to university) were increasingly weaned from human *Being*, being comfortable in their own skin, *being there*, and the innate recognition that the range of human emotions, and *existing*, was a natural part of human existence; *the irreducible given*. The result was stunted human beings whose psychological growth had been curtailed by years of emotional programming. This was exaggerated even more by the pushing of psychopharmacology onto students; the trade in psychoactive medications (e.g., anti-depressants, anti-anxiety, beta-blockers, pain killers, etc) flourished in university medical centres, where doctors were inundated with emotionally incontinent students. It was a veritable tsunami of artificially created psychopathology.

The real test of the infantilisation of students (or display) came in the autumn of 2020 during the COVID-19 tyranny when university students started/returned to university. In Scotland, students were ordered to stay in their halls of residents, not socialise with anyone and all lessons were done online. The icing on the cake for an indication of how much students had been subjugated and programmed was when the Scottish government told students that they could not go home for Christmas. The students and the National Union of Students Scotland complied for the most part, agreeing with the restrictions and, instead of questioning the ludicrous COVID-19 restrictions, lobbied the university and government for more mental health and welfare provisions. It showed how docile the student population had become.

David dozed off to the sound of the electric humming of the minibus. The seats on the bus were very uncomfortable; the hard, barely padded, black shiny plastic seats, that could be easily washed for hygienic purposes, did nothing for passenger comfort. David had put his jacket under his bottom and his fake fur winter hat against the glass as a pillow. That did the job for a snooze. He dreamt of sandy beaches and huge waves from memories of family holidays in the south-west of France, near the Spanish border, with his parents. His father took him and his younger brother out into the shallow surf and waited for the waves to come crashing in. The joy and playfulness of those moments were etched into his mind forever. So simple. They would sometimes go to the café after such beach adventures, before dinner, whilst his mother would prepare dinner in the mobile home they rented near the beach in the holiday park. His father would let him have a coca cola (but made him promise not to tell his mother) and his father would have a pastis or glass of wine. David felt decadent sitting with his father in the bar. He recalled the World Cup football tournament was showing on a widescreen television on one occasion. All the French holidaymakers were watching as France was playing some other nation (he could not remember which). His father, not a great fan of football, would chat in French with one or two of the hysterical French football fans. David could not understand what his father was saying, and he would ask him what he was saying afterwards. His father would reply that he was asking what the chances of the French were of winning and how they were doing; he had no clue what stage of the competition they were at, or the standard of the team. He would often finish off by telling the French chap that at least they were in the competition (the French), as Scotland had not even qualified. That was the extent of my father's stock phrases in the art of chit-chat when it came to World Cup football. He never was one for idle chit-chat – or, as he would say, he detested being lost in 'the they', as the German philosopher Heidegger might say.

David's father was a shy man, but confident. Or, rather, as his father told him, after the birth of David and his younger brother, he became more confident and grew into his psyche. Fatherhood can do that to a man. Having a child takes away the concern of self-consciousness, or narcissistic self-consciousness that people can have. Such pithy worldly concerns about how people see you, or what they think about you, dissolve under the weight of fatherhood. Indeed, worldly concerns, like Kierkegaard discussed, become less when you have such small, precious beings to care for and look after. Being a father, as David was told by his father, helps one endure suffering. Indeed, he told David that being a dad made suffering almost a pleasure. Working on the house doing DIY, working in the garden, fixing broken sewage pipes, building things for one's children; then, in the evening, body aching, sitting with one's children, cuddling up in front of the television was a joy, contentment personified.

David's father used to take him and his brother hiking up into the hills, where they would gaze at the breathtaking views. David and his brother were astounded at the panoramas. His father, often used to say,

'Look at that, you can't buy that. That can never be bought and it will always stay with you.'

Unfortunately, such things were taken away from the people. Under the auspices of Agenda 2030, sustainable development and the 'climate crisis' agenda, the country and rural places were now the preserve of the state and the elites, where the rules that ordinary people had to abide by did not apply. What with travel restrictions, access to such areas was severely restricted. The elite of society, of course, were exempt. They could travel where and how they liked. This had been in the programming for years, when they were building the 'fences' of the society for 2050. During the COVID-19 pandemic of 2020, when travel restrictions between areas of Scotland were brought in for the first time, notable politicians and celebrities flaunted the rules but were essentially let off.

As the minibus made its way up the A82 toward and past Tyndrum, the vast expanse of countryside made David's heart ache. The vast, empty, rugged mountainsides pierced his soul like daggers. The beauty of them was interspersed by massive wind farms on the high and exposed areas. Through this long valley from Tyndrum towards Bridge of Orchy, where the wind howled, stood miles of huge wind turbines on the hillsides and over on the hills above Loch Tulla. There were also the horrible shanty towns of workers' villages that were erected to house the souls that were sent there as part of the 'programme' to maintain the wind turbines, the protein farms and surrounding land.

On the long decent from Tyndrum to Bridge of Orchy, Danielle informed David that they would be stopping to pick up two more people. They would then double back to Tyndrum to get on the A85 for the last part of the journey to Oban.

The minibus drew to a halt outside what used to be the Bridge of Orchy Hotel. It was a hotel no longer, but the headquarters of this area's Department of Work and Well-Being. Many years before, when the economy was deliberately crashed, many businesses went bust. The government then commandeered all property under the 'Debt Forgiveness Scheme'. This meant that home and business owners who could not pay their bills and mortgages would be exempted from their debts, but would have to give up their properties and assets. Invariably, they were all moved into 'smart cities', urban areas that included the explosion of cramped, high-rise housing that sprung up during this time. The state takeover had engineered a perfect prison planet, a society of control; get the people out of the country and into the large towns and cities, where people could be far more easily controlled, and where the borders of such places could act as boundary lines where travel could be monitored and restricted.

Danielle exited the minibus via the sliding side door to greet two men, who were patiently wating in a shelter just outside the headquarters. They entered the minibus. One man, in his mid-50s, bald, with a short, rough, jet-black beard, sat two seats behind David. He beamed a warm smile to David.

'Hello,' he said kindly. 'Fergus is the name.'
'Nice to meet you. I'm David.'

The other man looked barely 18. Skinny, with a mop of brown hair and a grey waterproof coat that looked like it hung off his bones. He looked petrified. He went and sat right at the back of the minibus without saying a word, and stared glumly out of the window.

The minibus then did a U-turn and made its return journey to Tyndrum to join the A85 to Oban. It was approximately forty miles and would take around an hour. Driving back up the valley towards Tyndrum, Fergus piped up from behind and addressed David.

'Is this your first time into the Hell of the West?'

'Yes, this my virgin voyage,' replied David. 'I have been told it will be good for my character. And you?'

'Me!' Fergus guffawed. 'Dear God, no. This is my fifth tour of duty, son. They can't reform me or find me any meaningful work back in the metropolis, or keep me in any one place for long. I have been in Orchy for six months now, working on rail lines, dealing with deliveries for the camps and such like. Am sick of it. I need some sea air. My wife left me after the third tour… she could not stand the waiting or the uncertainty…'

Danielle jumped to attention. 'Ok, Fergus, that is enough. You know the social hygiene regulations. No revelations of personal or psychological information to other personnel. This could lead to emotional triggering and problematic moments that might have to be dealt with. Let's just get to Oban and the boat so we can get to the Western Isles.'

'Oh, pardon me, DOCTOR,' Fergus retorted. 'We can't have any inkling of human camaraderie, can we? I mean, we might all start crying and hugging each other. We cannot have that, can we? I mean, look at the perfect specimen of human social interaction back there.' He indicated to the young boy. 'He is fodder for the New World Order. Emotionless, psychologically stunted, mute and probably a eunuch.' He laughed.

'Ignore her, son,' he then continued quietly to David. 'She is just a bloody computer program. Her type is neither here nor there. Lost souls, flotsam and jetsam on the ocean of life with not a clue of what is, what was, or what will be. The day of judgement will come to her, mark my word.'

Danielle glowered in Fergus' direction.

'Don't worry, son,' he said in a fake hushed tone. 'Once we are on the boat, I will emotionally trigger you to fuck with

86

ordinary conversation. But I can see you can handle it and won't need psychological rehabilitation after it. What a joke. Look at muggins back there.' He indicated again towards the young man at the back of the bus. 'He probably has had years of cognitive restructuring. They have got him where they want him – docile, obedient, compliant and subservient. I will fill you in, mark my word. Don't worry, son.' Fergus reached over and patted David on the shoulder.

David liked Fergus immediately. A warm human being in a world of inhuman beings.

Danielle was the perfect protype of the dystopian socially engineered method; she was exactly how the state wanted human beings to engage with themselves and others. The 'psychology' of the state regarded every human interaction as potentially harmful, dangerous, emotionally traumatic and something to be highly regulated. In essence, however, it was a way to stop ordinary human bonding and social interaction; the state did not want people to form close, warm, trusting human relationships. Isolation on a physical and psychological level was much more preferable. This was the social engineering that was decades in the making. The masses had become, for the most part, hyper-introspective of their every emotion, thought and feeling. Spontaneity had been engineered out, people profusely feared each other; they not only viewed each other as bio-hazards and carriers of infections, but also as psychological hazards. But, of course, the human spirit could not be engineered out in a few decades with crude psychological techniques and even cruder psychopharmacological methods. History has proven that, time and time again. Even in the harshest of conditions of suffering, something always shone through to combat the oppression.

David began to feel sleepy again as he gazed out of the minibus window. Life had not worked out how it should, he thought to himself. It was not meant to be like this. It did not have to be like this. But it was. There was nothing he could do to change it. David drifted off to sleep, a deep sleep, where he dreamt that he was flying. In the dream, he was *in* the world, but *not of* this world. He was held in a power that everyone had within them, but most people had forgotten. The world was a test of some kind and this was entrusted to people to keep the channels open to this power. The next thing he knew, he awoke with Danielle shouting at him.

'We're here.'
They had arrived at Oban. The boat was waiting.

Chapter Nine

The Boat to the Western Isles: The Gulag Caledonia

It was a five-hour boat journey to Lochboisdale on South Uist. From there, we would have to drive and take a short ferry crossing to get to the Isle of Harris, the final destination.

Danielle, David, Fergus and the sorry young man with no name exited the minibus. They were met on the quayside by two employees of the Department of Work and Well-Being. The quayside was busy with delivery lorries with goods and construction materials being loaded onto the ferry, and other foot passengers (e.g., construction workers, technicians, civil servant types and people from other parts of the country being sent for Work and Well-Being placements in the Western Isles).

'This is Josh and Raymond,' Danielle beamed at us. 'They will be taking over from here. You are in good hands.'

Danielle hugged both Josh and Raymond. They seemed well acquainted with each other. The three of them had that 'right-on' air of well-heeled West End Glaswegian civil servant, respectable on the outside, a crumbling emotional wreck on the inside, with a very generous dash of dark perversity and low morals.

'Hi. How are you doing?' quipped Josh.

'Nice to see ya,' added Raymond.

'So, who do we have here, Danielle?' asked Josh.

'These are the virgin islanders, David and Neil,' Danielle responded. 'And, of course, not forgetting Fergus, a frequent flyer to these parts, as you well know.'

'You are in safe hands, everyone,' said Josh to the three newcomers. 'We'll take care of you from now. We are going to ask you to come with us onto the ship now, so we can place you in your cabin for the duration of the journey. You will have your own cabin, which we expect you to stay in, except for when you have some time in the refreshments area. You can contact us via the intercom system from within your cabin.'

Josh was very effeminate in nature, but tried very hard to be butch. Around 5 feet 6, he had a shaved head and a rough, blond stubble. His round, gold-rimmed glasses were very reminiscent of SS guards in Nazi Germany. The clothing was very casual: green army trousers and big brown boots and a black biker jacket.

Raymond interjected. 'Have any of you got any questions before we board? Have any of you got any concerns? We have a medical officer on board who can be called if you need one.'

'That will be just in case we lose the plot, eh, Raymond?' joked Fergus. 'To give us a wee sedative… calm us down. This poor bugger,' he added, pointing to Neil, 'has never been to the Gulag Caledonia before… He might need a few downers to get him through!'

'Oh, come on, Fergus,' said Raymond. 'Don't frighten our new recruit. This is a great opportunity to contribute to the greater good. The environmental projects out here are invaluable to the country. Many people learn a great deal about caring for the environment, and develop hugely in life and social skills, which make it easier to contribute to society in a more productive way.' He spoke like he was reading from a script he had recited a million times.

Fergus rolled his eyes and roared a huge laugh with his head back.

'You know what…' he said, 'you had almost convinced me there, Raymond. You could sell sand to the Arabs. I like your style. Wee Neil here does not stand a chance in the Gulag with the likes of you. You will bore him to death with your social integration clap trap. He will be hypnotised in no time, doing the mindfulness sessions in the morning before work, learning about his inherent toxic masculinity in the lifestyle classes. Just you stick with me, Neil, and I will get you through this.' He looked across at the young man as he spoke. 'I have some jokes that will give you some sweet medicine to carry you through the cold, windy days in the Gulag.'

Poor Neil was red faced, but looking mildly amused by the banter.

Raymond was a tall drip of a man. Around 6 feet 4, he was skinny with short, brown, wig-like hair, with a hairline that looked utterly artificial. He wore a long, waterproof coat with a hood, hiking boots and skin-tight jeans.

'Ok, sorry to interrupt this little chinwag, guys, but we have a boat to catch,' said Josh. 'Nice to see you, Danielle.'

'Bye, everyone. Enjoy your re-education, David,' Danielle quipped sarcastically.

90

David just glowered at her.

Danielle got back in the minibus and it drove off the quay into the distance.

'Ok, people, this way,' said Josh. 'Follow me!'

Josh and Raymond marched towards the ship, which was moored a few hundred metres away in the harbour. David, Fergus and Neil, all with their bags in hand, dutifully followed behind.

'Gulag Caledonia… I like that, Fergus,' whispered David. 'It has a real ring to it. A ring of truth. Do you think Josh and Raymond see it that way?'

'Oh, believe me, David laddie, these bastards come across as super nice, super friendly…' replied Fergus. 'Oh, we will help you in any way… we are there for you… But, believe me, they will stab you in the back in a second. Super slimy. Watch what you say. They will take meticulous notes, as will the instructors and foremen on the islands. Everything can be used against you, including your biometric data from your chip. Look at a woman and get aroused – *misogynist*. Say a bad joke – *bigot*. Make a fuss about freedom and liberties – *dissenter*. Nothing gets past these cunts, believe me. And yet, they… they are the scum, perverted scum. The ship moors overnight in Lochboisdale. There is a bar on the ship. All those bastards get pissed, fornicate, take fucking drugs, you name it. Fucking satanic bullshit, ritualistic in my opinion. All these environmentalist-loving pagan types are the fucking same… fucking tree huggers. Oh, let's worship nature, let's love what nature brings to us… Aye, with no fucking limits or borders. Anything fucking goes. Stay clear. Out here in the Gulag, there are no rules for those bastards. They get a free rein… on the upside, they are liable to turn a blind eye when we get our down time and they give us a bit of freedom, so to speak… as long as we don't rock the boat. Oh, don't get me wrong, they will never accept us as one of them. We are scum in their eyes. They want to keep us out of their privileged circle. You see, we are tainted, the unwashed. We are the faulty machines. Young Neil, there, he is prey to them, but I can see in the wee bastard some fire, eh Neil?'

Neil shrugged.

'Faulty machines,' continued Fergus. 'Aye, they think they can fucking straighten us out. Actually, they try to bend us out of nature. They are the benders, the manipulators of nature. Fucking fucked-up psychology bollocks. Trying to nudge us here, there, fucking everywhere. Man as God. God save our souls, David.

91

Lord, forgive them, they know not what they do. But, me and you, David, I can see you think differently. I see in you a hunger, boy. Your eyes have been opened, that is for sure. Once the genie is out the bottle, there is no going back. The light has been let in. With these cunts, the light has been snuffed out big time. See yon Danielle, fucking dead inside, eh? A fucking drone. A hater of life, and hater of men, no doubt. Fucking stone-cold bleak house. I have seen enough in my time to sniff them out at forty paces.'

Fergus paused for a moment and looked around him, as if checking no one else could hear. 'We are going to the Luskentyre branch, right? It's a cushy number out there for this lot. A law unto their own. They let their guard down. We see them, so, in return, we get a wee bit of leeway. Fair's fair. Human nature always gets in the way of a grand plan, eh? Ha ha! You cannot stop it. The cream always comes to the top. All this pretend perfection, the air of respectability they put on… aye, fucked-up like the rest. None of the psychology works completely in the end. Fuck, they couldn't even snuff it out of some folk in the Nazi concentration camps. So they sure as hell won't snuff it out in the Gulag Caledonia, boy. There is a guy I want you to meet when we get there. He will set you right… and wee Neil should meet him, too. In our down time, when the goons let us out for the day… you will meet him. Even the goons like him. You know why? They see in him what they actually fucking yearn for, what they are missing. There are some nice folk out there, where we are going. Don't give up hope, boys…'

They approached the platform to get on the ship. Fergus sang the tune of 'Hotel California' by the 1970s band the Eagles, but he changed the words.

'Welcome to the Gulag Caledonia…'

As they entered the boat from the boarding platform, they came upon a huge round foyer with four corridors leading off – two to the right and two to the left, numbered 1 to 4. Raymond disappeared down to the right, also sub-labelled 'Department of Work and Well-Being, Administration Department'. Josh, on the other hand, turned to the three men.

'Ok, people, we are down here in Corridor One, passenger accommodation. Follow me.'

They all walked down the windowless corridor past doors numbered 1A, 1B, 1C, etc, on the right-hand side of the corridor. They came upon doors 1J, K and L. Josh stopped.

'Ok,' he said. 'David, you are in J, Fergus K, Neil L. I am next door, in 1M, with Raymond. At the end of the corridor there is a TV and refreshment lounge, where you can access drinks and snacks from the machine. I am afraid you only have a limited time in this area of one and a half hours. Too much social interaction at this potentially stressful time of transition could be triggering for many reasons, so we try to limit social interaction with others and any leading or even radicalising conversations. Safety first and all that. We have your well-being at heart. We don't want to upset our new recruits, do we? There is also a viewing deck if you wish a bit of a sea view. So… settle into your passenger cabin and stretch your legs if you wish in the TV lounge. You can get in with this card, which will operate the door for entry.'

He handed each of them an electronic key to use for the lounge.

'These cards will tell us how long you have spent in the lounge,' he continued. 'When you have reached one and a half hours, an alarm will sound and a voice will emit from the ship's audio system, which will identify you and your room number and ask you to return to your cabin immediately. If you do not return immediately, security will come to escort you back to your cabin. The journey will take approximately five hours. Your electronic keys are also needed to access your rooms; to enter and to exit them. If you lose them, press the red help button in the corridor. Several are situated on the walls down the corridor. There are also help buttons inside your cabin on the back of your doors. Security will arrive and help you if you need any assistance to exit or enter your room. Your electronic key will not let you enter anyone else's cabin – an alarm will sound and indicate if you have entered somebody else's cabin. That is not allowed. We don't want any hanky-panky now, do we! If you don't exit the other person's cabin, security will arrive to escort you to your own cabin. Enjoy the trip. Happy sailing.'

The supercilious Josh then trotted off like a little pony into 1M.

What a prick, David thought.

'Ach, well, off to the cattle holding bay,' said Fergus. 'See you in the lounge later, maybe. I will give you a knock, or you give me a knock if you are going, boys. The snacks are not bad. The TV is shit, though. Scottish Broadcasting Centre propaganda. Scottish

Bull Crap Centre, more like! I am going to have a shit and a wee kip. My arse is killing me after that fucking minibus.'

'Ok. See you later, Fergus,' replied David.

'You can come too, Grasshopper. We don't want to leave you out,' quipped Fergus, looking at Neil.

'Aye... ok... cheers,' Neil mumbled.

David entered 1J by pressing his key card on the reader on the door. He entered a windowless room, about two metres wide, four metres long. It had an irritating, long, fluorescent strip light on the ceiling. There was a reclining chair in the middle of the room with a mezzanine bed folded up on the left-hand wall. Just inside the cabin door, to the left, was another door leading into a bathroom and shower with wash basin. Next to the reclining chair was a small table, on which was a reading lamp and a radio. On the back wall was a TV screen. The room was bare, soulless and suffocating. The lack of windows made it extremely oppressive. A dark, heavy feeling overtook David. He slumped into the reclining chair, staring blankly at the wall. There was silence except for the rumbling of the ship's engine. A tannoy sounded.

BING-BONG....

'This is Captain Fairbourgh speaking. We are leaving in approximately thirty minutes, at 10 am. The journey to Lochboisdale will take approximately five hours. We should arrive at around 3 pm. The sea is pretty choppy today and it is quite windy in the West, which might make things a little bumpy on our arrival in Lochboisdale. But sit back and enjoy the trip. Please listen to the following safety announcement...'

A high-pitched BEEP pierced David's ears, followed by the rat-a-tat of an authoritarian woman's voice.

'Passengers in corridors...'

David zoned out at this point. The woman's words were just sounds that became unrecognisable and filled the room with noise. He felt dizzy and had the perception of being glued to his chair, his body paralysed. For a while, time felt like it had stopped. He could feel the movement of the ship and the vibration of the ship's engine below him. The rocking of the ship became more pronounced and he guessed they were now in open sea. It made him feel quite sick. The lack of windows to locate landmarks or get visual cues made this disequilibrium worse. This thought, disequilibrium, echoed through his mind, recycling over and over. It penetrated every cell like a wake-up call to something bigger, dragging him to a new, dizzying height of realisation – which, up to that point, he had not been cognisant of. Cognitive dissonance had become a way of life.

Cognitive dissonance: This had been inculcated into people as a way of life over decades, starting with the dumbing down of politics and politicians. Of course, the old adage 'never trust a politician' was always in parlance, but now politics had mutated into pure theatre. As a measure of the level of cognitive dissonance, looking back and forward through history it was clear the theatricality of politics was subtly increased year by year. Such was the nature of this theatricality, that watching any political debate became nothing more than a soap opera, of politicians on all sides of the debate, those in opposition, those for or against a course of action, all carefully orchestrated for a common goal, a means to an end. Such debates raised the bile in anger and frustration in the unawares observer.

The unaware were drawn in by the sceptical, believing they were witnessing democracy in action, but feeling demoralised by the lack of justice conquering injustice. Of course, like any good totalitarian psy-op, the induced frustration, anger, fear, helplessness and disequilibrium was the required and desired result.

Disequilibrium: This orchestrated theatre within politics had been the *modus operandi* of the state for decades; the manipulation of people via the medium of fear and misinformation and propaganda. Of course, it disorientated people. The coordinates of reality were unreliable. Like sailing in a ship with no working guidance instruments, or the instruments being set at the wrong coordinates, and no way of seeing, fear as a way of being became a normal way of life. This fear lay below the threshold of perception, or rose to a level of fear and anxiety where a person could perceive and experience themselves in a state of distress.

Fear was and had always been a prime tool in the armoury of the state. It is a good way to control people; far more efficient than torture and official prisons (although, the threat of them could also be used). Generalised fear can control and manipulate vast amounts of people. Waves of manufactured fear and then hope cause chaos, disequilibrium, menticide and psychosis; a split mind, hooked on phantasms.

The menticide was promoted heavily over a few decades via the use of terrorism, pandemics, environmental emergencies, and orchestrated weather dangers. These were good enough to get people to fear the external, the world. The biggest trick was to get people to even fear themselves. Of course, getting people to see themselves as a biological contagion or environmental terrorist was a pretty good trick, but it didn't quite hit the mark. It was necessary to get people to hate and doubt themselves and their very existence, in every way possible. Inherent character flaws, however immutable (e.g., the colour of one's skin, being white, or sex, being male), were inculcated to be seen by people as dangerous, wrong, dirty, shameful, etc.

To get people to hate their very being, in the here and the now, and forced to comply with such a doctrine, for the greater good, and to be ashamed if one did not adhere to such a doctrine, had become the psycho-panopticon reality. It was the perfect prison, people cut off, stunted and drifting in a Godless universe.

The enormity of this situation, of David's present situation, was bearing down upon him like the force of gravity, pulling him down. He had experienced such inklings before, throughout his life, but at this moment, on the ship, the weight of this realisation was now too great to bear. The dam of any remaining cognitive dissonance had burst.

He had become merely part of the cattle herd of humanity, or what was left of humanity. Every aspect of his life at this point was being taken up into the care of the state. His day-to-day activity, his psychology, his movements, his socialising, his communication, every aspect of his life had had the guts of any resemblance of freedom ripped out. God knows how many tours to the Western Isles would be his fate. He might end up like Fergus, wisecracking his way through life. This was not a way to live. David did not feel up to the job of wisecracking or joking ever again, or joking towards his eventual death. It was no joke now. This joke wasn't funny anymore.

A terror came upon him. A terror never felt by him ever before in his life. He thought of his mother, his father, his wife and children; ordinary existence, innocent love, liberty and freedom. All that was now gone. The light of his being was becoming terrifyingly dim. A darkness engulfed him. His body was shaking uncontrollably against his will. He could not stop it. It was as if a power or demon had possessed him. He was unsure if his thoughts emanated from him, from the state indoctrination, or perhaps even a demon that was within him.

He was rooted to his chair. Tears began flowing from his eyes; huge globules of salty tears running down his face, soaking the front of his sweatshirt. Yet, he made no sound. He could not make a sound. It was like his voice box had been disabled.

The terror: nobody could save him now. As a child, he thought (as most children do) that his mum or dad would always be there to rescue him and his brother. David felt like a child. He wanted to be rescued – but he knew now that nobody would come… ever. That was when the resolution came to him in a blinding flash. It seemed so obvious, so clear. It calmed him, it made him feel at peace, reconciled to the inevitable: he would end his life. A logical conclusion to a meaningless world. He would be at peace then, be free, liberated from this hellish nightmare.

David felt calm, peaceful and heavy. And drifted into a deep sleep.

David's Dream

He found himself in a courtroom. He was the defendant in the dock. He was surrounded by several judges – he was not sure how many, maybe ten, maybe there was an infinite number. It was hard to tell. But they all looked like him, like doppelgangers.

One judge, who seemed to be the head judge, and sitting directly opposite him, peered over his glasses and looked at David sternly.

'Why should we spare your life? This is highly unusual. I mean, this never happens, ever.'

Before David could answer, a flurry of voices from the other judges echoed the first judge's sentiment.

Judge 2: 'It can't be, it never has been.'

Judge 3: 'This upsets the natural order of justice. He has to die. He has broken the code, there is no recourse to an alternate law. The law is written, as it always has been.'

Judge 4: 'Learned gentlemen, you know what is being asked here today from this defendant? To be delivered from evil. Yes. Where would yielding to such a demand lead to? Is this where we are at?'

Judge 5: 'Agreed, he has faith in justice, but justice cannot be shown to be given, under any circumstance. He has reached the end of the road. Yet, deep down inside him, he has a spark of light which indicates, really, a desire for redemption. How rude, how utterly selfish. We cannot possibly tolerate such impudence. There is only one possible conclusion. That is clear.'

Judge 6: 'He has offered himself up to justice. It cannot be seen for leniency to be shown. What would others think if justice was shown?'

David felt terrified. They were discussing his case for the right to live. Initially, at the start of this trial, he felt that a reprieve was possible, that it was within his grasp to walk free from the court, that such things were possible. But now, to his utter horror, it seemed like it was not possible. This was a nightmare, an utterly hellish nightmare. He tried to utter words to the judges to allow him to defend himself. It was like they could not hear him, or that there was no sound coming from his mouth. His words evaporated into thin air and came to nothing. He stood sobbing in the dock.

For a brief moment, he felt a glimmer of hope. The courtroom went dark. David shot up through the building, through floor after floor. The upward trajectory was easy and exhilarating. The fabric of the building did not touch him; he just went through it like a ghost. Anything was possible, absolutely anything, including saving his life. He felt this was possible, this WAS possible. 'I can do it,' he told himself, with an emphasis on the I. He had this power, this incredible ability. Just as he pierced the final floor of this immensely high building of the courtroom, his trajectory dramatically reduced and he came suddenly to a stop. Like Icarus who flew too close to the sun, now David, with his arrogance of superhuman ability to fly and pass through solid floors and stone, plummeted back down to where he had started.

With a thump, he landed back in the darkened courtroom. He could not see any of the judges. He was in the dock, but trapped in the dock with a series of straps, boards and mechanisms, from which there was no escape. He tried to struggle, but struggling made his capture even more secure. Terror set in. There was no escape... ever... this was for eternity. Imprisoned in the dark forever... the fear was too much. It was overwhelming. He wanted it to end, but even hoping for that was futile. He could not even lose consciousness. This was hell. Then the terror increased a millionfold and he was screaming from his hellish entrapment. A loud sound engulfed him, like some kind of cosmic din that would be impossible to measure by human means. He could no longer even hear his own screams. At that point he lost consciousness.

*****

BING-BONG... BING-BONG...BING-BONG...
BING-BONG...BING-BONG...BING-BONG.

David awoke, startled by the loud, ear-piercing shrill from the ship's intercom in his room. He was nearing his destination.

Chapter Ten

Land of Final Solutions

David was shaking, still terrified from his dream, or nightmare. It had felt so terrifyingly real. He had been out cold for five hours. Comatose. He could not quite believe it.

He stumbled to his feet, rubbing his eyes. He had been crying in his sleep, as fresh tears still lay upon his cheeks. *When the spirit is weakened, it tends to be drawn down into darkness*, he thought.

But he had come to his conclusion. This was it. He felt nothing about this final solution; not emotion, not sadness, nor fear. An odd state of mind, considering the enormity of his decision. It was what it was. If one lives in a world where human life, liberty, and freedom mean nothing, by the state, is it any wonder why some people succumb to such menticide and psychosis? All for the greater good, for those that do succumb, whatever that 'greater good' was.

David got up and went to the toilet for a piss. His bladder was full to bursting point. He was also desperately thirsty and starving. He had not eaten or drunk anything for hours. He peed for what seemed like ages, a smelly yellow urine.

The tannoy sounded again: BING-BONG… BING-BONG… BING-BONG. Then a female voice spoke.

'We will be arriving at Lochboisdale in twenty-five minutes. Please be aware that the TV and refreshments lounge will close in ten minutes.

David finished emptying his bladder, then went to the sink and splashed his face with cold water. He looked into the mirror. Looking back at himself was a broken man; red, tearful eyes, tired wrinkles around the eyes, and greasy, messy hair.

'It's over, no more. I can't do this anymore,' he said to himself.

He grabbed his electronic key from his pocket, exited the toilet and pressed it against his cabin door. He then hurriedly rushed down to the TV/refreshment lounge. Again, using his electronic key, he pressed it against the reader of the door of the lounge and it opened.

It opened to a large, open-plan semi-circular room. At the far end, in front of him, was a curved viewing area, with huge glass panes looking out to the front of the ship. Dotted around the room were several small tables, each with a swivel chair affixed to the floor. The tables were also fixed to the floor, of course. This was no doubt to facilitate non-mixing or socialising. Such things were frowned upon. To his left, as he entered the lounge, was a series of vending machines where you could get snacks and drinks. Above these, on the wall, was a screen pumping out the latest Scottish Broadcasting Corporation propaganda news; energy production was reaching news highs, crime was a record low, viruses were predicted, so special precautions had to be taken, etc. Nothing new, then.

David grabbed a couple of bottles of water from the vending machine, which did not require any credit, and a couple of fake cheese sandwiches.

He walked up to the viewing area and peered through the glass. It was a dark, late autumn afternoon. The clouds were low, and it was raining. The sea was fairly choppy, but nothing exceptional. He could see the port of Lochboisdale in the distance. It was nothing really to look at. Just a scraggy bit of coast with a couple of hills overlooking the village. The ferry slowly approached the harbour. It didn't look like there would be much fanfare for their arrival. There was a scattering of houses at the actual port and, behind them, masses of modern office/living cabins. Like many ports in rural places, the inhabitants were mainly from the state, living and working in administrative roles. Over several decades, due to United Nations/globalist initiatives, the number of local residents of these areas, whose families had lived here for years, had diminished and the government had taken over the properties. The rural areas were just run as a state asset, fulfilling the goals of sustainable development and the ecological goals. The state owned the land, air and water. It effectively took ownership of the air people breathed, the water people drank, and the land where people were allowed – or, invariably, not allowed – to go.

The bureaucratic panoptic gaze and influence had reached the very fabric of the living world. Its tentacles had reached far. Hardly a scrap of the world was free or liberated. The global medico-technocratic communism had gripped so many nations after the concocted COVID-19 virus pandemic in 2020. That event speeded things up for the globalists in what was known as the 'Great Reset'. Originally, the 'Great Reset' was regarded as a conspiracy theory, but it soon came to light that the globalist elite, the banks, and the science and technology companies, aided and abetted by its puppet politicians in individual countries (or, rather, departments; a sovereign country or nation was stretching it a bit in the definitions stake by 2020) had been planning it for years. Essentially, democracy had been gradually stripped away. Yes, sure, people voted, but deals were done where the desire of the masses was obliterated. Whole countries were sewn up like kippers by politicians and leaders, who did not represent the people who voted for them.

As part of the 'Great Reset', which was ramped up in 2020, most small to medium-sized businesses were made bankrupt, closed down, or the state made it impossible for them to operate due to ecological and bureaucratic policies. Shut down as a result of government dictates for the COVID-19 virus, coupled with years of increasing business rates and taxes, made running a business impossible. Only state-sanctioned or state-run business outlets, which included large corporations, were able to survive the cultural revolution of business slaughter. It made for a dull world. A monoculture, where difference, creativity, flare, colour, and vibrancy had gone. A soulless retail and hospitality industry.

Indeed, by the year 2050, food had become so bland that, for the masses, it was only eaten for sustenance. One could hardly describe eating as a gastronomic experience anymore. The common industries of the 20th and early 21st century, like sheep, cattle and fishing industries, were culled. Of course, a tiny fraction of these industries did exist, but it only served a minute fraction of the food economy; it served the palates of the elites. For the most part, the masses were moved onto synthetic protein.

'Meat' was grown in large industrial laboratories. It was made by growing muscle cells in a nutrient serum and then encouraging them to form muscle-like fibres. Other animal products, like artificial milk or hen-free egg whites, were created by yeast that was genetically altered to produce the proteins found in eggs or milk.

Grub farming also became a huge industry after the loss of traditional farming. Historically, entomophagy – the eating of insects – did exist. The most widespread insects and arachnids eaten around the world were things like crickets, grasshoppers, ants, caterpillars, and worms – such as the mopani worm, silkworm and waxworm – and the larva of the flour beetle. In the early 21st century, as part of the grand plan of the 'Great Reset', there was a gradual introduction of such culinary delights into the Western world; in the Far East and parts of Africa, the eating of insects and other such things was more common and widely accepted.

Entomophagy met the challenge of reducing human consumption of heavy animal industries and controlling what people ate. And it met the predicted need for the, at the time, predicted population of 9-10 billion by 2050 and how to feed them. Edible insects and the mini-livestock markets emerged in the West with government-funded scientific research into human-grade edible insects. These farming methods and structures became the economic backbone of the livestock industry. Even if people did not want to eat the insect, so to speak, the processing of the protein made its way into protein products to make the eating of insects and such like more palatable.

The materials from insects provided a complete protein that contained all nine essential amino acids as well as important minerals, making it comparable with fish and meat. The possibilities were endless for the production of food products.

The Western Isles were very suited to the protein farm industry. There was plenty of land for buildings and harvesting the protein. In fact, the Western Isles were world famous for the products that were produced there. Just like in previous generations, when food products gained great prestige from certain areas like cheese, or beef, mealworm protein burgers from the Isle of Skye, or Hebridean Insect Protein-based pasta, made its way across the world with great success.

David looked out onto the approaching, rugged-looking island. He was destined to be a resident there for six months (at least) to work in the bug factories and have his psyche straightened out. He had shown too much resistance, had questioned too much, had been too masculine, too rational, too concerned for actual injustices in the world and called them out. People like David, like his father before him, were anomalies, faulty machines, in an insane and completely engineered human world.

The fact that people in the preceding decades had given up their freedom so easily, that they saw eating maggots as a free choice and embraced such culinary habits so easily, was really debased. The majority of humankind had fallen so low, but embraced it, and the masses punished and shamed those who did not follow the herd.

The wilfulness and gullibility of giving up freedoms became especially evident with the COVID-19 events of 2020. David's father told him that people gave up their rights to breathe the air freely and use their natural respiratory systems as God intended. The wearing of face masks became compulsory for several years in public places to 'stop the spread of the COVID-19 virus' and, consequently, other viruses. There was little scientific evidence for their use and they caused great harm, but people kept wearing them. The vileness of the government at the time even mandated mask wearing for children in schools. Many children developed lung problems, bacterial infections, and psychological difficulties. Some developed anxiety issues from wearing masks; fear of infection, fear of people, fear of death, etc. The psychosocial development of children was severely stunted. Children were brought up in a world where people's faces were constantly masked. This discouraged ordinary social interaction and the ability to read people. It was one of the most fascistic things done to the human race. Political leaders, public health advisers and mental health experts were complicit in pushing the wearing of face masks. They turned a blind eye to the harms this would do to people in general, but especially for children. It truly was criminal and state-sanctioned child abuse. The fact that this policy was pushed by many political activists and politicians who were supposedly concerned with child welfare and mental health was quite incredible. Pre-2020, forcing a child to wear a face mask would have been an issue for the police or social services. The cognitive dissonance of the masses could not see this blatant contradiction in their political 'leaders'.

Another aspect where the extent of submission was clearly shown was the phenomenon of 'social distancing'. Due to the 'danger' of COVID-19, people were required to keep two metres away from each other in shops, workplaces and public transport. In shops, there were markings on the floor and signs everywhere telling people to socially distance. People were herded like sheep.

In essence, these measures were ritualistic, illogical (as they were not based on science) and humiliating. This was deliberate. The state wanted to break the psyche of people; brainwash them, drive them into psychosis. The stark reality that people were being initiated and broken in for a life of cultish

104

totalitarianism was clearly shown by the dictate of the psychotic leader of Scotland in 2020, Nicola Sturgeon.

These illogical rules delivered by Sturgeon and other leaders were a deliberate attempt to disorientate and control the minds of the masses, to short-circuit critical thinking. Their tactics were exactly the same as those employed by cult leaders or domestic abusers. Cult leaders change the rules or the narrative at a whim for no apparent reason – hence, the 'get married with mask', 'don't wear a mask when getting married' flip-flop. It made no sense – it was not meant to. People blindly obeyed, journalists did not question, political commentators and activists went to sleep. Cult leaders and abusers wanted to make the masses follow chaos. These tactics formed the basis for making the human subject into an object, of making people become alienated from themselves.

This abusive objectification and alienation that the totalitarian leaders of 2020 imposed on people, including children, was the greatest atrocity of humankind. It was dark and inhumane at its roots. Many religious-minded people believed its roots were satanic or occultist. It certainly had that feel. Indeed, it was difficult to see it any other way, even in 2050. Now, people were eating insects, and living like reptiles; operating on pleasure, pain, fight or flight. Higher humanity and its very being was destroyed.

Such were the musings of David as he looked out onto the approaching Western Isles. Everything was destroyed; meaning, connection, humanity, freedom, liberty and Being. Stuffing his face with his fake cheese sandwiches, consisting of garish yellow slices and hyper-processed bread, he was lost in a fugue state just looking, not thinking. Not thinking. *This is what has happened to humanity*, he thought. Thinking was lost in the mists of time somewhere, where people once existed, where people would meet each other, man to man, so to speak, fearless, naked, raw, exposed. All gone. Sucked into a medico-technocratic dystopia. There was no escape. David now felt he had come to the logical conclusion of what must be. Darkness. The end.

It was ok. It was not his fault. Evil had triumphed over the world. Those in power had fucked it up; those who did not fight, were complicit. It showed that those who gained positions of political influence should not be given too much power. Those who sought power were invariably drawn to, or seduced by, evil; known truisms for thousands of years. Not heeded. Ignored. Dismissed. The elites and those in power thought they could create a utopia for themselves. They failed. They had created Hell on Earth. They could go to hell as far as David was concerned. That is where they would go. David hoped he would not go to hell. He hoped, at the least, if there was nothing after death, just to have sleep, darkness. Silence… just silence. Stillness… nothing. That is all he hoped for now. Nothing.

David's daydreaming was suddenly interrupted by a tap on his shoulder.

'Come on, David,' Josh sternly hissed. 'Chop, chop. We are here. Let's get going. Assembly in disembarkation area, where we got on the ship… five minutes. Get your skates on.'

Chapter Eleven

Last Leg: Welcome to the Gulag Caledonia

Josh was in a terrible mood for some reason. David followed him out of the lounge and down the corridor, then slipped into his cabin to get his bag. Coming out of his cabin, he bumped into Fergus.

'Where the hell did you get to?' said Fergus. 'I never caught you in the lounge. It was all quite uneventful until wee Grasshopper had a mental breakdown.'

'What happened?'

'Oh, he was sitting staring out over the sea in the lounge. He started crying and kicking furniture and throwing sandwiches about the room. The goons quickly came and sedated him and carted him off. I tried to talk sense into him, but it was no use.'

'Where is he now?' David asked.

'Oh, he will be in the isolation section for those who lose it,' replied Fergus. 'Drugged up and waiting to be shipped back to the mainland for a nice stay in the hospital, getting the last vestiges of his brains scraped out and reprogrammed. Poor lad. Just collateral damage of the final solution of mankind. That is why Josh and Raymond are in fine fettle. They had to actually do some work other than wank each other off during the crossing. It is not good for them to lose people so early on. Not good for their "Back to Work and Well-Being" performance, hahaha… Come on, we had better get going to the disembarkation area, or we will be sent back to the loony bin at this rate.'

David and Fergus both arrived in the disembarkation area, where they had first boarded the ship. Ship crew were wandering around getting ready to dock. Josh and Raymond were sitting on a sofa in the centre of the area. They were looking extremely pissed off, busily conversing and tapping on their personal computers on their laps.

The engines of the ship rumbled loudly as it lodged against the harbour wall. David peered out one of the windows. Men wrapped up in waterproofs and warm hats and thick gloves were rushing around tethering the boat to the dock. Another man in a motorised vehicle was driving a set of steps up to the exit.

Two crew members were ready at the door to secure the steps to the ship.

Josh and Raymond got up. They approached David and Fergus.

'Ok,' said Josh. 'We will go down to the waiting minibus. It's about three-and-a-half hours from here, including a fifty-minute ferry journey. Then we will arrive at the Luskentyre community and your accommodation for the next six months. Unfortunately, we have lost Neil. He is not feeling well, so he is having to go back to the mainland.'

'He has no got the true grit for the Gulag yet, eh, Josh?' mocked Fergus. 'A wee stay in the mind-bending hospital will sort him though, eh?'

'Come on now, Fergus,' replied Josh. 'We don't make fun of mental health. That is highly insensitive and inappropriate. We hope he gets the care and treatment he needs, and he will be able to get back on track.'

'Back on track?' David said in a deadpan manner. 'What is that, Josh? What does that actually entail? Accepting his fate in the great scheme of all things for the state? Maybe he is sad? Maybe he is at the end of his tether for a life that will not be lived or realised? Maybe he feels entrapped into a system of which he sees no end, no resolution, no hope?'

Josh and Raymond looked astonished and flabbergasted at what David had just said. It was like they had just been fed something that they could not digest. Fergus smirked and slapped David on the back.

'Such negativity is extremely demotivating for all concerned, David,' Raymond whined back. 'We are all in this together, for the country, for the social and cultural programmes the government is trying to achieve. We all have to make sacrifices. It is tough sometimes and we have to double down and try to get through it.'

David shook his head and smiled in dismay. It was just the kind of non-response he was expecting. A non-response laced with a not insignificant dose of violent totalisation of the situation. No specks of light could get through such a response. It was like a sugary-sweet treacle spread thickly over social discourse.

'I am sorry to break up this philosophical discussion,' chirped Josh, 'but we have to get off the boat now. Our carriage awaits. Chop chop.'

Josh and Raymond proceeded to exit the ship, along with all the other foot passengers, down the steps, followed by David and Fergus. Stepping out into the fresh air of a dark afternoon, with the clouds, wind and rain, was utterly refreshing after being cooped up for hours on the boat. The wind and rain lashed at David's face. It felt like a cleansing. As he walked down the steps, he felt like a free man with not a care in the world. They walked toward the waiting minibus. Raymond got in the front, while Josh sat in the back with David and Fergus. Josh closed the door and the driver then took off from the port out onto the road bound for Harris.

David wouldn't need to put up with the likes of Josh, Raymond, or the folk at the Department of Work and Well-Being, for much longer. They were insignificant now. David was lost to them. There was no way to speak with people who espoused and oozed their ideological outlook. One may as well have spoken to a brick wall; it was impenetrable.

Society had, over many decades and centuries, rescinded in the nightmarish reality of direct communication (aided by the rise in science, man as God) as described by the Danish Christian existentialist philosopher, Soren Kierkegaard; the direct communication exemplified by Raymond's psycho-babble when describing the fate of Neil. The gift of indirect communication had been cast aside into the bin.

David reflected on this. He recalled how his father had recounted to him that the destruction of subjectivity (negative thinking, based on the infinite as opposed to positive, objective thinking, based upon an idea of man as God, the finite, earthly concerns) was borne over many hundreds of years of moving from an experiential philosophical towards a purely speculative philosophical method. Through the historical developments of the renaissance and enlightenment, where religion (Christianity) went from being an experimental or experiential practice to a purely speculative and essentially legalistic doctrine, detracted from the true meaning of the Christian church. Of course, it did not disappear completely.

Essentially, speculative or positive philosophical outlook negated the heart. The heart, and not the brain, is the area in which the theologian is formed. Theology includes the intellect, as all sciences do, but it is in the heart that the intellect and all of man observes and experiences the rule of God. One of the basic

109

differences between science and the spiritual man is that man has his heart, or noetic faculty, by nature, whereas he himself has created his instruments of scientific observation.

Positive thinking, based on the finite, the material, the speculative philosophical outlook, is based on the idea of certainty in sense perception, in historical knowledge, and the results of speculation. But, as Kierkegaard argued, all this positiveness is sheer falsity. The certainty of sense perception is a deception; it is approximation knowledge; it fails to express the situation of the knowing subject in existence. Such a method gives a person a semblance of certainty; but true certainty, based within the heart (with the help of the grace of God), rather than the brain, can only be in the infinite, where one as an existing subject person cannot remain, but only repeatedly arrive. Nothing historical can become infinitely certain for a person, except for the fact of one's own existence, which cannot become infinitely certain for any other individual.

The negative thinkers, on the other hand, have an advantage, as the negative (based upon the heart, the spiritual) is present everywhere (as existence is a constant process of becoming). It is necessary to become aware of its presence continuously. If one forgets or is not mindful of this, one can slip into positive or speculative thinking, which is to risk slipping into deception. The distinction between negative and positive (or speculative) thinking is exemplified by Kierkegaard, who describes the difference between direct communication (positive, speculative) versus indirect communication.

But people, over many decades and hundreds of years, came to think of such things as superstition or esoteric mumbo-jumbo. Of course, with the loss of religious sensibility in society and culture, as evidenced by hundreds of years of cultural indoctrination, people did not miss anything being stolen from them. How could they, when it was so elusive and ineffable? If one is only taught to see and value the material, of one's desires needing to be met, couched in pseudo-scientific certainty, then what need would people have of the transcendent?

Humankind became lost. Very lost.

Now, humans (the masses, not the elites who controlled the masses and who had enslaved them) had become mere cattle, objects, and treated their own existence like an object to be manipulated. The only thing that counted now was direct communication – dictates, orders, solutions, strategies. On the surface, it was harmless enough, but it separated humankind from Being, becoming, the infinite and the heart. It was done on purpose, David's father believed, by elites, over hundreds of years, intent on separating humanity from the source, from God. Humanity thus became withered and broken. But David mused how his father told him not to give up, or let things feel hopeless, as there was always a way, a hope, an order, a logos to things that would ultimately transcend the horrors that had befallen humanity, no matter what suffering people endured. If one gave up, then one was giving up for all of humanity. That was why suicide was regarded in Christianity as a sin.

Tears came again to David's eyes as the minibus drove out of Lochboisdale into the once wonderful free country that was once called the Outer Hebrides – now renamed the Western Isles. He had failed. He was giving up. He felt ashamed. There was no strength left in him. David felt like Meursault in Albert Camus' *The Stranger*, waiting for his death, but having even given up on the faith in his final moments. *So be it*, he thought. He had nothing left.

They drove along the narrow, meandering roads, roughly northwards up the southern Isle of Uist. This once wonderful place, long since largely rewilded on the back of Agenda 2021/2030 by the UN, now forbade small-scale crofters/self-sufficiency types, or just ordinary people, from growing a bit of veg and having a few chickens. The international governmental bodies found ways to make out that homegrown/reared food was dangerous. The result was that only government-sanctioned food supplies were possible. Growing your own carrots became a crime, as did having a few chickens for eggs. They did not want people to be self-sufficient or independent from the clutches of the state.

The few people that were left to exist on these islands either worked in the protein plants, or the wind or wave farms. Island life had changed considerably in a few decades. Any sense of community or island life had been amputated. First the churches were attacked due to the COVID-19 crisis of 2020; they withered. The clergy struggled to maintain any kind of church community, especially since many islanders were forced to move elsewhere, or reskill to work on the new protein farms and green energy projects which flooded the islands. Family life was also attacked. Initially, in the early 2020s, islanders rejected the Scottish government's queer theory sex-education agenda. The revolt did not last. Hate crime

111

laws banning any criticism of queer education in schools got rid of the last vestiges of dissent from concerned parents and people of a religious persuasion. They always come for the family. Not many people can withstand such a threat. The assault on community, family, livelihoods (e.g., small and medium-sized businesses) and any kind of self-sufficiency turned life into a drab, grey, homogenous, timeless reality.

As David looked out the minibus window, into the greyness of the late afternoon light, with the homogenous buildings that housed the grubs and maggots and mealworms lining the route, and the wind turbines raping the landscape wherever he looked, the sense of meaningless he already felt was compounded. *How could humans create a hell on Earth and destroy so much goodness?* he thought to himself. He was reminded of a book his father left for him and his brother, with a note inside the front cover which read:

> 'The defence of Truth, the value of parrhesia (fearless speech), is central to the heart or hesychasm. God is accessible to personal experience, because he shared his own life with humanity. All these things that I write, and what is written in this book, have been under attack for a long time, but in your time, it will seem as though they have been obliterated. But a flame will linger always in the heart of man. It's knowing where to find it, how to find it. That is what is the catalyst for change. It can never be extinguished. To my wonderful boys who came into my life with the grace of God and changed my life forever. I will love you both with all my heart, forever and ever. I will always be with you. Nobody or nothing can ever take my love away from you, not even death. Dad.'

The book, *The Triads* by Gregory Palamas (1296-1359), an Orthodox Christian monk, was an exposition on hesychasm, the noetic faculty of the heart, the key to Christian practice. For David's father, it highlighted key points which were pertinent to the ravages of a secular society, whereby religious sensibilities diminished and withered. This had the effect of cutting people off from themselves as well as from each other. It plunged people into a barbarism one would never think possible in an enlightened society. One such example David remembers hearing his father rage about was how the Prime Minister of New Zealand, in the early 2020s, fought for a law whereby babies that survived an abortion procedure would not be allowed medical help. In other words, even if the baby was living after the procedure, breathing, lying in pain, it was against the law for a doctor to assist the baby. It was a most cruel, vile and, for most people, unforgiveable act of law. It reflected how lost humanity had become that people campaigned for this, and how people just stood by and did not offer any protest.

A passage from the book that came to David's mind described how evil transforms virtue into vice, what is called impassability, the state in which the passionate part of the soul finds itself in a state of death. The activity of this passionate part of the soul completely blinds and gouges out the divine eye and, as a consequence, does not allow any of its faculties to come into play. It is with this faculty of the soul that we either love or turn away that which unites with ourselves, or else remains a stranger to ourselves. Those who love the good transform this power and do not put it in the service of evil or death, but instead activate it towards the love of God and their neighbours.

David feared that his soul had been killed, that his divine eye had been gouged out. He felt a terror in his chest that he was irredeemable. It was terror where there was no escape. Nobody was coming to help, ever. He looked over at Josh. He felt sick. The guy was a robot. Brain dead. One could grab somebody like him by the throat, squeeze and squeeze, demanding him to see sense. Somebody like Josh would not flinch, even if one did this to them. They would let themselves be killed; such were the effects of menticide or brainwashing by the state and the darkness that had afflicted them. Death was preferable to any light being let in. Fallen man.

The fragility of man, when faced with another, an Other, is too hard to bear for some. The ethical demand that one is confronted with is too raw, too real, too human for some. In that one moment, Being towards death and Being in life co-exist and coalesce at the same time. A moment in eternity which illuminates the divine eye or noetic faculty, the heart. The heart aches in such moments. Eternal Beings existing for a moment, hurtling through time and space, to the inevitable end, death. It was this exquisite realisation, this experience that had no equal; but, at the same time, for many, it was a terror of such profundity. It was in that moment, when terror dominates, that people turn and the divine eye shuts.

David closed his eyes and wished for death. He longed for the end. He wanted to be extinguished from existence once and for all. He didn't care anymore. There was no point. Oh, how he had tried... how he had tried. Even if he tried to resurrect his soul, it would fail; every time he grasped at hope, he would be dashed against the rocks. Every action was met with failure. It was as though his action, his will, was futile.

David, like his father, had suffered from depression in his life. It was a particular malaise or haunting spectre that appeared most fervently in the late 20th/early 21st century as the rise in secularism in the Western world took an even greater hold. People began to develop an uncanny inability to withstand the vicissitudes of life, unlike in earlier times when the 'black dog' was tolerated as an ordinary facet of life, perhaps even a spiritual trial that had to be accepted and gone through, akin to the ideas of St John of the Cross and the 'Dark night of the soul'. The rise of the cultural hegemony of mental health within an increasing secular society was a phenomenon that went into hyperdrive during the late 20th century with the increasing role that psychology and psychiatry (as well as psycho-pharmaceutical products) played in inculcating the masses into seeing their experience (cognitions, thoughts, moods, emotions) as essentially problematic, pathological, and an issue that had to be resolved. But the only way it could be resolved, the only method that was available, especially after the death of God, was a solution-focused, psycho-objective 'therapeutics' which erased and negated all other modes of dealing with, and conceptualising, experience.

The Fabian socialist Bertrand Russell, in *The Impact of Science on Society* (1953), wrote:

> '...it is to be expected that advances in physiology and psychology will give governments much more control over individual mentality than they now have even in totalitarian countries. Fichte laid it down that education should aim at destroying free will, so that, after pupils have left school, they shall be incapable, throughout the rest of their lives, of thinking or acting otherwise than as their schoolmasters would have wished... Diet, injections, and injunctions will combine, from a very early

114

age, to produce the sort of character and the sort of beliefs that the authorities consider desirable, and any serious criticism of the powers that be will become psychologically impossible.'

By the time David was in school, this philosophy had taken hold, whereby the ethos of all state schools was permeated by this psycho-technocratic philosophy. David recalled sitting in a circle with classmates aged 6 or 7, all discussing their moods, thoughts, fears, etc. Heavily prompted by a teacher, they were encouraged to discuss their families (e.g., their mums' and dads' mental health) and what strategies could be employed to cure their minds of the aberration of experience. Of course, these group confessionals served as data collection points for the state to gain a lens into the family home to garner some dirt for future purposes. The surveillance via therapy was never meant to be truly therapeutic. Only as a means to gain control.

In these groups, children were singled out by the teacher if they were not participating in a satisfactory way; if a child was not forthcoming on the state of their inner mind, or of the state of mind of his or her parents, it would be noted that the child was hiding something. The local council social services department would make a note of this 'reticence'. It was an indication of non-compliance. These records would follow a child throughout their lives into adulthood and affect their chances of gaining employment and other things. It was essentially the beginning of a social credit system under the guise of a benign therapeutics. On the surface, most parents of children generally only saw these developments as well meaning and caring. Most people said, 'What is so wrong with helping with mental health?'

David recalled how his father objected to this blatant social engineering and enculturation. He occasionally mentioned these issues to other parents at the school gates. The other parents would either stare at him, eyes glazing over, thinking his father was a crank, or they would gush enthusiastically about how the Well-Being programme was great and how their child was able to monitor their moods and cognition and devise strategies for self-regulation and mood enhancement.

It was utterly monstrous how human experience had been reduced to such a base common denominator. To get children to see their own experience as an object to be monitored

115

and manipulated was brainwashing and child abuse. This abuse was carried out with very little opposition and supported by professionals and organisations supposedly with the goal of improving the well-being of children.

The result of such state ideological intervention was children growing into adults with a stunted and shallow personality, whereby any difficulty encountered in life, within the domain of the psychological, would be labelled as pathology and in need of state intervention, e.g., medical treatment, talking therapy, medication, etc. The psychic limitations implanted into people, on a mass basis, were truly an achievement on a grand scale.

Of course, the programming did not work on everybody. People like David and his brother, who had enlightened parents, were able to negate the conditioning. But it came at a price. People who did not succumb to the system became, in the eyes of the majority, oddballs, outsiders, weirdos, eccentric, and were regarded by the state as extremists or even dangerous. For the most part, such individuals were controlled by being prevented from getting jobs or promotion, or being the first to be made redundant if a company was laying off people. There was also increased state interference from social services if such people started families, e.g., health visitor checks.

David and his brother were examples of children who had managed to get through life pretty well; but, like many outsiders like him, they never really fitted in. Things were often difficult for them both. In primary and high school, the teachers labelled them as problematic, as having behavioural issues, as confrontational. Even at university, some of David's professors suggested he was not enculturated enough into the system and strongly suggested he change his attitude or act more accordingly to the demands of the system. Looking back, it was difficult to know if these were friendly hints, or sinister warnings.

Sitting in the minibus, being driven against one's will to a state-enforced Work and Well-Being placement in the Western Isles, they could have been both hints and warnings. Either way, whatever path one chose in life, individual sovereignty, liberty, and autonomy were prevented and curtailed. The perfect control society. A living, breathing panopticon everywhere one went. The land where you walked, the air that you breathed, the work you did and the food you ate all had state interference; one could not escape its tentacles. From the moment you were born until you

116

died you were recorded, chipped, monitored, controlled, medicated, programmed, punished, etc. It was never ending. And, to top it all, one was expected to work for it… for the greater good!

The most infuriating aspect of the world was the cognitive dissonance of people, displayed most perfectly by the likes of Josh and Raymond, the perfect models of the regime. Of course, years of education (brainwashing) and psychotropic medication had a great effect of numbing one to what was going on and significantly eased any dangerous self-reflection.

David began to daydream. The rain outside was drizzling down, with low cloud, and he was aware of the constant hum of the electric minibus. Everyone was silent. Fergus was asleep. Josh was engrossed in his electronic notepad. Notes maybe. A report about Neil, perhaps. How he had intervened to stop the crisis, how his interventions had improved things, or not, what could have been done better, what could he have done, how could he improve the next time there was a crisis. The never-ending professional self-reflection, self-improvement, monitoring, and administration. This was part of everybody's working life. Squeezing unnecessary blood out of a stone.

Such bureaucracy crept into the world over many decades; in social services with care plans, risk assessments, care reviews, etc, and these migrated into schools and educational settings. As David found out in his university post, bi-monthly meetings with his boss were essentially self-criticism and reflection sessions. They became so repetitive, inauthentic, and almost like theatre. He was asked questions about his progress, how could he improve, was he thinking about diversity, inclusion, global citizenship, sustainable development, etc. As David found out, such a system had migrated into the so-called land of the free radical activist types. Their circle jerk (self-reflection) meetings were just an excuse to monitor each other's thinking, and punish those who were straying from the accepted line. Of course, there was the danger that, if one did stray from the party line, the group would turn on you, like a vicious pack of dogs; or, even worse, they would report you to the authorities for your indiscretions. The atmosphere of paranoia, guardedness and inauthentic behaviour was thick in such situations. One dare not put a foot wrong. One lived in a constant low-level fight or flight situation. It was exhausting. Just to live became an exhausting effort.

117

People just withdrew from each other and from themselves. Ordinary human interaction became rarer and rarer. It was part of the plan. Renegades like Fergus, or people like David who did not fit in, were obvious targets for the Work and Well-Being programme; all for the greater good, for the safety of others. It was the ethos of social hygiene which had been extrapolated from the bowels of history, in other times when the state had to get rid of the undesirables. In 2050, it came under the guise of Well-Being (for the social greater good).

David felt drowsy. He felt his eyes closing and a bit of drool escaped from out his mouth. He wiped it away and shoved his coat under his right ear and leant against the window. He felt a strange sense of self-disgust, like he was nothing more than livestock, being shuttled around against his will, drooling, imprisoned, soulless. He was off to the slaughter. He was nothing but a worthless piece of organic flesh coming to its logical conclusion. He did not matter, nothing mattered; he did not care, nobody cared for him. He shut his eyes and felt happy about death. He was content. He had not felt as happy in a long time. He prayed for blackness, nothingness, non-existence, before falling into a deep sleep...

BOOM!

David woke with a start. He did not know where he was for several seconds. He was on a car ferry on the sea and he could see land ahead with huge wind turbines blotting the landscape. The sea was very choppy with waves banging against the front of the ship, which might have accounted for the noise that wakened him. He rubbed his eyes. They were wet, almost like he had been crying in his sleep. Was such a thing possible? Maybe it was. He had hoped not. How embarrassing. But it was not beyond the bounds of possibility.

'Where are we?' he asked Josh.

'On the Berneray to Leverburgh ferry,' replied Josh. 'We will be arriving soon. And from there, it's only about another half hour to our base near Luskentyre.'

The light was really fading now. This added to David's sense of growing unease and claustrophobia; at least with daylight there was a sense of escape from oneself out into the world. When the light fades, that disappears; the world disappears, then all one is left with is oneself, the fear of being, the fear of existence. The presence of Being can be a terrifying presence. After all, it is the intersection of the noetic faculty/the heart and the presence of the demonic. The awareness of the presence of Being had, for many, many decades, or even centuries, been cultured out of humanity. Some may have argued against such a notion by citing the example of (a watered-down and neutered) Buddhist mindfulness. But this was simply used to inculcate into people a narcissistic humanist vision of humanity; that the individual was God, that he was the centre of things, that he was important. It was just pure self-indulgence, with no reference point beyond the narcissistic 'me'. Of course, more enlightened religious types would point out that such a self-centred practice was an open invitation to indulge sinful passions and, in the worst-case scenario, demonic attack, by encouraging the egotistical inflation. People scoffed at such supernatural ideas. But, of course, why would a Satan reveal himself as something to be feared? That would be pointless. The years of the genre of horror cinema depicting frightening demonic scenarios was just a ruse, a dummy pass to keep people off the scent. After all, Eve was offered a lovely juicy apple by the serpent. And so, it was and is with humans. Feed them the sugary-sweet juice of egoism, of self-indulgence. They won't be able to resist. They could not resist. The fall of man.

The ferry manoeuvred into Leverburgh harbour. The huge engines roared, trying to stabilise and orient the ferry in the choppy waters so it could let the vehicles disembark. The ferry and harbour crew worked frantically to tether the ship to the harbour side. The crew on the harbour side looked like a real hardy bunch. One man, who must have been in his seventies, wiry, around 5 feet 6, grabbed a rope and coiled it around a cast iron post. David stared at him, transfixed. The man's face was etched with lines, and big bushy auburn eyebrows set off his orange bobble hat and luminous jacket. What was most striking about this man was his piercing blue eyes, which defied age and time. It was almost like he was supernatural.

The ferry was tethered and the ramp descended onto the harbour floor. There were only two other vehicles on the ferry. Two agricultural work vans. They drove off first, followed by the minibus. As they drove slowly onto the harbour, they passed the harbour crewman with the piercing blue eyes. David looked at him. The man instinctively looked up and saw David. For several moments, which felt like an eternity, they both stared at each other. Those blue eyes revealed something that David could not quite comprehend. It was like looking into a window to another world, a world far from where they both were. David could not make up his mind if he felt comforted or frightened, or both. It was both unsettling and comforting. He wanted to hold onto this moment for a little longer, but they drove onward.

The man with the bright blue piercing eyes just looked and never dropped his gaze. It was not threatening, however. It was almost as if he saw into the depths of David's soul and could see something that others like Josh, Raymond, or Mallory or Jones from the Department of Work and Well-Being, could not see in him. He had a depth and presence that was ineffable; he was awake. David didn't meet many awake people. Josh et al. were predictable. Just like machines. The man with the piercing blue eyes was not predictable, nor was he a machine. Humans are not machines. Humans are ineffable. That was what had been cultured out of human interaction. This was deliberate. The deliberate destruction of the human, the ineffable, mystery, ordinariness, depth, simplicity, Being.

They drove away from the harbour, then up through the village of Leverburgh itself. From there, they turned left at the junction heading towards Tarbert on the A859. David felt as if he was being deported or exiled as punishment for simply being a human being, one who did not fit in, or as some kind of faulty machine that was being sent away to be fixed. In other times historically, dissidents and those who did not toe the party line were put into prison, or concentration camps, where many died. Exiling people for life (e.g., to Siberia) also happened; this was an excellent way to deal with people who did not fit in. So, people like David and Fergus were essentially being exiled, albeit with the promise of it being only a temporary work/re-education placement, for the good of their Well-Being, of course. David looked back at Fergus.

'You doing ok, Fergus?'

'Living the dream, buddy... living the dream,' replied Fergus, not breaking his empty stare out of the window. It seemed that the wisecracking Fergus that David had first met only a few hours ago had melted into the dark waters of inevitable melancholia. Jokes can only go so far. When the reality of things is too close to the bone, for one's own situation, it is hard to joke about it.

120

David noticed an eery silence had engulfed the minibus. Something that he could not put his finger on. It was almost supernatural. It was thick, permeating the fabric of existence itself. Interestingly, it had a duality about it that was equally hard to decipher. On the one hand, it was utterly awful in its demeanour, like a spectre injecting a poisonous spell upon the whole of reality. On the other hand, it was an unveiling, the revelation of perhaps something else, something truly other that was always omnipresent, as the presence of the spectre waxed and waned. It was a curious and terrifying experience. It reminded David of the German philosopher Friedrich Nietzsche, who wrote that, if one looked into the void long enough, something would speak back to you. David often pondered what this meant. What could Nietzsche have been trying to say? David fantasised that Nietzsche the atheist, who went insane, may have been confronted with something that contributed eventually to his insanity, something that did not conform to his vision of the 'Overman', his vision of man as the God, master of the world and all its domains.

What if supernatural evil, the Devil if you like, as a force did exist and was in constant battle to force its essence onto reality? Then it would be wise to convince the world that it did not exist. What a trick that would be. That would be an ingenious coup. How many people have been driven insane by such a situation, by sensing something of this fabric of reality, the duality of good versus evil, on the level of the supernatural, but had been corralled into a psychiatric hospital, a prison cell, or just ridiculed by society?

But still, trundling onwards to their final destination, it was clear nobody was coming to help this time. That was a former terror that now had been bypassed. It was an ever-reinforced fact now. Who would argue otherwise?

They turned left off the A859 onto a small road towards Luskentyre beach. David was struck by the immediate light pollution emanating from this road, which was lined with huge lamp posts with great big lights, illuminating the whole area. On the right, dominating the landscape, was an ugly metallic forest of wind turbines. There were also rows and rows of buildings consistently dotted along the route accompanied by wire fences and more ugly, intrusive lighting.

They drove slowly along the road for a couple of miles until they came to an area where there were numerous buildings on either side of the road, again behind fences. The minibus turned off the road, following a gravel path between several rows of buildings until they came to a large car park, where there were a number of minibuses and even more off-road quad bikes parked outside a large, plastic-looking two-storey building with huge windows and a roof covered with solar panels.

Josh looked up. 'Ok, welcome to your new home,' he announced. 'Let us get you settled in.'

He opened the side door of the minibus and got out, followed by David and Fergus. Fergus got down on his knees and kissed the ground as if he was praying. He got up, laughing and guffawed, 'Welcome to the Gulag Caledonia, David.'

Chapter Twelve

Induction to camp life

It was now completely dark, apart from the artificially hyper-lit area of the camp and the surrounding area. There was a surreal air about it. From what David had heard from his parents about the Outer Hebridean Islands, he had always thought they were a beautiful, magical place, peaceful, quiet, healing. However, from what David had seen on his drive up to the camp, especially what he was now seeing in this artificially lit and state-commandeered land grab all over these islands, it was more like ecological, sociological and psychological rape. With the lights bearing down from all sides, up and down, one had the feeling one's brain was being fried. He just hoped that, wherever he was sleeping, the lights would not protrude into his room.

Apart from David and his other travelling companions, there was not a soul around. It was fairly windy and, in the background, there was the distinct hum of something. *The wind turbines*, he thought. Or it could have been the sound of boilers. On a nearby building, steam was pouring out of a large box and rising into the air, to be blown away by the wind. There was the distinct feeling that this place had no life, no soul. It was dead. No sense that this was a community that one would wish to settle into. David felt straight away that he needed to escape.

There was a lull in the wind, and David could hear the sound of the sea in the distance. They were near a beach. Luskentyre beach. He caught the scent of the sea, seaweed and all things that one gets by the seaside. This smell transported David to memories long ago. Of family holidays by the beach, camping, swimming, making fires and cooking on them. Bodysurfing. The warmth of the sun, sunburn, salt. He remembered one summer holiday down the west coast of France, between the Spanish border and Bordeaux somewhere. He recalled himself and his younger brother with their father in the very wild shallow surf, with lots of other bathers riding the waves – or, rather, being carried by the waves, wonderfully, violently towards the shore. He remembered the laughter, of both him and his brother and his father. His younger brother was gripped onto his dad like a sea limpet, while David held his father's hand with great commitment, accompanied by a glorious fear of being washed away. Wonderful memories, of a different time. *Could It have been just a dream?* he thought. *Where has that world gone?*

David was roused out of his daydreaming by Josh announcing, 'Come on. This way, guys.'

Raymond and the minibus driver got out and started hooking the vehicle up to the recharging station. David and Fergus got their bags and trudged behind Josh into the foyer of the large building, which had a huge glass frontage. There was a long counter in front of them, and a back wall with an assortment of different sections: screens showing real-time video footage of different parts of the camp, and a control panel with what looked like different switches, buttons and levers. It could have been anything: a central heating system, electric power controls, etc. Below the panels were several microphones on a desk, with computer screens which were switched on. On them were small square mini screens, around six, showing what looked like individual rooms and larger rooms with individuals in them. The twig dropped for David – this was the centre of the panopticon. Security could monitor and observe everything in this camp area, including individual rooms and communal rooms in the camp, and respective buildings, etc. No doubt there were several of these stations within each camp and other buildings. They ran a tight ship. No privacy, it seemed. Nightmarish. Privacy was a luxury of earlier times in human history.

A man behind the counter sprang to life. 'Ok, guys, here are your welcome packs,' he said. 'Each bag contains a set of pyjamas and toiletries, for example soap, toothbrush, shampoo, conditioner, dental floss. You also have an electronic key card which will allow you to enter and exit your rooms and communal areas. You can't get in or out of your rooms without them. Don't lose them. There is a lanyard attachment if you want to put them around your neck for safe keeping. There is an information pack about this centre. This tells you all you need to know about the centre, where everything is, such as the canteen, games room, gym, education rooms, library, etc. You also have a booklet outlining your timetables. This details where and when your classes are, when and where your work placement is, what is permitted for your leisure time and curfew rules, and when you can leave the camp area, for instance to visit the bleak wilderness out there. Don't get caught out after hours down the beach, or I will get angry!' joked the man. 'The number of times I have to let people in, or go and fetch them from far-flung parts of this inhospitable bloody island in all weathers, does my bloody head in.'

Josh laughed. 'Yes, I remember you had to get someone to come and fetch me from outside Tarbert one night in the torrential rain, when the bus broke down.'

'Yes, I remember that well,' said the man. 'I have no clue why people want to wander around this desolate bleak wilderness at all times of the day or night. It escapes me.'

Josh and the man behind the counter were exchanging banter about essentially having little freedom and privacy like it was normal. It really was quite shocking, the level of submission to having God-given inalienable rights being taken away. This was an example of how a lack of freedom and privacy had become normalised and integrated into the mindset of the masses. They saw nothing untoward or sinister about being infantilised by the state, of being monitored and checked up on in a myriad of ways, twenty-four seven. The guards were even monitored. They monitored themselves like prison guards. They had swallowed the rhetoric, hook, line and sinker, with no questions asked. They had become stick men with no inwardness or subjectivity. You could always tell such people by their eyes – well, at least David could tell. This type of person never really listened to you, or heard you. There was a distinct lack of presence. Of course, this was the result of social programming over many decades. What with the secularisation and attack on religion over many years (or, as some would say, hundreds of years), the rise of a humanistic technological/scientific *modus operandi*, where man was God, the inculcation of a mental healthism or mental hygiene movement in all walks of life, it slowly, bit by bit, dehumanised people where they truly could be present with each other.

This social engineering was ramped up to the nth degree in the COVID-19 crisis of 2020-2025. This comprised social distancing laws, compulsory mask wearing in public, laws banning the mixing of households, hospitality settings like restaurants and bars being mostly shut down and made bankrupt, and having to abide by a strict electronic medical passport system, table service only and no mixing of guests inside, most work being put online/remote, including much of school and education. Ordinary human interaction that had occurred for millennia was obliterated in a few short years. It truly was nightmarish and dystopian. But people like Josh were perfect fodder for the machine. Compliant

125

and unquestioning, like a drone. 'All for the greater good' was the battle cry of these people.

The utterly surprising thing was that, during the COVID-19 crisis of 2020-25, educated people, and *highly* educated people, were also seduced and/or readily submitted or went along with the dystopian dictates, despite there being no science behind them. There was no scientific reason or data to back up what the governments of the world were dictating to the people at the time. And yet, they willingly helped plunge humanity into the darkest ever period in its existence. Some people said it was the end times, in biblical terms. Mass vaccination programmes were rushed out to the public; these were experimental mRNA vaccines which, in the proceeding years, showed that mortality risk, lack of fertility and susceptibility to illness were all increased. In essence, these vaccines were nothing more than a subtle form of population control; genocide without the gas chambers, and people willingly gave up their personal sovereignty under the guise that it was for your health, and freedom. And here David was, existing in this hyper-surveillance, tracked, monitored world and now a camp, where daily work, education, and free time was dished out to him from the state, not under the banner that he was prisoner, but that it was for the greater good, that it was for his own good.

There was no freedom. There was no autonomy, no way out. Well, there was one way out. The big one-way system out of this dystopian shit. It was a way that many people took these days. Suicide rates were astronomical. In 2019/20, the suicide rates in the UK were approximately 11 per 100,000. In 2050, it was around 38 per 100,000. The demographics were shocking. Men, women and children were well represented in the suicide figures. Children under the age of 16 made up more than 16 per 100,000 in the population; of that, half were below the age of 10. Of course, the government essentially turned a blind eye. It either employed cognitive dissonance or pretended to care by offering computerised psychological treatment. This was therapy with an algorithm. Real psychotherapy, between a therapist and a patient, had been devalued to the point that a fully technological approach was the only method left. If a person was lucky enough to meet an actual human being, it would be solely to get them back on board with the party line. Again, another example of not being heard, or listened to, in the true human sense of how people should interact.

Josh, who looked a bit awkward with such faux joviality, perhaps because it was in front of another state worker, looked David's way.

'David,' he said, 'your key worker should be arriving any minute soon… they will give you the finer details of what is entailed here and show you to your room… Fergus, Aidan is your key worker, like last time. He will meet you in the morning and I will show you over to your room… Ah, speak of the devil… here she comes.'

A woman, in her early thirties, entered the reception area. She was around 5 feet 5 with a small, frail build, like a bird. She had short, elfin-cut, brown hair and big brown eyes. She looked Mediterranean of origin, or Middle Eastern. She walked in with an attitude that belied her physique; like she did not give a fuck… She had a self-assurance that was quite off-putting. David noticed the tired cultural cliches of freedom and emancipation of the Brave New World – multiple piercings in both ears, and neck tattoos that protruded above the collar of her thin yellow luminous jacket. David noticed something else that repulsed him – she wore a ring on both thumbs. For David, that was a sure indicator of mental disturbance. David's mother was a practitioner of traditional Chinese medicine (which was now outlawed, like many traditional healing methods). She often joked with him to never marry a woman who wore thumb rings, as this was a sign of mental instability as the rings disrupted Qi flow, or something, around the body. It was an interesting theory and, strangely enough, most people (men and women) whom he had met who wore thumb rings always had a 'story' of some kind. *Maybe there was something in it*, David thought, looking at his new key worker.

'David, this is Louisa,' chimed Josh.

'Hello,' replied David looking at Louisa.

'Hi,' she replied, not even looking at David, still with her hands in her pockets. She had the air of someone who would rather be elsewhere.

'Oh, hello, Louisa. That smile would make the angels weep,' Fergus said sarcastically.

'Back again, Fergus, I see,' Louisa replied. 'What a surprise.'

'I couldn't stay away, Louisa. I missed this wonderful, soulful atmosphere far too much,' retorted Fergus, whilst simultaneously winking at David.

'Ok, David, come with me… I will show you to your room,' Louisa quipped tight lipped.

David picked up his welcome pack and bag. 'Cheerio guys…' he said to Josh and Fergus. 'Wish me luck.'

'Aye, you will need it, David… you will need it big time…' said Fergus. 'Keep your sense of humour in here… you will need that, too… Not too many comedians here… comedy is banned here, from my experience of the Gulag.'

Louisa turned around, hands still in her pockets, and started walking out of the reception building.

'Come on, David… Let's get you settled in,' she said while walking.

'Bye, David. See you later,' quipped Josh.

David followed Louisa out of the reception building and then left down a paved path, that took them between rows of single-storey buildings approximately 30 metres long by about 10 metres wide. Louisa walked quickly ahead of David, still with her hands in her pockets. David, stiff from the journey and with his bag of belongings and welcome bag, was struggling. He felt irritated that his 'keyworker', supposedly assigned to him for the duration of his stay at the Luskentyre camp, was so disinterested in him, and still had her bloody hands in her pockets. She did not even offer him a hand with his bags. David stumbled and dropped his welcome bag. It fell right in front of his feet and he went tumbling down onto his chest and hands with a clatter.

'Fucking hell,' he cried.

Louisa turned around and looked at him, almost with glee. 'Are you alright? Have you got two left feet tonight?'

'I'm bloody exhausted, to be bloody honest…' David replied angrily. 'I have had a shitty few days… and, to be frank, I just want to get my head down. What is your role here, again?' he asked sarcastically whilst picking himself up off the ground.

'I am your key worker,' replied Louisa. 'I make sure you know the ropes here, where and when to go places, where not to go, and make sure you are keeping up with your work and educational assignments… I'm here to keep you in line with the aims of the programme.'

'Oh, right… the aims of the programme?' said David, getting to his feet. 'What does that mean, exactly? What are the aims?'

128

Louisa, seeing that he was on his feet and walking again, quickly turned around and began marching ahead again, still with her hands in her pockets.

'The aims of the programme are to turn you into a model citizen, to build you back for the greater good, so you can contribute to society in a meaningful way again,' she explained. 'There is so much at stake, David. We have reached so many economic, environmental, and psychological targets for the last few years. You can contribute to that. We all can.'

She sounded just like a machine spouting out state-speak. It was so abstract, devoid of anything meaningful or concrete. Nothing that he could get his mind around.

'The suicide figures are pretty bad...' said David. 'Is that what you mean... getting the figures down?'

Louisa abruptly stopped, turned around and looked at him. David kept walking until he was level with her, face to face, less than a metre away, staring at her with a wry smile.

'Unfortunately, the mental health crisis has been attributed to a number of things, including faulty genetics,' she replied coldly. 'It is unfortunate, but perhaps we will have to wait a few years until this gene is bred out, or better medicines are found.'

'People are killing themselves because of the miserable social conditions,' said David. 'You know, lack of freedom, liberty... people are miserable... why can't people get their head round that?'

Louisa became steely eyed. 'Listen, talk like that gets you nowhere here. Look at the likes of Fergus. He is like a boomerang... we keep throwing him back to the mainland, but he keeps coming back because he spouts this freedom, liberty nonsense. He is what we call a repeater. He never learns. Good mental health comes from community inclusion, participation, sacrifice. The planet is so fragile. We all need to do our bit.'

'Ah ok, gotcha... loud and clear.' David was now very clearly getting angry. 'Ok, where is my bed? I need to get some food and sleep and do my bit for the greater good. I am on board, big time.'

'Good to hear,' Louisa replied dryly. 'Come on, it's just down here.'

She turned and walked another 100 yards, David following behind, until they reached Building 131 on the left.

129

Louisa slipped her electronic card into the reader and the glass-fronted door clicked open, opening inwards.

'After you,' she said, indicating to David to walk in first.

He entered into a reception area with a central corridor off to left and right. There were tables and chairs, and a few uncomfortable-looking sofas at the far side against the window.

'You are down the left-hand corridor, Room 12A,' said Louisa. 'The canteen is back up the path to the main reception, go past it, on the right. It is called the Claymore canteen. It is now shut for dinner, but they have left you some food in your room. You can heat it up in your microwave. You have a basic kitchen in there for your personal use. Breakfast is served in the canteen from 6.00 am until 9.30 am, Monday to Friday. Lunch is 12 pm to 2 pm, Monday to Friday. Dinner is 5 pm to 7 pm, Monday to Friday. Weekends, you are given foodstuffs to cook yourself up a gourmet surprise. Ok, so tomorrow is Friday. You have an induction meeting at 9.30 am, back in the reception building you arrived at. That will give you the low-down on what is on offer for you here. After that, you are free for the weekend and can do as you please until Monday. That is when your classes and work placement in the mealworm unit starts. All clear? Any questions?'

'Aye... where is the pub?' David joked.

'Yes, there are social cafeteria areas in the camp,' replied Louisa seriously. 'There are leisure facilities, including a cinema. Some alcohol is served, but it is limited to ten units per week and no more than four units per day. Outside the camp there are establishments... Let's say that you can indulge yourself there, but I will leave it up to you if you want to venture there. There are some fucking weirdos out there,' she laughed. 'Plus, drunkenness on the camp is not tolerated. It can lead to a longer stint on your placement. We are trying to get people to be more responsible.'

'Weirdos?' asked David. 'How do you mean?'

'No-hopers, broken machines... folk stuck in the past, thinking some god is going to save them... the islanders that time forgot. Some do a bit of old-style farming for the upmarket meat trade. There is still a demand for that, you know... cattle, lamb, fishing, mussels, crabs, etc. Some folk never change. But they come in handy, sometimes. We employ them on a temporary basis if we have a lot of work on and get them on the wind farms or protein farms. We exist in peaceful co-existence. They will never be allowed back to the mainland... they would not survive a day...

130

It's the same up in Sunderland and the Scottish Borders. Weirdos still hanging on to old ways. Sheep shaggers.' Louisa gave a short laugh. 'Anyhow, I must be off. Settle in and I will see you at the induction tomorrow. Be sharp. I am wanting to get off this island tomorrow for the weekend, for a weekend of partying, and I need to catch a plane from Barra to Glasgow.'

'Alright for some,' David said.

The perks of being part of the system. A bloody electric minibus for the masses, a small plane for the privileged. Partying? David had heard stories of how the 'elites', or those who toed the state party line, partied. As someone with a critical eye on society coined it, a deconstruction of moral values was a key ingredient in the 'partying' of those with the privilege. An anything goes approach, pleasure on demand. A hysterical Faustian pact with the Devil.

'Yes, well, I deserve some time off,' Louisa quipped.

And off she trotted out the door of Building 131 almost with a skip in her step. Her hands were now out of her pockets. She was waving her arms up and down, as if she was dancing. Or was she just trying to provoke him? The latter, David suspected. *There goes the salt of the earth*, he thought mockingly. David had met many people like her during his research. They were soaked in a peculiar narcissism that tried to disguise itself as a human right. Such people could not see past their psycho-somatic needs moment to moment. Like primitive species, such as reptiles, they reacted to their internal psychological and physiological rumblings and external stimuli (e.g., the virtual communication world, their shallow social interactions) and computed how they could get on top of things and recalibrate to achieve 'homeostasis'. It really was a dire drop in human evolution.

It was based upon what David's father had coined 'The Eternal Method'. This was the epitome of the modern or postmodern world. A world without God, without humans. So many had pharmaceutically engineered their moods and even their bodies, and modes of communication were purely functional to serve self-absorbed demands and desires. From the moment a person woke up, to the moment they went to sleep, the 'moment' was obliterated in a series of process-orientated initiatives, where there was a forward-thinking tension to get from state A to state B. There was no dwelling within what was, no free-floating absorption in the here and now. A discontentment and detachment

131

from what was, to a desire to what could be, was at the forefront of the transhuman of 2050. Years and years of social engineering had designed people to become like this. And people willingly put on their chains in the name of human rights, whilst consigning their humanity to the scrap heap. A true tragedy.

David stood silently in the entrance of Building 131. For a moment, he felt stuck to the floor and could not move his legs. All agency seemed to have evaporated. A spark of insight occurred to him; this was the effect of a mental breakdown. He was breaking down, coming to an end, towards the end. He had never thought the onset of suicide would feel like this. He had always seen such a thing as a conscious decision. But he now saw that a darker, ineffable force took over in these moments of impending self-destruction. Insanity via biochemical malfunction. Or was it more sinister? Demons? The Devil? *It did not matter*, he thought. The only thing he knew was that he was approaching the end and he was glad. What more could be done or said on the matter? What point was there in fighting the inevitable?

After what seemed like an eternity, David found the strength in his legs to make them walk. He walked slowly down the corridor towards his accommodation. Bright strip lights blinded him from above. Those bloody lights and light pollution everywhere. As he walked slowly down the corridor, he heard faint noises from the rooms left and right. The sound of someone speaking, running water, some music. Others like him. He wondered what they would be like. How they would be. David felt almost panicked. He was forgetting what human beings were. It was as though he was partly already departed from the Earth. The thought of human beings felt foreign to him, like a menacing force. David felt sick. He needed to get into his room. He came upon it, 12A, on the right-hand side of the corridor.

The door was already wedged open. He walked in and shut the door. Before him was a large, open-plan room, like a bedsit. Immediately to his left was a wet room with toilet and sink. The main bedsit area had two large, double-glazed windows with curtains. In the left-hand corner of the room was a small corner kitchen area with worktop, sink, overhead cupboard, two storage base units, a small electric oven and 4-hob electric cooker, fridge and microwave. Next to this was a small round table with one chair. In the middle of the room was a sofa facing the left-hand wall, on which was fixed a telescreen monitor. A side unit on the wall had a radio and an intercom system. On the right-hand wall was a wardrobe and single bed with duvet, pillows and a small bedside table.

Small, functional, private. *It was not bad*, David thought. Better than he had imagined. He dropped his bags onto the floor and wandered over to the kitchen area. On the worktop there were three plastic containers with a note on top of them. It read:

'Please find your dinner. Vegetable curry and basmati rice, with a desert of chocolate cake. Heat the curry and rice in the microwave for three minutes each. Fresh water and fruit juice are in your fridge. Additional foodstuffs, pots and pans are in your base unit cupboards. Dishes, cups, glasses, knives and forks are in your overhead cupboard.'

David opened the vegetable curry. It looked edible. Opening the fridge, he took out a small bottle of orange juice. He opened it and drank the whole bottle in several gulps. He stood in the silence of his room and looked around, having digested the contents of the bottle. *What am I looking for?* he thought. It dawned on him that he was looking for 'opportunities' for the final cut, so to speak. Nothing in here, and anyways, it would not end in the camp. It would be a place where he would be free. A free man. He did not even want them, the state, to find his body if possible. A hard call, but he wanted it to end in a place away from the 'system'.

He opened one of the velux windows. The air that came in smelt of salt and the sea. It was wonderful. In the distance, in the darkness, he could hear the crashing of the waves on the nearby Luskentyre beach. He stood there listening to the sound of the sea and breathing in the salty-smelling breeze. Looking to the sky, between the gaps in the clouds, he glimpsed several bright stars shining through. He thought of his family. His brother, who was living in the hellscape of London, his mother, now deceased, and his father, who had disappeared into the bowels of the state years previously. Maybe they were all dead. Maybe they were now stars in the sky looking down on him. Deep down inside him, he longed to be united with all of them, his family. Was that a futile fantasy? Not if there was an afterlife. But David was a sinner. He was going to commit a sin. Would he be forgiven? He was past caring, as he could not tolerate existing anymore. The pull of extinction was so strong, so sweet in its allure. Why?

On the topic of suicide, David's father had things to say. He said that we were all going to die, so why rush it? David had found an error in that argument. What was the point in prolonging life if it was a meaningless hell, if one was just putting off the inevitable? David felt kind of proud with his philosophical reasoning skills to outwit his father in these moments. It felt reasonable enough... but, of course, David's father would attest to the fact that human reason, the human workings of the brain, was a blunt and often faulty mechanism, it blurred the heart... But now, such arguments were of no use; they could not save him now. David's heart went to the inevitable place... the end.

His head dropped and he sighed. He felt exhausted. It was like his whole organic being was slowly being turned off. Everything was an effort. Even thinking. He shut the window and pulled the curtains closed and turned toward the kitchen area. He grabbed the container with the vegetable curry and tore off the lid. He grabbed a fork from the overhead cupboard and fell onto the sofa. Like an animal, he scooped the cold curry into his mouth without thinking. The taste of the dish was irrelevant. It was merely for sustenance to take him into the final act. That was all. David felt a sense of self-disgust. Slurping down this curry. He imagined if his mother could see him. What would she have said? David would have felt ashamed of himself and how low he felt he looked. It was as though his basic humanity was being squeezed out of him. *A tragedy*, he thought. Not just for him, but for everyone like him.

He got up and threw the carton and fork into the sink. He grabbed a glass from the cupboard and poured himself a glass of water to wash the curry down. He let out a huge burp and wiped his mouth with his sleeve. He walked over to the bed, sat down and undid the laces on his boots and kicked them off. He then stood up and unzipped his jacket and threw it to the other side of the room, almost in anger. He pulled back the duvet and got into the bed. He reached over to the light switch controls and switched off the main light. Then, pulling the duvet over himself, he curled into a ball under the covers.

He prayed to God. He prayed that he would not wake up. He prayed for death. He did not want this life anymore. He prayed incessantly in anger that he would not wake up. He had never prayed with more surety for anything else in his whole life and he felt completely at peace with that decision. It was liberating. It was a relief. He wondered why he had never ever thought of this solution, ever before. The feeling was like an exotic sweet nectar that he had tasted for the very first time.

He fell into a deep sleep.

Chapter Thirteen

Re-education

David awoke. Just an awareness that he was awake. Nothing more than that. For several moments he did not know who he was or where he was, and he had no memory of his personal history. These brief moments seemed to stretch for intolerable hours. It was like he had been cut off from some kind of essential source that needed to be present in order to be fully human. The terror was utterly palpable and inescapable. Little by little, tiny fragments of knowledge and memory came to him… his name… his location… his past… his life… and the realisation that he was still alive, after going to sleep hoping he would never wake up. He felt ashamed to be thinking this thought. It felt wrong in so many ways, but he could not put his finger on why he felt the shame. Why should he feel shame for wanting to die? Why would such a notion come to anyone? Shame for all the feelings he could feel? Fear, yes. Anxiety, understandable. But shame? What a fucking idiotic feeling to have. *Christ! I can't even dwell on the idea of my own self-inflicted demise without some super-egoic annoyance badgering me to my last breath. What the fuck is all that about?* he thought.

An in-built panopticon monitoring every 'infraction', whereby he was not free to indulge the basest of ideas. Hell, even George Bataille, the French philosopher, masturbated in the bedroom of his mother, as she lay dead, motionless on the bed, on the day of her death, without remorse or guilt. Was that not worse than thoughts of suicide? Bataille was able to short-circuit all morality, social convention, and decency and get away with it; a kind of dark, base queering of reality, that many would aspire to in the decades after the death of Bataille. This kind of morality seemed to have been achieved in 2050.

Why should there be social rules or standards, conventions, expectations? The outlandish ideas of Bataille, built on the back of people like Friedrich Nietzsche and his idea of the 'Superman'… the 'you can be anything you want', giving birth to the rise in humanism, queer theory, and accentuated the fall of man… or so it seemed, David mused. Any yet, even after all that 'liberatory' philosophical history that informed the modern world and destroyed the religious sensibilities of the world, shame still permeated his whole mind and body with the thought of suicide.

Something in him, morality wise, would not break, or relinquish from his very being, somehow.

It reminded David of his life's past adventures, or misadventures, when he had attempted to mingle in the world and to live the vision inspired by the likes of Bataille. His futile attempts at the great liberation embarrassed him. He recalled a party, many years before. He'd been invited to it by a friend of a friend. Some guy, who was pretty high up in the legal profession, was friends with a female friend of David at university when he was doing his PhD. She was kind of arrogant and portrayed herself as a free spirit... no ties, no responsibilities, that kind of thing. She was a committed hedonist with very little moral fibre. She rented a flat from this legal guy. She gleefully hinted at the fact that she got the flat rent free due to the favours she dished out to him. She did not go into detail, but it was clear that it was a very suitable arrangement, even though the guy was married. She even boasted that, if the arrangement went tits up, she would inform her 'friend's' wife about their little arrangement.

At the time, when David heard this story, he felt it was a bit low of her. Anyhow, she invited David to this party at this guy's house. It was a gentrified tenement building apartment in Gayfield Place at the top of Leith Walk, in Edinburgh. On arrival, it all looked quite ordinary. Champagne was offered by a female host, with the usual *hors d'oeuvres*. The main room where guests mingled was full of glamorously dressed people guffawing, talking loudly, and engaged in conversations of serious one-upmanship. The bottom line was that it was pompous. David immediately regretted going. His friend, who knew the host and several of his friends, almost seemed embarrassed to be with David, which made him hate being there even more. He took advantage of the free drink and sampled copious amounts of expensive red wine and cheese and biscuits. Why not? As the evening wore on, people became more and more inebriated. Some people were openly smoking marijuana. On a visit to the bathroom, some girls were at the huge double sink area outside the toilet cubicle, cutting up cocaine and giggling and sniffing it up their noses, whilst looking down their noses at David as he passed by. Maybe it was David's sense of insecurity or paranoia, or maybe he hit the nail on the head with his perception.

The evening gathered pace when the party moved to another room where there was a DJ, plush sofas, and dark corners.

David saw the host sprawled on a sofa with a young man, pawing him and sticking his tongue in the young man's mouth, much to the mirth of his wife. David's friend was sitting with a couple, a male and female. The female informed David's friend that her boyfriend was a 'slave' and she encouraged him to make my friend feel comfortable. He took off the boots and socks of David's friend and began suckling on her toes. David's pissed, stoned, and wasted friend then proceeded to kiss the female partner as she fondled her breasts. Meanwhile, people danced to the music in various stages of undress, while people sexually cavorted to varying degrees.

On another visit to the toilet, the upstairs one, as the ground floor one was occupied, David passed a bedroom where he glimpsed three people on a bed completely naked; two women and a man. Whilst draining his bladder, David felt sick and vomited up what seemed like several pints of red wine. He had had enough by now and left the party. He picked up a kebab on the way back to the hostel he was booked into, just off the Royal Mile. The kebab settled his stomach and rejuvenated him back to some sense of normality. As he walked back to his hostel, he felt a sadness and longing. The narcissism and inauthenticity of the guests of the party he had just left grated on him. He remembered gatherings and parties when he was a child at his country home. Ordinary folk. Extra-ordinary ordinary folk.

He lost contact with his friend not long after that. He realised he had little in common, other than a liking for getting drunk. A man she was dating died a horrible death, a jet ski accident in Thailand when he was on holiday with her. David contacted his friend when he found out, but she was perfectly fine. She seemed unperturbed by the event. Just one of those things. The relationship was not going anywhere, anyhow. She quickly changed topic to how well she was doing in her job. David knew then that their friendship was going nowhere, and that it had possibly been as superficial as his previous doubts had indicated to him.

David looked at his watch; it was 8.41 am. He had to get ready for his induction meeting. He slowly sat up in bed and threw off the duvet. He had been sweating heavily in his sleep and felt damp on his torso and legs. *No matter*, he thought. He was not going to any party, so there was no need to wash. He could not be bothered, anyway. He got up and found his boots and sat on the sofa to lace them up. Hunched over, his diaphragm seemed enlarged; he always suffered bloating when he was stressed, except he did not feel stressed. He felt tired. He coughed and spluttered, as though something was caught in his body. A foreign entity. He stood up and coughed his way to the kitchen sink and ran the cold tap, cupped his hands and splashed his face with the icy cold water. It felt good. Healing.

The intercom sparked into life with an automated voice.

'David. It is 8.45 am. This is a reminder. You have an induction meeting at 9.30 am in the main reception building in room 8.'

David guessed that the bloody intercom system and automated voice would be a frequent guest in his new 'home'. *How quaint*, he thought. No doubt it would listen into his room, too – just for his safety, of course. He wandered through to his wet room/toilet and took a piss in the toilet. It was yellow and smelly. Dehydrated. He did not bother washing his hands; like the former British Prime Minister Winston Churchill of the 20th century, he did not piss on his hands. He found his bag, a rucksack suitcase, and unzipped it. He rummaged around for some gloves and a hat. Just in case. Locating them, he grabbed his bag and went to his wardrobe and opened the door. In it, hanging up, were three sets of dark blue work overalls, and a heavy and a light waterproof jacket and waterproof trousers (all dark blue), and on the floor of the wardrobe were two pairs of black wellington boots. *How kind of them*, he thought.

He threw his bag on the top shelf of the wardrobe. He took the heavy waterproof jacket from the hanger. He put it on. Pretty good fit. *Almost like they expected me*, he thought. He shoved his hat and gloves into the side pockets, grabbed his key card from the worktop and walked towards the door. The key did not work the first two times. Maybe he was on house arrest for an infringement? House arrest or social isolation was a method of control in 2050 if one had broken some rule or other; carbon quota, social credit infringement (e.g., mixing with the wrong kind of people, which led to a curfew, etc). Maybe because he had spoken to Louisa in a disrespectful way? Maybe. The key card worked on the third attempt.

David quickly made his way through the building to the outside. It was a grey, blustery morning with a bit of drizzle in the air. There were a few people about. Several men in dark blue waterproof jackets were walking about looking purposeful, and two yellow luminous-jacketed women in an electric buggy driving down the pathway towards him. They came straight for him, playing chicken with him. He moved at the last minute. They just stared at him like he was a piece of shit. He continued towards the reception, walked past it and, on the right, was the Claymore canteen. He got his key out again and used it on the door to enter. It was a huge room. On the far left-hand side of the room was a large counter where people were queuing and gathering their breakfasts on trays. The rest of the room had rows of seats and tables set up as little booths, one table and a seat either side of the table. The partitions between the booths meant that you could not really speak to the person next to you, and with a solid partition on the table, you could not see the person on the opposite side of the table.

This was the social engineering policy on 'social distancing'. It was a hangover from the COVID-19 crisis of 2020-25, where people had to keep two metres distance from each other in public, and gatherings of people inside and outside were highly regulated. Face masks had to be worn everywhere. This inhuman policy had massive ramifications for social interaction. Family relationships broke down, romantic meetings and potential meetings fractured and stopped occurring, and mental ill-health soared. A new way of human interaction developed. Close relationships were rare, people were suspicious. People lived very individual and solitary lives. People came to see each other as mere objects, as commodities to satiate their own desires, whims, and narcissistic needs. An authentic closeness or attunement was short-circuited by the tactics of applied behavioural psychology; by the Pavlovian shock (pseudo-threat) of catching a virus, which made people very fearful. This was attenuated by propaganda of various strands and hues; menticidal via waves of hope, fear, ever-increasing confusion, chaos and deliberate misdirection. This was most notably seen in the climate agenda propaganda; people were frightened, encouraged and shamed into not travelling anywhere. Therefore, families that were cast across the world lost contact and never saw each other again. The narrative that humans were bio-hazards was continually pushed, even after COVID-19. Scare narratives were pushed for every cough, sniffle and sneeze. One could not breathe heavy without it being regarded as a bio-threat.

If one was to dare to breathe freely, or shout loudly, one was regarded as a bio-terrorist. And so it went on.

Obviously, people mixing and meeting in ordinary social ways had to be obliterated – or, at least, made very difficult and awkward. The individual booth set-up was just a mechanism so that close contacts or friendships would be made difficult. On the partition wall of every booth was a screen broadcasting the Scottish Broadcasting News. Speakers placed throughout the large room piped in the sound of the news. It was all the usual stuff: environmental updates; greenhouse gases modelling predictions; weather updates and global temperature estimates; and CO_2 predictions. There were industry updates; protein manufacturing grow/production, product updates; wind energy production, etc. It was constant and incessant. It was pseudo-science gibberish with no end in sight; menticide. The narrative was that the environmental crisis was being won, but we must do more, that people must up their game, that more sacrifices had to be made. We were all in this together. It was the new religion. All the while, humans were treated like cattle and their 'eco-system' of interpersonal relations was destroyed and kept permanently in check from ever re-emerging. The Claymore canteen seating set-up was just a reflection on that.

David walked towards the serving counter and waited his turn. Nobody was chatting to each other. Just silently standing, waiting. Nobody really looked at each other in the face. It was as if these 'inmates' had part of their soul taken away. David grabbed a couple of croissants and a banana and took a mug of coffee from the drinks dispenser. At the end of the line, a woman scanned David's key card to register his breakfast. He then took his tray to find a seat. Walking down the row to find an empty seat, he spotted Fergus sitting motionless in his booth, staring at his telescreen. David stopped and tapped him on the shoulder.

'Hey Fergus, how are you doing?'

'Bad night's sleep, buddy… no feeling too great…'

Fergus' personality had changed. He was quiet, placid. He did not even look up when David spoke to him. Suddenly, a canteen warden appeared next to David, almost from out of nowhere.

'Could you find a seat as quick as possible and move along, please.'

David looked at the warden for several seconds.

'Are you saying that exchanging morning pleasantries is not allowed?'

'We can't have bottlenecks in the canteen,' said the warden. 'Lots of people to get through, lots of cleaning up afterwards. You can chat out in the grounds while you're going to your placements.'

'Whatever, buddy… see you later, Fergus.'

Fergus moved his head and looked at David. He tried to give a smile. Spittle formed at the corner of his mouth. He tried to mouth a few words, but instead just raised a fist as if to say 'keep up the fight'.

David quickly moved to an empty booth and sat down. He felt agitated by the interaction. Social interaction was a problem issue that needed to be dealt with and had been targeted through social engineering since the COVID-19 days. David understood that. But it looked like it would be highly controlled and ramped up in this camp, or at least monitored. And Fergus? It appeared he had been medicated in some way. Probably. Perhaps because he was acting in a way that they disapproved of. Or maybe it was self-orchestrated, so he would be given some medication to dull the reality of his situation; another stint in the Western Isles, with life unlikely to change much in the future. It was bleak, very bleak.

He wolfed down his croissants and dipped them into his coffee, as was his way. The attractive presenter on the telescreen was presenting the weather. It was going to be bright sunshine, but a bit blustery today. That was nice. His father told him that the weather on the Western Isles could be one day wild and stormy, the next day beautiful sunshine. Both were beautiful. David could never understand why people had some romantic notion of hot sunshine and spoke negatively about the Scottish weather. The seasons were exquisite in their variance. David recalled taking walks with his father, younger brother and their dog in the Borders up hills in all weathers. They used to get to the top of some famous hill and his father would get his flask out and give them some juice and a sausage roll, and he would sit and gaze out onto the land and sky. David used to watch his father and wonder what was going on in his mind. He seemed immersed in some profound depth of the human soul, maybe sad… maybe prayer. After this quiet and silence, his father would take photos of David and his brother, or all three of them together. David would make funny hand signals, like some kind of American rapper. David's brother would copy and do the same, not knowing what they meant. He just copied his brother.

The voice and smiling face of the female newsreader on the telescreen was beginning to annoy him. She was so fucking happy, chirping her nonsense to the masses. Did she realise that there were people in this very country sitting in rows, in booths, not allowed to talk to each other, and had been sent involuntarily to work and re-education camps? Of course, those in the media, the intelligentsia (writers, artists, poets, social commentators, academics) were well versed in living by lies, and had been doing it for so long they had forgotten what was truth and what was fiction. The incessant swallowing of lies does funny things to people. It turns them quite mad, quite inhuman. You can see it in their dead eyes; just like the dead eyes of the woman reading the news. Dead. The light goes out. It really is quite disconcerting.

This is what happens in totalitarian regimes when free speech is supressed. The world was warned of this process by the likes of 20th century authors Alexander Solzhenitsyn, Czesław Miłosz, C.S. Lewis, and Stanisław Ignacy Witkiewicz. People screamed and echoed their warnings long into the 21st century, especially during the COVID-19 ruse. It fell on deaf ears for the most part. The dumbing down over many decades of people in the Western world had done its trick. People readily took rushed experimental vaccines to protect them from threats which were not really threats (statistically speaking) and which compromised their natural immune system. Many people died. The deaths were denied and covered up by the state. Many elderly people passed away with state-sanctioned genocide under the guise of medical care and altruism. It really was a terrible episode in human history. A history which David and his brother were born into. The architects of this history had their fate sealed in sin and the consequences of sin. 'Just following orders' was no excuse. Civil unrest became the norm for several years, whilst, at the same time, the architects redesigned society to become the optimum control society, whereby human labour, movement and ownership was monitored, controlled and coerced to fit the state's agenda.

David looked at his watch. It was 9.15 am. His induction meeting started in fifteen minutes. He slurped his coffee down and wiped his mouth on his sleeve. He stood up and scanned the room, at the people sitting at their little breakfast booths. He could not get out of his head how they looked like chickens pecking on

143

their food from the ground. David's parents had chickens. It must have been those memories that sparked that image. David recalled the wonderful eggs they got. That all was stopped, of course. Keeping your own chickens or other poultry was banned, the reason given was that they spread disease. Only government-sanctioned poultry farms were allowed. A few years later, people were not even allowed to grow their own fruit and vegetables. Some pseudo-scientific reason was given that fruit and veg spread bacteria, or something like that. It was nonsense, of course. The state just wanted to control the food supply and did not want anyone to attempt to be self-sufficient or evade state capture/control. Prison planet.

David felt sick. A nausea welled up inside of him. A terror, even. Things were truly horrific. The meaningless of it all. The meaningless lives of the people here in this room. There was no start and no end to this meaningless. It just always was. Of course, there were memories of other times… times that were reinterpreted by the state as dangerous, foolish, selfish times in human history. Nothing was ever of any value or goodness from the past.

He needed air. He got out of the canteen as quickly as he could and found himself in the fresh air. It was drizzling rain. He stood with his back against the wall of the canteen. His breath rose up in front of him. The mountains, the sea and countryside in the distance looked wild and pleasing to his eyes – the parts without wind turbines, that was.

'Hi, buddy… settling in?' Fergus said, having just exited the canteen, his stupor appearing to have lifted.

'Aye… just taking in the scenery,' replied David. 'Any day trips you can recommend? Sightseeing?'

'Yes, buddy…' said Fergus. 'Out the camp gates, turn left. Go down towards the beach. It's not far; a five or ten-minute walk. There is a shop, a few houses, a church, a pub, a crematorium. A wee haven of civilization. There are some good folks down there. Reverend McDade, his nickname is Lazarus… he is always popping about… sometimes in the pub… There you will meet some hardy folk. The camp personnel don't mix too much with them. They like to buy some prime cuts of beef or lamb from the shop, though. Although they speak badly of them, they come in useful. Some of these bastards even go to the pub… but they are not really made welcome, if you know what I mean. The locals

144

don't take kindly to colonisers and collaborators… you cannot blame them, eh? This place used to be beautiful until they bastardised it with wind energy and these fucking maggot farms.'

'Thanks, Fergus… I will check it out… a few pints maybe, and a swim…'

'Just don't get caught out by the curfew,' said Fergus. 'The bastards at reception give you a hard time if you are late in and smelling of booze… goes on your record. It results in an extension of stay on the island…'

'I think I might like it here, Fergus,' said David. 'I think I would like to stay… I mean, there is nothing back in Glasgow for me now. I hate the fucking place. Fucking pokey flat, concrete jungle. No job. No family. Meaningless universal basic income. Am I meant to become rehabilitated to like that, to enjoy it, to desire it?'

'Of course you are, sonny boy…' replied Fergus, laughing. 'Of course you are… they want you to devour the ideology of the Brave New Normal. Me and you, David, are fucking dinosaurs. Hey, don't give up, though… they get sick of folk sometimes, and just leave them at places like here in perpetual exile. I knew a guy in Sunderland at one of the camps there. He settled there on the condition that he did not return to the city, to civilization and infect the masses with his liberatory philosophy… You can't control everybody's mind… human history has shown that… no matter what they throw at us…'

'You talk a good talk, Fergus,' said David. 'You are almost convincing me… I think I will stay… It's a good idea…. Where are you off to now?'

'Am off to the medic's office to get my back checked out… bloody sciatica. If I am lucky, I might get off working in the maggot factory for a few days.' Fergus winked.

'Hope you get your wish,' said David. 'I'm off to my induction now… pretty sure that will be a barrel of laughs.'

'Oh, you mean your abduction meeting?' said Fergus. 'Abducted into the cult… haha!' He laughed for a moment. 'You will be educated in the fine arts of conformity, toeing the line, unquestioning and living by lies.'

'Aye, well, I feel pretty much abducted already by some dark shit…' replied David. 'I don't think they could top the number being done on me.'

145

'Oh, that is crazy talk, laddie,' said Fergus. 'You've got Island blues… the comedy club you are about to go to will cheer you up. Let's meet later and you can tell me all about it… I need a good laugh… the shit they teach the folk who lead the inductions… incredible… walking fucking lobotomies. They have been programmed with the most up-to-date, logic-resistant software. Just sit quiet… take notes… act like a good little boy…'

'Thanks for the advice. I will try to see it as a comedy show… I will have to get going, or I will be late… See you later…?'

'Yes, you don't want to be late… haha!' Fergus joked, talking to David like he was a 5-year-old child.

David smiled and gave a little chuckle. 'See you, my friend. Take care.'

He took off and walked down the path towards the reception building. *Just get this over with, then I can start living the rest of my life. Then I will be free*, thought David. He wanted one more shot at the fuckers. He would relish the onslaught of bullshit he was about to receive. He could just imagine what guff he would be fed. He was in the belly of the beast, so to speak, at the heart of the state apparatus machine, where faulty machines were sent to be fixed. This was the ideological mechanic's workshop. Most people conformed blindly. They had blind faith. They never questioned, even if the evidence to the contrary was put right in front of their noses. It happened so many times throughout history. Bullshit stories were put out by the mainstream media that were so full of holes, the masses did not even notice. Governments and pharmaceutical companies put out experimental medicines, untested, onto the masses, and even when people were harmed or even died, including family members, people still blindly accepted that the government could do no wrong. So strong was the pull to the cliff edge; people willingly jumped off to their existential and, sometimes, literal death. Truly depressing.

He entered the reception building.

'Excuse me, where is room 8 please?' he asked the man at the reception desk.

'Down there…' said the man, pointing to his left down a corridor. 'Room 8 is on the right.'

David walked slowly down the brightly lit corridor. He noticed a sign hanging from the ceiling that read:

146

The door was open. On his left, he was confronted with a semi-circle of approximately six chairs with folding tables. A large desk to his right sat in front of the semi-circle, with a white digital board behind it. The room was otherwise empty. David took a seat on the edge of the semi-circle nearest the window, the furthest from the door. A young woman, mid-20s, with long blonde hair scraped into a pony tail, wearing a white blouse, black flared trousers and black high heels, walked in. She had a bag with papers or documents with her. She stunk of perfume. It wafted over the room towards David.

'Hello,' she said. 'My name is Becky. I am here to fill you in on the details of your stay here... your work placement and educational modules.'

She sat perched on the large desk, legs crossed, with one high heel swinging loosely from her foot.

'I thought Louisa was going to be here?' David replied.

'She had a flight to catch back to the mainland and it was re-scheduled,' said Becky. 'You will see her Monday, I think.'

She took a thick A4 document from her bag and held it up.

'Ok. This won't take long. I have a few things to give you. Here is your personal educational workbook. It contains all of your medical psychosocial and educational modules that you will be taking for the next six months. It covers everything from psychological well-being and resilience, social relations and relationships, and their boundaries and rules. It also covers environmental topics such as protein farming, wind and wave farming, ecology and sustainable growth. There are sections on responsible health, on what medications and inoculations you must take and keep up to date on. There are also sections on looking for employment. It outlines what level of understanding you are expected to reach, and you can chart your progress in the back and note your assessment scores that you receive every week.

'Assessment is based on attendance, commitment, participation level and interaction style. You will have a meeting every week with Louisa, your key worker, to go over all these in detail. You will discuss what concerns you are having, or any feedback you have. She can give you pointers on how you can improve and progress. Louisa will draw up a personal care plan and risk assessment for you. The personal care plan will take into account any special educational or physical needs you have. The risk assessment will identify any triggers or well-being needs that you require, such as mental healthcare, counselling etc.'

David's heart sank. The bureaucratic well-being speak that Becky was coming out with was a way of speaking and thinking about the world which had been decades in the making. It was empty, shallow, meaningless. Based upon a postmodern bastardised version of education and therapeutics mixed in with the worst application of an Aristotelian poesis, of progress, striving for an outcome, to get from A to B; an abstract notion of a human being and his relationship with other people. The meaning of this was forever in some non-existent future – or, at the very least, a human-constructed future; an idea of being human that had little to do with being human, actually human. In the Aristotelian model of praxis, being human, or meaning, could be boiled down to the doing or dwelling within being for the sake of the action at the moment; no hope for progress, a future, invaded this space.

Obviously, it was far more complex than that, but the general idea was of a medico-psychosocial pedagogical ideological structure which took the humanness out of the human. The result, in 2050, was the likes of Becky spewing out this well-being education nonsense, thinking it was for the greater good, not knowing the immense violence she was committing in the name of humanity. People often referred to historical events, crimes against humanity like the Second Word War and the Nazis, or other genocides in history. The perfect crime against humanity was when people willingly carried out this crime, desired it, and even felt it was good for humanity; the perfect crime. Where were the witnesses? If anybody did call it out, they were called mad, bad, a danger to public health. That was how depraved the world became.

'What is the aim of the programme, the objectives?' said David. 'I mean, what am I meant to be turned into? What I am trying to say is... what was wrong with me before I came here? I lost my job on a spurious complaint against me, couched in the most questionable ideological terms. I ended up unemployed, unemployable, tagged, tracked, traced by the state, controlled in every way imaginable, judged before I could argue my case. And now... now I am being told by you that my well-being needs will be catered for here? It is quite ironic, no?'

David could feel his anger rising, and his voice grew louder. 'Who are you,' he continued, 'the state, to define the parameters of life in such a microscopic way? At the same time, be so far removed from my life and the events that occurred in it up until now? Did you know that my father had been taken away from me, my brother, my mother, when I was just a small boy, just because he would not take an experimental rushed mRNA gene therapeutic (falsely sold as a vaccine) with carcinogenic plastic in it? Just because he wanted to have control of his own bodily integrity? He was fucking worried about the consequences on his own fucking body and wanted to be there for his fucking kids and wife. And me – yes, me – I identified bullying within political activist groups, terrible bullying of men… God forbid, you would have thought I had raised the demons of hell when I mentioned that one to my boss. And now, separated from my own wife and kids, as the only way the state would not take my kids into care was if my wife went away and had no contact with me… and I ended up in a fucking concrete block… existing… unable to travel, unable to fucking be… I feel nothing less than cattle. And you… you sit there now… telling me that you are going to cater for my *well-being*… Jesus Christ… do you see what you are saying? Do you understand what you are into here? What we are both into here?'

David gathered himself. He was becoming angry and flustered. He suspected it might not do him any favours if he kept going and really lost his cool. He felt at the end of his tether.

Becky looked red faced, flustered, furious.

'I won't be spoken to like that,' she said contritely. 'I will have to make a report to Louisa about your outburst. Perhaps you have anger issues that could be better dealt with by some specific anger management techniques. We have the staff here to deal with such things. I will leave your workbook here. Ok, I think we are done here. Have a good weekend and I hope your work placement and education classes go well.'

Becky then hopped off the desk and began to walk out of the room.

'You see, Becky,' said David, calling after her. 'I just reached out there to you, but you refused. You took the position of the state. You never questioned it. No self-reflection. No second thoughts. There is no conversation between us if you operate like that. No dialogue. It's not in the algorithm, is it? No room for it. Just shut down, does not compute. Do you not understand you are turning away from humanity in your every utterance… Humans are bathed in language, the word – not as information, but as in the soul, for God's sake…?'

Becky turned round and gave David a cold look.

'That is a fairy-tale world, David.'

She turned back and was out of the room in a flash.

David remained seated. He felt so lonely. There was just silence. You could hear a pin drop. He could hear faintly the wind outside, almost calling him. He felt his breath and his chest rising up and down… counting down to his final breath. Getting close. He raised himself up from his seat and walked out the room. He left his workbook on the desk. He would not be needing it. And he walked slowly out of the room, through the reception building and out the door. He walked up the path and through the gates of the camp. He stood for a second and wondered where to go. Reverend McDade popped into his mind. And he turned left to go down the outsiders' settlement.

Chapter Fourteen

The Reverend McDade

He felt like a free man walking down the road. It was a blustery day with flecks of intermittent drizzle in the air. The smell of the sea air was beautifully intoxicating. It was so quiet, apart from the sound of the wind, and the sound of his feet touching the ground as he walked. And then, the sound way in the distance… the sea, or so David thought it might be. He could see the sea and the island of Taransay and its mountains beyond it. A strange feeling came over David. He could not put his finger on it. A mixture of fear, joy, or the 'perception' of a presence of some kind. His mind was empty of thought, but was accompanied by a sweet immediacy, which was at the same time quite unsettling. Looking up into the sky, the clouds were breaking and the sun was peeking through intermittently. The rays of the sun broke through in any case, streaming downwards, with several rays illuminating the land and the sea and Taransay in the distance. It was quite beautiful, quite surreal. He almost felt human and alive again… free, even.

The road was long and straight in front of him. Fergus said that it was a five to ten-minute walk at most to the hamlet. Initially rising up slightly from the camp gates, the road progressed into a gentle decline towards his destination. Up on the hillside, on his right-hand side, there were numerous large wind turbines spinning around in the wind. They polluted this beautiful place, scarring the land wherever you looked. It was a tragedy in so many respects. David recalled his parents telling him about their honeymoon in the Outer Hebrides, many years before. He remembered how they told him about the wonderful beach at Luskentyre. David's father told him that it was like a Seventh Wonder of the World, that beach; it reminded him of the Bible story of the parting of the Red Sea. It was like some unknown force was keeping the ocean at bay, as it gave the illusion that the sea was higher than where you stood at some parts of the beach. It seemed to defy the laws of nature.

David kept walking slowly down the road. He was curious as to what he would encounter at this small hamlet of 'outsiders', as Louisa, his key worker, had labelled them. Back in Glasgow – or Scotland, in general – there were, of course, outsiders, but they existed within a sprawling concrete metropolis, where people just existed within the technological bureaucratic grid of the state. It could not really be called living. The souls of most people were dead. The dreadful had already happened.

It was pleasing to the eye for David to see some sheep roaming wild on the roadside and verges, munching on lush green grass. Some glanced up at him as he walked by them, looking quite startled at a human being suddenly in their midst. In the distance, he could see grassy mounds with patches of sand dune. As a child, David loved going on family holidays to the beach – any beach; the first glimpse especially, the beginnings of nature's intersection of sea, beach and land. Indeed, seeing these sandy oases comforted him. He felt, in many respects, as though he was coming home in a strange sort of way. Well, he was in the purest of respects going back home, to the source, he realised. The purest, most uncontaminated, way of Being, returning to the primordial soup from whence he came. There was something quite poetic in it all. He caught himself and realised his acceptance, his being towards death and his reconciliation with this; this was a huge achievement. He thought about the stories of the Samurai gladly ending their own life, or Christian martyrs never yielding to their oppressors right until their death.

He approached the end of the long, straight piece of road and advanced towards a right-hand bend, which sloped downwards to a left-hand bend. On the right of the corner was a house. A modest-size dwelling with one storey and chimney stacks at either side of the gable ends. It looked cosy. It had been whitewashed. The front door, at the centre of the house, had a cross on the wall above the door. For some reason, David felt kind of shocked to see it. Such overt religiosity was rarely seen; but then again, the Outer Hebrides had a historical reputation for being deeply religious. He guessed that Reverend McDade might live there. He could have been wrong, but it was an excellent deduction, he decided. To the right-hand side of the house, he could see a wire mesh enclosure with four or five chickens of various colours; white, black, brown and ginger. The person who lived here was something out of the late 20th or early 21st century, he mused. People on the mainland were not allowed to keep livestock or poultry unless they had a government licence, and it was very difficult to get one. It was a way for the state to keep you tethered to their teat for everything; they did not want anybody to be self-sufficient in any way.

To the left-hand side of the house, the theme of self-sufficiency continued. On a grassy patch was a series of nine raised beds for vegetables. There was also a greenhouse at the head of the rows of raised beds. *This person was hardcore*, David thought. Chickens, vegetables, the cross; the epitome of everything the state wanted to get rid of. No wonder Louisa called this lot down here outsiders. They were *out of timers*.

As David rounded the bend, he noticed a stone structure to the back of the house. It was a small chapel, with two stained glass window panels on the near side of the building. A large wooden door sat in the front, below the high apex of the roof. Again, there was a large cross on the wall above the door. *A church*, he thought. It was a beautiful little building. A sanctuary in a fucked-up world. Indeed, this little set-up here appeared very idyllic.

David continued on down the road towards what looked like the hamlet, an assortment of wooden buildings and portacabin/caravan-type buildings dotted around the area, interspersed with little interlinking roads. It looked kind of like a chalet encampment of the holiday campsites David and his family used to frequent when he was a child. At the top right of this settlement was a grassy area with gravestones. *This must be the cemetery*, David thought. This had been preserved. Most cemeteries on the mainland had been closed down; the few that remained were reserved for the elites of society. The masses were just burnt, without a coffin, in an incinerator and put in a plastic bottle for whoever wanted to keep the ashes. Directly in front of him was a large, double-storey wooden structure with a Wild West-style veranda/porch area at the front. A huge sign across the front on the building read:

Luskentyre Café Bar & Shop

It was a most comforting sight. David almost felt excited to see what might be within this building. It had been so long since he had been out and about mingling with ordinary people in ordinary places. He walked the remaining 100 metres or so between the residences of one of the few remaining outposts of normality in this part of the world; it had that feeling of being pushed to the edge of the sea. It was like the people here were hanging onto this little piece of land that sat right on the edge of the sea. Even the sand was invading the area, giving it the feeling of being under attack by natural forces. As he walked by, he caught a face or two glancing out of their cabins, almost like they knew he was arriving. Of course, he did feel a bit paranoid, but it was quite possible that they had cameras set up to see people coming.

David was used to living in a world of cameras and constant surveillance back on the mainland. Cameras were everywhere in every town and city. Facial recognition software plugged into the smart grid tracked your every movement. Again, the masses accepted this totalitarian creep into their lives without a peep. It was like they did not care. They did not care that their liberties and privacy were being constantly breached. Like victims of abuse, they had developed an incredible ability to employ cognitive dissonance and even went to great lengths to defend their abuser, the state, saying that it was necessary to 'keep us safe'. Their obsessive desire for 'safety', fear of life, and fear of death had been carefully orchestrated for many decades; with the dying away of religious faith in Western society, people had nothing else but their own lives and fixed time on Earth. It was a genocide of souls. And the people volunteered themselves up for the culling. The injunction in the Bible, 'Fear not', was old news. People lived in fear, subjugation and under tyranny. They wanted it.

David reached the wooden steps of the café/shop building and walked up them. To the right was the door for the café and bar. It was a large, panelled door with black metal studs, like something you would see in an ancient castle. A sign on the door read:

BEWARE: STRONG LANGUAGE MAT BE HEARD HERE

He was not sure what to expect, or who to expect. He felt nervous for some reason. He did not know whether to knock on the door or just walk in. There was a sense of being on the edge of some meeting with destiny and that, once he crossed that threshold, it would never be the same again. David turned the big, wrought iron ring handle and turned it clockwise. The door opened and he stepped into the bar. To his right was a long bar along the wall with pumps for a myriad of beers and lagers. The wall was adorned with a very impressive array of spirits. The bar had a row of high stools for customers wanting to sit. Large windows to the back of the room gave a nice view of the island of

Taransay in the distance, and you could see the sea before it. The centre of the room had an assortment of sofas, coffee tables, tables and chairs, and on the left-hand wall was a huge wood burning stove, which was already lit and glowing away. A spiral staircase at the far right-hand side of the room went upwards. A sign indicated that this was for the toilets and dining area. *Very cosy*, he thought.

Two men, who looked like workmen with luminous waterproof jackets hanging on their chairs and big boots, were deep in conversation about something or other. An elderly woman with white, curly hair sat by the wood burning stove. She was knitting something extremely colourful. Another man at the window to David's left was sipping a huge coffee-type drink, reading what looked like Dostoevsky's *Crime and Punishment*. What was striking about this serious, bespectacled, straggly haired, skinny-looking man was that he was smoking a cigarette. Cigarette smoking had been banned in indoors hospitality venues way back in the early 2000s. The walls all around the room were filled with old postcards from all around the world, with bank notes from the many different countries in the world, currencies that no longer existed since the development of a global currency, which was largely digitised. Physical cash still did exist, but only small outlets and businesses accepted it generally.

David took a seat at the bar on one of the high stools. The barman was a large man and wore a checked shirt, jeans that were of a large size, and braces holding them up over his stomach. He had a long, grey, straggly beard and a skinhead haircut. He looked quite scary.

'What can I get you, pal?' the barman asked.

'What do you recommend?'

'What is your poison? Lager, ale, something stronger? Or coffee, tea?'

David pointed at one of the pumps, which indicated it was a real ale of around six per cent proof.

'I like real ales…' he replied. 'What is that like? Harris Hop real ale?'

'An excellent choice,' the barman remarked.

The barman poured him a small glass and offered it to David to taste. David took the glass and savoured the cold, reddish/brown liquid with a lovely white froth on the top.

'That is lovely,' David remarked. 'I will have a pint of that, please.'

'A pint of Harris Hop coming right up, sir…'

'Good choice… but strong. Watch your head,' a voice came from the left of David.

David looked towards where the voice emanated. A man was coming down the final few steps of the spiral staircase. He then sat on a stool, a few seats down from David. David immediately recognised him and felt sort of embarrassed. It was the man he'd seen working on the harbour when he arrived on the Western Isles, the man with the piercing blue eyes, red beard and bushy red eyebrows.

'Aye, well, I feel I need a strong drink, to be honest,' said David. 'It has been an interesting few days, to say the least.'

'Yes, I know… I recognise you from the Gulag Express at Lochboisdale harbour,' retorted the man.

'Yes, I recall seeing you, too…' David sheepishly replied.

'So, you are new to the island, eh?' said the man. 'A gulag virgin, eh? Well, Grasshopper, you have a lot to learn… those bastards up there, the camp commandants… they make out they are all for their Great New Society vision… But it's funny, they are down here like a shot, sampling our fine beers and lagers in the smoky interior and buying fine cuts of lamb, beef, venison and the like at our shop. They make out they are all eco-friendly and the like, but they can't restrain themselves from the pleasures of normality, the fruits of the Earth we should all be able to enjoy freely…' He gave a great laugh. 'Fucking hypocrites, the lot of them!' he guffawed. 'Yer no one of them, are ye?'

'No… just an inmate, so to speak.'

'Aye, good… ye can never tell,' said the man. 'The name is Noel, by the way… pronounced NO-ELL.'

'Nice to meet you… I'm David Campbell… or, at least I used to be…'

'Here is your pint, sir,' said the barman. 'Like all our first-time customers, the first drink is on the house.'

'Thank you very much, much appreciated,' David replied, surprised by the gesture.

'Not at all,' said the barman.

'David Campbell, nice to meet you,' said Noel. 'So, how are you settling in up there?'

'I don't feel settled at all up there… I never will… I *won't* settle up there,' David intimated darkly. 'I can't see myself staying too long… I don't think I am suited to state re-education and re-integration into what they call society. I fear I am a lost cause… a bad student…'

'Aye, well… join the club,' replied Noel. 'We are all bad students here, eh, Arthur?' He looked towards the barman.

'Yes, we are indeed…' said Arthur. 'We are all bad students… I would not have it any other way.' He winked at David.

'Me neither, Arthur…' said Noel. 'Bad students, we are… sinners too, no doubt… Speak of the Devil… here comes Reverend "Lazarus" McDade!' He pointed out of a window, where a man in long, black overcoat and grey flat cap was walking along the veranda of the door to the bar.

The door opened and in walked the Reverend.

'Good morning, all,' he bellowed loudly as he entered the bar. 'It's cold out today.'

He took a seat in between Noel and David.

'What can I get you, Lazarus?' asked Arthur.

'I will have a black coffee, please…'

'Coming right up.'

'How is Noel this fine morning?' said Reverend McDade.

'Very well, thank you…' replied Noel. 'Let me introduce David Campbell… just new on the island… the latest recruit to the camp.'

Reverend McDade immediately turned to David, instinctively knowing who Noel was referring to.

'David Campbell? How very nice to meet you. Peter McDade, but folk call me Lazarus on account of the fact I am a minister of the Church, which the state thought was dead.' The Reverend outstretched his hand to shake David's. 'From the Campbell clan in Argyll?'

'Hello,' replied David, shaking the Reverend's hand warmly. 'No, I don't think I am from that famous clan. Born and bred in the Scottish Borders, near the Cheviots… I don't think I have any Campbell warriors in my blood… it would not do much good today, anyway.'

'Ah, from the Cheviots…' said the Reverend. 'Reiver territory… you never know, you might have picked up something of the lawlessness or the rebel in you…' He gave a light chuckle. 'What about your father? Is he from the Argyll, with a surname like that… did he not tell you the roots of your surname?'

157

'Well, certainly I feel like a rebel these days…' said David solemnly. 'Unfortunately, I have not seen my father for many years, not since I was a child, when he was dragged off by the state in front of my eyes as he refused to take some silly vaccine… He was regarded as some kind of public health risk, I was told… So, maybe I get it from him…' David felt almost annoyed at Lazarus' questioning.

'I am sorry to hear that, son…' replied Lazarus. 'Many families were unnecessarily and cruelly split up around the time when you were a boy… terrible times. Crimes against humanity. And many people went along silently and complied like bloody idiots. Dark times. What about your mother?'

'She died… only my younger brother and, err… me…' David stumbled over his words.

Just sitting next to this old minister was making David leak out words he did not want to say and feel emotions that he did not want to feel. Lazarus was a striking sight. With his long, black overcoat and thick, long white beard and long, white, curly hair on the back and sides, whilst bald on top, there was an imposing look about him. He had a craggy-looking face that made him about mid-70s, with blue eyes and white eyebrows. Lazarus had an air of calm and being centred or grounded that was quite uncanny. He was about 5 feet 8 but seemed taller than he actually was. David's legs were shaking. He did not know if he felt uncomfortable, sad, or just angry. He took several huge gulps of his beer and finished his pint.

'Can I have another one, please,' David indicated to Arthur.

'Coming right up,' said Arthur.

David felt the need to keep moving, to keep distracted from something that he could not identify. His pint arrived on the bar and David immediately grabbed it and took a long gulp. He handed the barman his credit card to pay for the drink.

'Many thanks,' said Arthur.

'So, your father imprisoned by the state, your mother dead, and just you and your brother now, and now you're stuck here at the behest of the state,' said Lazarus. 'Whatever happened to your father?'

'As far as I am aware, he disappeared like many dissidents into the psychiatric system,' replied David. 'He was eventually forced into exile, as his ideological stance was a public health risk…' He put down his pint glass on the bar. 'Bloody state… Why the fuck did people go along with such bullshit?' he angrily spluttered.

'I know… I understand,' said Lazarus. 'It is quite incredible what cognitive dissonance people sunk into. It had happened many times before, though… Nazi Germany to name just one… It should not happen again, so the saying went… but it happened, alright… Such evil never goes away… it just changes its clothes to suit the fashions.'

'Just shows it is a pointless endeavour to have hope, to care…' replied David. 'Humans are so idiotic… You are a minister of the church… How do you get through this? How do you reconcile this madness with your God and faith?'

David was feeling very irritated now. He wanted to escape… the conversation was painful for him.

'Faith, you ask?' said Lazarus, looking at David in some surprise. 'I will quote the great St Gregory Palamas… *Every thought which strives from below towards Him who is transcendent and separate from the world comes to a halt once it has gone beyond all created things. Yet, it is false to say that beyond the accomplishment of the divine commandments there is nothing but purity of heart. There are other things, many other things. There is the pledge of things promised in this age. There are also the blessings of the age to come, visible and accessible through this purity of the heart. Then, beyond prayer, there is the vision that cannot be spoken of, the ecstasy in the vision and the hidden mysteries…* I love that quote.'

'Very nice… please excuse me while I go for a pee,' said David sarcastically. He felt nauseous.

David went to the spiral staircase to go up to the toilets.

'Go easy on him, Father,' Arthur said quietly when David was out of earshot. 'He has just arrived here. He has the haunted look in his eyes… I have seen it before… the light has gone out, replaced by hopelessness.'

Lazarus just shook his head. 'Calm down, Arthur. Sometimes, it takes a bit of suffering to wake people up.'

Noel, who had been listening to the conversion, was looking perplexed. He got off his stool and sat next to Lazarus.

'This sounds crazy… far-fetched, and an incredible coincidence,' he said. 'But I have to say it, or I will burst… please tell me I am going mad… I mean, it might be nothing… it might be just my eyes playing tricks… It struck me just now, as he got up and went to the toilet… His mannerism, his sarcasm, the way he moved, his bloody face… I clocked him at the ferry port yesterday when he arrived on the island… I knew there was something about him I recognised.'

'Spit it out, man!' Lazarus said, getting increasingly impatient. 'Use your words, stop blethering… What are you trying to say?'

Noel shook his head, as if in disbelief, and continued. 'He has a brother, their father was taken away and put in a psychiatric institution and disappeared into the public health system and then into exile. He is from the Borders, and his bloody face… he is the spitting image of Thomas bloody Rutherford on Taransay! Thomas had two sons, he refused the bloody COVID-19 vaccine, he went into a psychiatric hospital and was then forced into exile, and he's from the Borders… He looks like a bloody older version of David. The auburn hair, the blue eyes, the physique…' Noel leant in closer to the Reverend. 'Thomas Rutherford is his DAD!' he whispered.

'He has the wrong surname… how could Thomas be his dad?' Lazarus responded in a hushed voice.

Noel continued. 'He changed his bloody surname when he came to the islands… he was Thomas Campbell when he came here, but for many reasons, he changed it… But he told me… lots of folk changed their name for various reasons in those times… they tried lots of ways to evade the prying eyes of the state…'

'He told me he changed his name, too,' Lazarus retorted. 'He never told me it had been Campbell, though. I kind of wanted to respect his privacy… Dear Lord… it is uncanny, now that you mention it… the physical resemblance, the biographical details… You do know he was coming over for dinner here today, before church? I should speak to him before he leaves… perhaps forewarn him… It could be nothing, just coincidence… Campbell is a common name, lots of kids lost their parents to the state machinery… I fear, though, in this case it is not just a coincidence… Oh, Dear Lord… what are the chances?'

'Ssshhh…' whispered Noel. 'Here he comes.'

David came slowly down the spiral staircase, holding onto the banister firmly. He felt a bit dizzy. The two pints of beer had gone to his head. He felt he wanted more beer, and also he felt the need to have a smoke. He took up his seat at the bar.

'Can I have another pint, and a pack of cigarettes and a lighter... you do sell cigarettes here? You can hardly get them on the mainland,' David asked Arthur.

'Super Strike reds?'

'Full strength ones... yup,' replied David.

Arthur poured David another pint and fetched his cigarettes and lighter. David paid with his card. He hurriedly ripped the plastic wrapping off the cigarette packet and fetched out a long, white cigarette with a yellowish filter tip. Placing it in his mouth, he lit it and drew in a long inhalation of nicotine and assorted chemicals. It felt good. His head buzzed and he felt for several moments even more dizzy, but it felt kind of nice.

'David,' said Lazarus, 'I am having lunch later with a friend, before we have a small church meeting. You are welcome to join us.'

David looked directly at Lazarus. He had heard the words, but it was like his brain was unable to compute their significance or meaning.

'Sorry, can you say again?' he said.

'I am having a late lunch with a friend, upstairs here,' replied Lazarus, pointing to the spiral stairs. 'Maybe a few others will join us. Then we have a church meeting, up at the church – at the house on the corner, just up the hill there. You are more than welcome to join us. If it is convenient, of course. I don't know if you have anything planned?'

'Oh, I don't think I have anything planned...' said David. 'I have not much on today... Very kind of you... I am not sure I will be very good dinner company, though...'

'Ach, well, we have all sorts here...' said Lazarus. 'No pressure... just good food and interesting conversation and contemplation... maybe go easy on the beer, if you want to join us...' He winked kindly at David.

'What time are you having lunch?'

'Around two o'clock... upstairs. Four-thirty we go to the church.'

'Ok...' said David. 'I will go for a wander and check out the area, and come back later, then. Very kind of you.'

David did not know what else to say. He just wanted to escape the social pressure he felt. He felt he was being pulled off his logical course that he had already decided. He was annoyed that, even in his final hours, he could not get enough peace to recollect his being and life. *Hell is other people*, he thought to himself, recalling a quote from Sartre.

'Great,' Lazarus joyfully replied. 'I will see you here, then. I recommend the beach. It is a wonderful walk down there. I must dash now and set up the church and do a few chores, and will see you later.'

Lazarus got off his stool and turned to Noel, giving him a wink from his left eye.

With that, Lazarus exited the bar and went off up the hill to his house at quite a pace.

David sat in silence, smoking his cigarette, and when he was not smoking it he took large glugs of beer from his glass. He finished his cigarette and lit another one. He felt he was on a mission.

*****

Meanwhile, Lazarus had reached his house. He rushed in through the front door, through the hall and into his office, which was wall-to-wall books and papers. A large, wooden desk and leather office chair took up the centre of the room, overlooking the window. He sat down in his chair and grabbed the telephone, scrolling through his contacts until he found Thomas Rutherford's number. He pressed the 'call' button. It rang for what seemed like an age. Eventually, someone answered.

'Hello,' said a voice.

'Hello… Thomas, it's Peter… Lazarus, here. I know you are coming over and joining me for lunch today… you are still coming, yes?'

'Yes, I am,' Thomas replied. 'I am just about getting ready to leave. I was having a bit of trouble with the motor on my boat, but I got it fixed and I am ready to go. I am looking forward to our lunch and church meeting. It is still on, yes?'

'Yes, yes, yes… but that's not why I am calling,' said Lazarus. 'It might be nothing, Thomas, but I thought I should check… just in case… It's probably a coincidence… can I be frank?'

'Yes, of course…' said Thomas. 'You sound worried… is everything alright?'

162

'Well, yes… well, I don't know how else to put it… May I ask, you changed your name years ago… your surname? Out of respect, I never asked you why you do this, or asked what your previous surname was…'

There was silence on the other end of the phone.

'You are scaring me, Peter…' said Thomas eventually. 'I changed my name partly to evade scrutiny, partly to forget. Many did change their name to forget. You know that. Why do you want to know my old surname?'

'Please, what was it?' begged Lazarus, almost crying.

'It was Campbell… it was Campbell… What is going on?'

'Oh, dear God, Thomas…' replied the Reverend. 'I hope to God… I don't know what to hope… fuck it… I have met a young man. He has just been sent to the camp here… just arrived. He says his name is David… David Campbell… He is from the Scottish Borders… Late thirties… auburn hair, blue eyes, a younger brother, mother dead. He says his dad was taken away by the state for refusing a vaccine and disappeared into the psychiatric system, then into exile. Tell me I am going mad, please, Thomas… could it be your son?'

There was silence.

'Are you there, Thomas?' Lazarus asked.

'Yes… I am here… Let me sit down… I think it's my David… it's too much of a coincidence… Those facts… where in the Borders is he from?'

'He said the Cheviots… is that where you were from?'

'Fuck… Yes, it was… I am leaving now, Lazarus. Where is he now?'

'I met him in the bar…' replied the Reverend. 'I invited him to lunch… he is a bit down, in a bit of a sorry state, what with being assigned to the camp here…'

'Ok, I am coming over,' said Thomas. 'I will see you in the bar as soon as I can. Thank you, Peter…'

'Don't thank me,' replied Lazarus. 'Just get your arse over here as soon as you can… part of me hopes I am wrong, partly right… Now that I have suggested it… he is the spitting image of you, Thomas… It's like looking at a fucking mirror…'

'Ok, I am on my way. Keep him there! Keep him there! See you soon. Bye.'

The phone went dead. Lazarus sat in silence, his heart beating ten to the dozen. *There is a God*, he mused to himself.

A woman came into his office.

'Peter! What is the bloody commotion?' his wife asked.

'It's Thomas Rutherford…' replied Lazarus. 'Or, I should say, Thomas Campbell… I think it is his son, David. He has arrived… at the camp. I met him just now in the bar. Thomas thinks it is him. He is the spitting image of Thomas. I don't think it's a coincidence.'

'Oh, Peter…' said his wife. 'My, that IS big. Is Thomas coming over?'

'Yes, he is on his way. I have invited his son, David, for lunch.'

'Peter, if it is his son, I don't think they will be up for lunch, or your company…'

'Ok, ok, ok, I was thinking on my feet…' said Lazarus. 'If it is his son, of course I will leave them to it… I have got a few things to sort out here, then I am going down to the bar. I am meeting Thomas there in a bit. I have never done a father-son reconciliation thing before…'

'Go easy,' said his wife. 'It might well be painful, joyful, angry for both of them… How wonderful, if it is him…'

'I hope it is wonderful…' Lazarus said.

*****

'Hey, Arthur, do you have music here?' David asked.

'Over in the corner,' replied Arthur. 'A vintage jukebox. I am sure you will find some stuff on there that rocks your boat. All stuff on there, late twentieth century, early twenty-first, the works… it's free.'

'Great, thanks.'

David wandered over to the corner of the bar and found the vintage jukebox. He scrolled through the electronic screen. Names of bands his mother and father listened to flashed before his eyes: Queen, Status Quo, AC/DC, Oasis, the Rolling Stones, Bob Marley, the Cult, Stone Roses, Pink Floyd, the Verve, the Brian Jonestown Massacre… They brought back so many memories, happy memories, memories of driving in the car with his father with the music blaring out of the speakers as his dad nodded his head to the music. David picked several songs by the late 20th century band the Verve, a favourite of his father. The first song he chose was called 'The drugs don't work'. The lyrics *'like a cat in a bag, waiting to drown, this time I am coming down*' struck a deep, emotional chord as the singer uttered them. David knew, then, that the nearby ocean was going to be his final hoorah. He wandered over to the bar, sat down, and downed what was left of his pint.

'One more for the road, please, Arthur,' David said almost joyfully.

'Coming right up.'

'Better go easy on the booze, if you want to be standing up later,' Noel interjected.

'Aye, well, I think I will prefer to be lying flat on my back, to be honest,' said David.

Arthur and Noel just looked at each other, not knowing what to say.

'It's getting me down, my love… just waiting to drown… you live your life, I am better off dead…' rang out from the speakers rigged up to the jukebox. There was a depressing air in the bar. David just sat smoking and drinking, staring at the bar. 'Catching the Butterfly' by the Verve was the next song that came on.

'Brilliant song,' he uttered.

David moved his head side to side, swinging left and right on his bar stool. He felt quite insane in a freaky, psychedelic kind of way. His heart was pumping in his chest. It was like the life force inside of him was trying to signal something to him. He had never felt so alive in his life, yet so close to death. It was exhilarating. *Why hadn't I thought of this before?* he wondered. All those people struggling to live in shit with no hope of changing it. Humans had become nothing but a herd, sheep, cattle. The state agenda had won. It would not be long until the human race would obliterate itself, he mused, in his darkened mind.

'There is no real truth… let me sleep tonight… There will be no lullabies… I just can't make it alone, oh no no no…' rang out 'Space and Time' from the jukebox.

The lyrics felt so apt and appropriate for the moment, like they were encouraging him down into his mood, confirming his destiny. He wandered back over to the jukebox and put on some more tunes. A selection from Pink Floyd, another group his parents enjoyed listening to. He wandered back to his seat, conscious of being watched by the few other people that were in the bar. He must have looked weird, or odd, or they were just annoyed by his choice in music. The first song that came on from

Pink Floyd was a dreamy song called 'Marooned'. How apt. That was how David felt – marooned in his existence as a human being.

Time passed in a strange way as David sat at the bar. He thought that space/time must do funny tricks to reality when one is fast approaching one's demise. 'Another Brick in The Wall (Part 1)' by Pink Floyd came on. David realised he had been just another brick in the wall, the world, the state, by the control state. Just an animal of no importance; recorded, jabbed, monitored, controlled, used, hated. That was all life was. Anyone who thought any different was fooled by some notion of freedom. *Even religion was fool's gold*, he thought. There was no hope, really.

He lit another cigarette and sucked in that hot, dry, nicotine loveliness. Pink Floyd's 'Goodbye Cruel World' came on. He waited for the lyrics *'there is nothing you can do to change my mind'*. He sat staring at the beer mat on the bar.

Hebridean Ale
1912-2012

How sad, he thought. Whole industries and companies destroyed and consigned to the memory hole. 2012. The year he was born.

David was roused to attention. He must have been dreaming for what seemed like an age. The lack of music awoke him. The silence felt horrible, like it was tearing into his flesh.

'Another one?' asked Arthur, holding up David's empty glass.

'No... you're alright...' replied David. 'I'm going now, thanks.'

David stumbled to his feet and ran his hands through his hair in an attempt to make himself presentable.

'I am off now! Nice meeting you all,' he called as he turned to look at Noel and Arthur.

He grabbed his cigarettes and lighter and stuffed them in his pocket.

'See you later, David,' chipped Noel.

'Aye... we'll meet again... some sunny day,' David said in a sing-song way, like the famous song by Vera Lynn.

He began to make his way to the door, but then looked back. 'Where is the beach...?' he asked. 'I am going for a walk, like the Reverend suggested.'

'Turn left out the door, then left again down the path,' Noel said. 'You can't miss it. The most beautiful beach in Scotland... the world.'

'Cheers, Noel. All the best.'

'See you later on?' Noel chipped.

'Aye...'

With that, David walked to the door and left the bar. He felt kind of sad. They would be the last words he would ever utter to another human being.

Chapter Fifteen

Revelation

David walked slowly down the path to the beach, in between the grassy, sandy, craggy mounds, and onto the Luskentyre sands. It was beautiful. The wind was blowing gently, and the sun was shining through the white fluffy clouds and blue sky. The beach was deserted. He took his shoes and socks off and rolled his trouser legs up and headed left, up onto the beach and walked on the glorious sands. They were perfectly smooth and there was not one piece of litter on them. The ocean was a supernatural blue that defied reality. David's parents had walked these sands on their honeymoon many years ago, before he had been created in the womb out of love. They must have dreamt about the possibilities of children, family life, an extraordinary ordinariness that defies the eternal method, the reductive man, man who dares and desires to be God to control life – and, in the cosmic scale of things, a moment's happiness on the mortal plane. And, of course, it was like that for a short while, but things were brewing in the world that had been planned for a very long time, which attacked such extraordinary ordinary fundamentals; fundamentals which coursed through the hearts of everyone – or, at least, was a capability we were born with.

But, with the eternal method, the rosy and juicy apple of the Garden of Eden, sold by the serpent, humanity was very slowly deconstructed, cut off and re-engineered to live in a different manner. The simple joy of walking along a beach, feeling the wind, hand in hand with a loved one, from here to there, never fearing from this life to death and into eternity; an inescapable destiny of being born to die. Such profound sensibilities had been gouged out in a sustained – what many would call, satanic – attack of the human mind and reality. Whatever it was, it stripped the sovereign rights of Beings born to live to die. It sucked the joy, ordinary pain, suffering and exquisite release into mortality and into eternity. It had been corrupted, and most people did not even notice. Nobody even knew such an anti-method ever existed.

No matter. David walked slowly up the sands, looking into the sky and mountains in the distance. As he walked, he could taste his mouth more than he had ever tasted himself before. Indeed, he could sense every fibre in his being like he had never

168

felt before; his arms, legs, stomach, and his heart. It was like his fleshly reality was wanting to sing loudly one last time.

He walked to the grassy sandy hills at the edge of the beach where it met the land and where the beach curled left. He sat on a grassy sandy tuft and looked out to the sea. Huge, wet, salty tears began dripping down his face. He was making no noise. There was no sound but the wind and the sea. It was perfect. It felt right. He had found his place for the final act. He was sitting completely still and looking out. His mind felt calm. He was just soaking up the final moments and entered what seemed like a timeless daydream state…

*****

Lazarus entered the bar, huffing and puffing. Flustered and looking nervous, he scanned the room.

'Arthur, where has young David… is he still here… has he gone out?'

'He went for a walk on the beach…' replied Arthur. 'I think he needed to clear his head. The booze was going to his head, I think. He looked in a rough way… singing Vera Lyn "We'll meet again some sunny day" as he left…'

'What!!' Lazarus cried out in desperation. 'I… I am going to go find him… I think he needs company… I should have thought… I was not thinking… people like him are vulnerable when they arrive here…'

'I thought he was just miserable… who wouldn't be as a new inmate up the road?' Noel quipped.

'Ok,' replied Lazarus in an authoritative tone, 'if he gets back when I am out… if I miss him, tell him to stay… Tell him I have something very important to discuss with him…'

'Did you speak to Thomas?' enquired Noel. 'Is he coming over?'

'Yes, I bloody well did!' Lazarus was losing his composure again. 'He thinks David is his son… he is on his way… Ok, I am off… Keep him here if he comes back when I am gone. If he is on the beach, Thomas is coming over on his motorboat… I might be able to introduce them to each other at the jetty, if I find David down there… What do folk do or say at such reconciliations? This is too much for one bloody day.'

169

'Calm down… I will come with you,' said Noel, getting off his chair and putting his black leather biker jacket on.

They both left the bar and headed to the beach.

*****

David rubbed his eyes and dried them with his sleeve and stood up. He walked purposefully to the shoreline and walked down to the water. On his way, he took off his jacket and threw it down. Then he took his jumper off, followed by his trousers and T-shirt. Then his pants were discarded. He looked to the sky and said, 'Lord have mercy upon me.' He walked straight in up to his neck. The water was freezing cold as he stood there. The water lapped up around his neck and the salty water came into his mouth. He took a large mouthful and held it there. And walked a little further. He could no longer touch the bottom. He let his head sink below the surface. Holding his breath under the water was easy at first… then the pangs for the desire to breathe came. He inhaled. A searing pain struck into him. His body convulsed. He tried to dive his head downwards. His mind and body were screaming in pain, panic and fear. But he wanted this. The pain eased and, for a few moments, he felt he could breathe underwater. His body felt airy, but heavy. And then it went black.

*****

Lazarus and Noel arrived onto the beach. Noel spotted David's boots and socks on the sand and footprints leading up and along the beach. In the distance, they could see the motorboat of Thomas Rutherford approaching the shoreline, making his way to the jetty to moor his boat.

'Where the fuck is he…?' Noel said exasperated.

Lazarus scanned the beach to their left. Way in the distance, he saw the trail of discarded clothes on the beach.

'There… up there!' Lazarus shouted.

They both started running frantically up the beach. As Lazarus ran, he looked over at the fast-approaching Thomas Rutherford and made a gesture with his hand to head to up to where they were running. Thomas clocked them and changed direction.

'Up here!! Thomas…! Up here!!' roared Lazarus.

Thomas looked to where they were running and, in the water, just out of the shallows, he could see a white figure of a human body floating just below the surface. He felt frantic.

'Please, God, no! Please, no!' he screamed into the wind.

*****

David found himself outside his body, looking down at himself floating under the water. He realised he was dying. He felt ok. The only thing he felt was that he hoped his brother and his father (if he was still alive) would not be too upset about this death. There was nothing to fear. All was ok. Death was natural and nothing to be resisted.

Suddenly, he turned around and could see a shaft of some kind projecting upwards from the water, like a kind of corridor or passageway projecting from the sea, jutting upwards towards a bright white light. He headed towards it instinctively, thinking to himself, *I am out of here.*

Immediately, he found himself within the white light. He was in the light, but also part of the light. He knew where he was. He sensed the presence of God; he knew God was here. Excited, he felt he needed to ask the big question. Of course, David had no body, no voice, but somehow was able to communicate to the light the question:

'What is the meaning of life?'

'Love,' was the response.

However, it was not communicated in a voice, but again via a kind of telepathic communication. David was struck by how the message was delivered. Although he understood it as LOVE, the message had a far more profound meaning than the English language could convey, than any human language could convey. The message was profound, but it was a message or meaning he felt that he had always known or been contained within him, but which he had forgotten. He felt he had regained a lost message or meaning. It was so profound. He was bathed in LOVE, this light. With no body, in the light but also part of the light. He felt he had arrived home. But to stay was not his destiny. Not just yet. That was not the plan.

Suddenly, he was transported almost at light speed back down the tunnel. He recognised this journey. He had done this journey before. The recollection was unmistakable. He realised that

171

life was a test of sorts, a challenge that had to be dealt with, a cross to bear so to speak. He was heading back to his body, back into his body. It was not his time yet. And then it went black.

*****

Lazarus and Noel had reached the shoreline where David had entered the sea. Lazarus took off his long overcoat. He kicked his shoes off and ran into the water, scanning desperately all around looking for David. He swam a little further out where he could not touch the bottom. He scanned the sea below, looking for David. He spotted him hanging a couple of metres below the surface. Lazarus dived and grabbed him around the chest. He was heavy. Somehow, he managed to get David to the surface, but he was struggling. Lazarus was on his back, trying to keep David's body above the water. Noel was now in the water. He got behind Lazarus and tried to add some support by kicking his legs furiously to help keep them both afloat. Thomas's boat arrived alongside and he threw them a rope.

'Wrap it tight around you and I will drag you to the shallows!' Thomas shouted.

Noel wrapped the rope around himself, Lazarus and David and made it tight.

'Right, pull us in!' gasped Lazarus.

Thomas pushed his pedal throttle and Noel, Lazarus and David were thrust against the side of the boat as Thomas dragged them to the shallows. Lazarus and felt the sandy ground beneath them and they stumbled onto their feet. Noel untangled the rope and, between them, they dragged David out of the shallows and laid him onto his back on the golden sands. Thomas powered his boat so it grounded onto the sand for a few metres and tipped to one side. He fell out and stumbled to his feet and ran to David and the others. Lazarus was busy doing CPR on David. He was shouting.

'For the love of God… don't give up, you bastard…! You bastard…!'

Noel sat exhausted nearby, crying and rubbing his eyes.

Thomas fell to his knees and grabbed David's wrist.

'He still has a weak pulse…' he said. 'I hope to God we are not too late.'

David emerged from the black and could see another blinding, bright white light. Suddenly, he felt a searing pain in his chest and stomach area. He tried to lurch forwards and upwards, but fell to his right-hand side, where Thomas was holding his hand. Thomas helped him over onto his side. David was sick and brought up the seawater he had swallowed. He coughed up what seemed like a gallon. David did not know where he was, who he was or what reality was. He was absolutely terrified. He could sense the Reverend's face at his left shoulder, looking down. He did not recognise what he himself was. He could sense the arms and stomach of Thomas, which he was leaning against, but he did not know what they were.

Lazarus was making sounds from his mouth, but David could not recognise what they were – or, indeed, what language was. He struggled in terror to try to grasp what was going on, in between painful coughs. He slowly pieced bits together… 'I am a man… this is Earth… I am David… I tried to kill myself… I am alive… That is Reverend McDade...' He began to recognise that what Lazarus was speaking was English.

Lazarus tearfully spoke to David. 'What happened, David…? Dear God… It's ok… We got you, son.'

'I think I died… I think I died…' David rasped, barely able to speak as his throat was so painful.

Thomas hoisted David so that he was sitting more upright. He cradled the younger man in his left arm, with David leaning against his chest, much like how a parent would cradle their baby.

David could feel the presence of this person, but wondered who it could be. He turned his head slowly to the right and slightly upwards. Looking down at him was a face he knew. He could not place it. Thomas was rubbing David softly on the head with his right hand, looking straight at him intently. He was crying, silently, with huge tears running down his face.

'It's him…' Thomas whispered. 'It's my David…'

Lazarus had tears in his eyes. He looked penetratingly towards both Thomas and David. Noel stood up and began wandering around, rubbing his head. 'I can't believe it… I can't believe it,' he was mumbling.

David squinted in the sun and gazed at this familiar old face, at the blue eyes, auburn balding hair and red beard, looking down at him. An emotion welled up within him. An emotion that he had never felt in all his life; grief, pain, sorrow, joy and exhilaration all wrapped into one. A growing realisation of who this person was that was cradling him arose within him. David tried to speak, but could not find the words…

'It's ok… it's ok, I am here, son,' Thomas said to David in a soft voice that only a father would say to his infant.

'Daaaaad!!!!' rasped David, grabbing his father, sobbing and coughing.

David held onto his father's coat with one hand and, with the other, placed his palm on the elderly man's cheek, almost to check if he was real. He cried and sobbed, his head tucked into his father's chest. Thomas cradled his naked son, just as he had when he was born…

*****

I heard a voice say to me
Take the hand of God
I tried to reach
But I failed
And I wept
My tears formed an ocean
And I floated over the waters
Into the arms of the beloved.

Bruce Scott, 04/04/09